CW01336876

So Close to Heaven

Far From Home: A Scottish Time-Travel Romance, Volume 11

Rebecca Ruger

Published by Rebecca Ruger, 2025.

This is a work of fiction. Names, character, places, and incidents
are either a product of the author's imagination
are used fictitiously, and any resemblance to actual persons,
living or dead, events,
or locales is entirely coincidental.
Some creative license may have been taken
with exact dates and locations
to better serve the plot and pacing of the novel.

ISBN: 9798262385140
All Rights Reserved.
Copyright © 2024 Rebecca Ruger
Written by Rebecca Ruger

All rights reserved. No part of this publication may be repro-
duced,
distributed or transmitted in any form or by any means,
or stored in a database or retrieval system,
without the prior written permission of the publisher.
Disclaimer: The material in this book is for mature audiences
only
and may contain graphic content.
It is intended only for those aged 18 and older.

Chapter One

The wind blew across the open moor, cool and relentless, tugging at her jacket as Ivy Mitchell trudged along. The hills rolled out before her, a soft and endless green divided by low stone walls and peppered with the vibrant blooms of summer heather, while the air smelled of rain that hadn't fallen yet.

At the crest of a small knoll, she paused, taking it all in—the sweep of the hills, the muted light of an overcast sky, the open space—and for a moment, she felt something she hadn't experienced in a long time.

She felt close to heaven.

Not the heaven of sermons and hymns, not the bright, unreachable place painted in church windows as she'd known on Sundays with her grandparents, but the heaven she'd known otherwise as a child, barefoot in soybean fields under an endless stretch of sky in southern Indiana, the sun warm on her shoulders, the world vast and full of promise.

She felt now the same as she had then, that she was just a tiny little blip in a great big world, and that she was free to be who she was, or whatever she wanted. She'd only known that feeling while with her grandparents at their fourth-generation farm. At home with her thrice-divorced mother—who was as different from her salt-of-the-earth parents as corn was from cotton—Ivy knew little peace, and even less security. To this day, Ivy was forever grateful for how long it took her mother to find Husband No. 4, as that meant Ivy was dropped off at her grandparents' farm every weekend while Daisy Mitchell was on the hunt. The saddest day ever was when her mother announced her intention to wed again, this time to Kurt Ledger—fittingly referred to as Junior, since everything about him was small, or lesser than: his brain, his ambition, his patience, and pretty much anything else that mattered. For several years before Daisy wed Junior, Ivy happily spent every weekend at the Four Corners Farm, showered with love and attention, with a sense of normalcy and constancy that she'd rarely known elsewhere.

Today, almost two decades later and thousands of miles away, Ivy had taken the train north on a whim, craving exactly this open space, the quiet in a world made turbulent once again. This would also be her last solitary hike in Scotland, as she was scheduled to board a plane in a few days and return home. Her boots crunched along the narrow trail winding up the hillside, the path marked only by a weathered wooden post that might have been standing for decades or even centuries,

She moved steadily upward, her hand drifting absently to her belly—one part of her recent turbulence. It was no longer small, though it could still be hidden under her jacket. The baby had grown enough that she'd had to purchase several pairs of elastic waist pants. She'd found a perfect pair of joggers, a good quality brand of organic cotton, and discovered that one size larger than her normal size four gave her plenty of room and comfort.

Seven months along already. She wasn't sure how the weeks and months had flown by so quickly. The doctor said everything looked good—healthy and normal. She should have felt reassured by that.

She felt instead as if she was nine or ten again, and it was late Sunday afternoon and her mother was due to arrive at any moment to take her back home—to the chaos, the instability.

She felt, on occasion, that same dread. Subsequently, sometimes, she caught herself feeling a quiet sort of relief that her grandparents weren't here to see her like this—alone, unwed, and knocked up on the other side of the world. It wasn't that she wouldn't have wanted them here. God, she would have given anything for one more day with them. But Ivy couldn't help feeling she had somehow faltered, been careless when she should have known better, that she had more of her mother in her than she would have ever hoped or imagined. For that, at least, she was grateful her grandparents had been spared the heartache of watching her stumble. They would have worried for her, and hurt for her.

And yet...

"No baby is ever unwelcome," her grandmother had always said whenever whispers spread through their small town about another unmarried girl expecting.

Ivy certainly didn't see her baby as a mistake. It was a life, and part of her life now.

And yet, it brought with it another sort of chaos.

What now? was wondered just as often as, *How am I going to do this?*

She had come to Scotland almost a year ago, a final-year veterinary student on a study abroad program she hadn't been able to pass up—a semester of coursework, rural outreach, and hands-on experience working with the great draft horses and hardy cattle—the Highland coos—she'd only read about previously. It was supposed to have been a brief detour. Four months, maybe six, and then back to the States to finish her clinical rotations, sit her boards, and start the long road toward her dream of becoming a veterinarian.

Having found refuge at her grandparents' farm in those dusty summers spent barefoot and sunburned, riding the backs of patient old plow horses, sneaking into the cool barns with a battered paperback and snacks in her pockets, Ivy had learned early that animals didn't ask questions or take sides. They didn't judge or use her as a pawn or weapon; they didn't drink too much or shout down the walls in fits of rage. They were soft, gentle, welcoming, and exactly what Ivy had needed.

Becoming a veterinarian wasn't only a dream. It was as inevitable as breathing.

Though her grandparents had left the Four Corners Farm to Ivy and not their daughter, Daisy—more chaos there— they had never meant for it to tie her down. They had always said she could have both: the farm and her dream. It was the farm, after all, that had made the dream possible. Without the inheritance they had left her, Ivy would never have been able to afford college, much less time studying abroad.

She hadn't simply abandoned it, hadn't left the farm to fall apart. Four Corners was in good hands. Her grandfather had built a team over the years—people he'd trusted, people Ivy now trusted, too. Hal Whitaker, the old farm manager, knew every field and fence line better than he knew his own children. Maria Sanchez handled the books and logistics with a sharp eye and a sharper tongue when necessary. Nate Jensen and Brett Chojnacki kept the machinery running and the crops rotating like clockwork. Even in her absence, the farm had been and would continue to be planted, harvested, and cared for just the same as it always had been.

It was still home. It always would be. But for now, it was a home waiting for her to find her way back.

And yet...for so long she'd put it off.

Nothing about Scotland had felt temporary since the moment she arrived. Not the craggy hills, not the serene misty mornings, not the friendly people or even the rousing town life. And not the guy with the crooked smile and charming accent who had shown Ivy her first taste of true attention, and what she thought was genuine affection.

It *was* genuine, she still believed; it simply hadn't been the lasting kind.

Ivy picked her way carefully across a rocky patch, her boots scraping against stone.

She'd met David Newlands on her first Saturday night in Edinburgh. Despite the thrill of Scotland, she had been exhausted, overwhelmed, and more homesick than she'd expected to be. Some classmates had dragged her to a small pub tucked off a crooked side street, a place with creaking beams, a low fire, and a cover band playing American-made music.

She remembered fumbling her way from the crush at the bar, balancing two pints awkwardly, when someone had backed into her hard. She'd sloshed half the beer down a bar patron's back.

Mortified, anxious, she'd looked up as the man had turned around, ready to apologize—and found herself staring into blue-green eyes and an uneven but electric smile.

David had plucked the half-empty glass from her hand, handed it back to the bartender, asking for another, and had quipped to Ivy, "First round's on me then."

It had been that easy, that fast.

He had a way of laughing that made everything around him feel warmer, lighter. His voice was rich, his r's rolling just enough to curl against the ear, and he had an effortless knack for drawing

Ivy out of her shell without making her feel small for needing the coaxing.

By the end of the night, they had traded numbers, shared a cab, and had made plans to meet up again the next day.

And the day after that. And the one after that.

Coffee dates, wandering through secondhand bookstores, ferry rides out to craggy shores where the sea foam slapped against the rocks. A week later, Ivy wasn't thinking about the semester but about David. He was magnetic, clever, teasing, and just reckless enough to make her feel young and alive and bold in ways she hadn't dared before.

They had kissed for the first time on the North Bridge, the wind tearing at their jackets, the city lights spilling below them in a haze of gold and stone. David had cupped her face in his hands and said, with the kind of certainty Ivy had always craved, "You are wildfire, Ivy Mitchell. Scotland's lucky to know you."

It had been exactly what she needed to hear. Maybe exactly what she had been waiting her whole life to hear.

A wry smile tugged at her mouth now, as she trudged onward.

The dream she'd begun to imagine with David had ended the moment she told him about the baby.

He hadn't been cruel; he'd been shocked. There was some—wisely cut-off—attempt to blame her for the unexpected pregnancy, though that had been panic speaking, she still allowed.

He hadn't shouted or stormed out. He had simply gone still. Shock, then reason.

"It's not the right time," he'd said, as if they were considering getting a pet or rescheduling a flight. "I have...other plans... so much ahead of me. We both do," he'd been quick to qualify.

A few weeks later, he'd accepted a job offer in London. He hadn't asked her to go with him.

After many long nights, crying lonely tears, Ivy had exchanged a handshake and an impersonal last kiss with David before he'd left. A neat, civilized end. David had already moved on, she'd felt, had probably begun to do so on the very day she'd told him she was carrying his child.

She didn't hate him. She was only sad that he'd not lived up to the promise of what she thought he was, and that *they* hadn't either.

He wanted a life that didn't include her, maybe never had in terms of longevity as she'd dreamed. She wanted a life he wasn't willing to make room for. She absolutely didn't want to be with someone who didn't want to be with her.

She thought about him, here and there, since then—*what ifs* and *maybe one day*—but not with any true sadness. More often, she thought, *Oh my God, I'm going to have a baby.*

Her boots scuffed to a halt at a rise in the trail. The ground leveled out into a wide, open moor. In the distance, the hills rose higher, gray-blue and mist-laced against the pale spring sky. Somewhere beyond them, the true Highlands stretched wild and unreachable.

Her hand drifted again to her belly, smoothing gently over the small, solid curve.

A now-familiar sense of unease swept over her, wondering if she were strong enough, sensible enough, mature enough, to raise a child by herself. She would find out, she imagined. This was her last weekend in Scotland. She had a flight scheduled for Monday evening to return home. It was time to get on with her life at Four Corners Farm. She would miss Scotland but wanted now to be surrounded by the familiar, by people she knew and who cared for her, by her own things and in her own place.

The wind picked up again, sharper, threading through the thin layers of her jacket. It carried with it a scent she couldn't quite place, something that reminded her of rain, but oddly seemed more ancient.

Ivy frowned, glancing around. She shifted her weight, unsettled by the way the land seemed to blur at the edges. The air had gone still, seemed suddenly heavy. A prickle of unease climbed the back of her neck, but now it hadn't anything to do with her anxiety over becoming a single mother. Maybe she was just tired. Maybe the weight of everything—school, the pregnancy, the thought of leaving Scotland and any hope of David changing his mind—was finally catching up to her.

She turned to start back down the trail.

The mist thickened without warning, rolling in low and fast, rose up so quickly that Ivy frowned at it, confused. It curled against her skin, clammy and cold, and for a second Ivy could barely see the trail under her boots. She paused, waiting for the fog to lift — but instead, the ground shifted beneath her. She froze but knew she hadn't slipped or mis-stepped. The land itself tilted subtly, feeling strangely as if the earth had just drawn a breath.

Ivy staggered, lifting her arms to steady herself, and held her breath, puzzled, as she glanced behind her. The trail she'd been following, the narrow ribbon winding between the low stone walls, was gone.

Her stomach gave a slow, sick twist.

The hills were still there, but rougher now, and the stone walls appeared broken and scattered. The grass was longer, thicker, and wild. Farther down, the line of trees looked different, older, thicker, and more plentiful. The air smelled different too, sharp and raw.

Somewhere beyond the nearest rise, a noise broke through the mist. It was distinct, harsh—an unmistakable metallic clash, like metal striking metal, followed by a ragged surge of voices raised in something that sounded closer to anger than conversation.

Ivy went still, straining to listen.

Another clang of metal rang out, closer this time, and another burst of rough voices reached her. The ground vibrated faintly beneath her feet. Ivy took a slow step back, her heart hammering, every instinct screaming at her to run, that something was... so not right.

***

The smoke was still thick in the clearing, hanging low where the trees opened up just enough to let the sun spill through in pale streaks. One of the English wagons had burned hot—its oil casks or pitch stores catching flame—and what was left of it lay in a scorched heap of blackened wheels and snapped axles. Ash clung to everything: the grass, the brush, the folds of plaid wrapped around the Highlanders who had done the damage.

The ground was a churn of hooves, broken crates, and blood—English and Scots alike. A pair of bodies lay near the tree line, blood covering unmoving chests. Another had been dragged toward the ridge where a makeshift triage had begun to take shape. Someone groaned behind the wreckage of a cart, but the sound was weak and growing fainter.

Alaric MacKinlay knelt with one hand braced on his thigh and stared down at the lifeless eyes of a MacKinlay lad, Onlay, whose mother was Alaric's cousin. He closed the lad's eyes and rose to his feet, rolling his shoulders to ease the tension, and had to force himself to unclench his teeth, disheartened by the number of MacKinlay casualties in a strike that should have caused them no harm.

He turned just as his captain came striding across the ruined path.

"Too long we're standing still," said Mathar MacCraith, spitting to one side. His voice was rough, wind-chapped from years of shouting over the clatter of battle and storms. "Ye ken the bastards that ran willna regroup?"

"They might," Alaric said. His tone didn't shift. "But we've lost too much blood already. I willna kill my wounded dragging them half-alive through the forest just to ease yer worry."

"They'll nae live long if they're caught still breathing when the next wave rides through." Mathar's jaw tightened. "We need to push hard now, ride 'em down, and leave nae one to bring word back to Stirling."

Alaric looked past him, toward the ridge where Calum was trying to keep a man's chest bound with his own belt, and Duncan sat white-faced and grim while someone stitched a long cut along his thigh.

"We hold the edge," Alaric said quietly, "and will move when all are ready."

Mathar exhaled sharply through his nose. "If they circle back, then we—"

"Then we'll bleed where we stand," Alaric said, turning from him. "Nae running like frightened stags."

He didn't raise his voice. He never did. When he spoke, men listened—not because he shouted loudest, but because he didn't waste breath on bluff or panic. His words were unflinchingly decisive.

They'd been at this since autumn—raiding patrols, upending wagon trains, slipping into English-held towns in the dark to cut a single tether and scatter the beasts. It wasn't glory they were after. Alaric had no taste for banners or speeches. They were a blunt edge in the king's war—a disruption. A wound that wouldn't stop bleeding.

Not all Scots were resisting anymore. Many had bent the knee when Edward's last truce passed. The Bruce was fighting still, but his name was spoken quietly, like a prayer or a threat, depending on who was listening. Alaric and his men had never stopped. They didn't need declarations and they didn't want a truce. The war hadn't ended for them, not when the English still marched their roads and fed their fires on Highland wood.

"We give the wounded an hour," Alaric said. "Those who can walk, walk. Those who can ride, ride."

Mathar gave a tight nod, his mouth still thin with disapproval, but he didn't argue further. The man was fierce, loyal, and twice as stubborn as most. He didn't ever hide any dissent, but he always followed orders.

Alaric rubbed the back of his neck, the grit of ash and dried sweat crusted beneath his fingers. He didn't like the feel of the place—too quiet now, the birds not yet daring to sing again. The

English had fled south, but that didn't mean they wouldn't come back with twice the number.

They had maybe an hour before that risk sharpened.

Maybe less.

A quarter hour later, Alaric crouched beside the makeshift litter where young Ruaidhrí lay half-conscious, pale and sweating, the shaft of an arrow protruding just below his ribs. The boy's tunic was soaked through with blood, and his breath came in short, wet gasps. Nearby, a knife and several lengths of boiled linen had been laid out on a flat stone, along with a thick iron rod being slowly heated over the embers of a burned-out cart.

"Keep his shoulders down," said Tàmhas, their barber-surgeon, already peeling back the bloodied fabric. "He's a wiry one, and this'll make him thrash like a fish on the line."

Alaric didn't answer. He planted his knee firm beside the boy's hip and set both hands across his chest, gripping hard across the collarbones.

Ruaidhrí's eyes fluttered open, wide and dazed. "I'm nae ready for dying," he whispered hoarsely.

"Ye're nae dying," Alaric said, not unkindly. "Ye're being patched. Hold still, or ye'll give the man more work than he wants."

Tàmhas grunted, already slipping the small curved blade beneath the edge of the arrowhead, feeling for resistance. The tip had lodged shallow, but it had torn something—muscle, maybe an organ. The blood was dark.

The boy let out a broken cry as Tàmhas worked the arrow free, his body jerking beneath Alaric's hands.

"Hold him," Tàmhas barked. "Ye let go now and he'll tear himself open from the inside."

"Aye and am I nae?" Alaric muttered, tightening his grip. Ruaidhrí's heartbeat thudded beneath his palms like a panicked bird. Sweat beaded on the boy's brow, and he made a strangled sound when Tàmhas pressed a cloth into the wound, then reached for the iron.

The stink of burning flesh hit fast. Ruaidhrí screamed once, high and raw, then went limp.

Tàmhas nodded once. "Guid. He's out. That'll save us both some misery."

A moment later, Alaric stepped back, scrubbing a forearm across his mouth. The heat from the iron still hung in the air, mingled with the sourness of fear and blood. He handed Tàmhas the fresh bandages without a word, then turned to scan the edge of the trees again.

Movement caught his eye—just a flicker, something low and tight to the ground. His first thought was a wounded man, dragging himself for cover. But it wasn't.

Half-shadowed behind a spruce at the edge of the clearing, a pair of wide, stricken eyes met his. Not the red-rimmed eyes of pain or fury. Not the hard, narrowed gaze of an enemy.

These were strange. Clear, but panicked. Eyes that didn't belong here at all.

They blinked. Froze. Then vanished behind the tree.

With deceptive nonchalance, Alaric let his gaze wander away from the spot. He reached for the rag tucked through his belt and began wiping his hands, his posture unchanged, his eyes flicking across the camp as if nothing had caught his attention at all. He waited until he'd made an internal count of ten before he moved, passing behind a half-toppled wagon, where one of the older men sat being stitched with blood-darkened thread. The man's knuckles were white on the water skin beside him, his eyes were pinched closed tightly, and he maintained a rigid wince, but made no sound.

Taking a long route across the edge of the wreckage, Alaric circled slowly toward the trees, allowing the battle scene to fall behind him. His bloodied boots found a quiet path between roots and brush as he stepped into the tree line. He moved carefully, not slow, but quiet—hunting not like a predator, but like a man who had hunted long enough to know when silence mattered more than speed.

The trees closed around him, dimming the light.

He curled his fingers around the hilt of his sheathed blade but did not draw as he moved silently through the thickening forest, circling toward the place where she'd first been seen and then vanished. She hadn't gone far, he realized a moment later, creeping up on her figure still crouched behind the trunk of an old spruce.

He knew exactly when she realized his presence behind her, just a few yards away, naught between them but low scrub and brush. She didn't twist around anxiously, didn't bound to her feet. One hand, visible beyond her shoulder, fingers splayed against the rough bark, shifted almost imperceptibly, those slim digits tightening into the skin of the tree. She moved only her head, turning with a measured deliberateness that suggested she was terribly afraid of what she might find behind her, mayhap afraid to trigger an action or reaction, like a hare holding perfectly still hoping the wolf would pass by.

Her eyes, wide and unblinking, locked on him. Carefully, she twisted one foot on the ground, pivoting, and rose from her haunches. Her hands were clenched in anxious fists.

She was young, though not so young as to be mistaken for a lass. Her face was flushed from effort or fear, framed by a fall of burnished hair—gold, copper, something in between—that caught the light through the trees. There was a delicateness to her features, the kind found in noble courts or carved into chapel stone, not in the wilds of a ruined supply trail. Her eyes—green shot through with brown—watched him closely, frightened but holding steady, like a hand trying not to flinch as the arrow was drawn.

She was beautiful. Beyond beautiful, actually, which creased his brow anew. He didn't trust beautiful. Especially not when it showed up silent, wide-eyed, and inexplicable on the edge of a battlefield.

He let his gaze pass over her strange clothes—tight breeches that clung like a second skin, a pale pink tunic that surely offered little warmth, and a soft green coat stitched through with odd seams and buttons like bits of horn. Her boots were near spotless, short at the ankle, strange in shape. The entire lot looked costly, made by hands not meant for work.

And she was, quite obviously, heavy with child.

"Late to catch the convoy," he said flatly after a long moment, his voice cutting through the space between them. "Though I expect they'd nae have left ye behind if ye'd been worth the bother."

She flinched at the sound of his voice. At the same time, her eyes widened.

"Ye a camp girl?" he asked, brow lowering. "Someone's kept thing?"

She moved her hand to her belly, the gesture protective, her breathing shallow.

She said something—soft, uncertain, the words strange and fast, bending in ways no tongue he recognized ever had. Not Gaelic. Not French. Closer to the butchered English of the border.

He stared at her a moment longer. Her gaze didn't break, though he could see the effort it cost her.

"They'll have to stop, to tend their own wounded. Ye should be able to catch up with them." He glanced at her swollen belly again. He had no idea about the appearance of such things, having left to fight before his wife's pregnancy had begun to show, but decided she was neither newly with child nor about to give birth at any moment. She was clean and appeared healthy, though, so must have been well taken care of, which suggested she was a well-favored whore and robust enough to hike away to find the lover who might not have given her a second thought.

Judging her no threat, and deciding she was not his problem, Alaric turned his back on her.

Chapter Two

"Wait!" Ivy called out plaintively after a full ten seconds had passed.

She lurched forward a bit but jerked to a stop when he turned and faced her again. He was possibly the scariest person she had ever encountered. But then, this—whatever was happening—was even more frightening. But this man...who was he? *What* was he? A chaotic trio of descriptors flashed across her brain—*brute, Viking, medieval warlord*. Viking wasn't fitting, though, not really; this was Scotland, after all, and he didn't have blond hair.

The man before her looked like something summoned from another century, some brutal, half-mythic past. Massive and still, he loomed like the embodiment of a warrior king—or a warlord—from the darker chapters of a history book. Easily six and a half feet tall, he was broad in the shoulders and heavy through the chest and arms, the kind of muscle that didn't come from gyms or workouts, but from survival.

A length of worn plaid was slung over one shoulder, and beneath it was a thick linen tunic that was stained with sweat and splattered with blood. Across his chest and belt hung leather straps and weaponry—swords and daggers, looking dull but not unused.

His face was as fierce as the rest of him: high cheekbones, a strong jaw darkened with several days' worth of beard, a straight nose with a slight crook that looked suspiciously like it had been broken at least once. His skin was sun-worn and weathered, tanned in a way that said he lived outdoors, lived rough and dangerously.

And his eyes—wow. His eyes were a searing, golden-brown, sharp and unblinking, like he was assessing every inch of her. Not with lust, not simple curiosity, but with what looked like cold suspicion, disdain even. Obviously, he didn't trust her and was not inclined to pretend otherwise.

He didn't move toward her. Didn't threaten her. And Ivy was too engulfed by confusion to be bitten by so much fear. Her brain scrambled for an explanation for this man—for what she'd witnessed in the last half an hour! —anything that made sense. Ren Faire? Movie set? But this man and what she'd seen, none of it felt staged.

He looked real. So real. As if he'd stepped off the screen of *Braveheart*—if *Braveheart* had been cast with men who'd actually killed people for a living.

And all the while, he was staring at her like *she* was the strange one.

She realized he was waiting for her to say something, that she'd called to him but then hadn't said anything, had only stared in wild wonder at him.

Ivy blurted out the most pressing question, the first thing that came to mind. "Who *are* you?"

He narrowed his eyes at her, the question in them obvious: why did she want to know?

His answer, whatever it was, had her repeating her question, slowly now, enunciating, as if hearing was the issue and not a language barrier. She thought she recognized the sounds he made as Scots Gaelic, but she could only pick out one word, a name: MacKinlay.

"I don't understand," Ivy said helplessly, closing a bit of the ten feet of space between them. "Do you speak English?"

A rustle behind her had her stiffening again and whirling, but it wasn't more danger, not exactly—just three younger men emerging from the trees and brush beyond. Kids, actually, as not one of them seemed to have graduated from his teenage years. Though they were armed as well, none looked nearly as lethal as the first man. One of them—a stocky, ginger-haired boy who couldn't have been much older than seventeen—stopped short when he saw her and favored her with a curious frown. The way he scrunched up his lips added to the expression of surprise.

As the redhead said something in Gaelic to the man with the intense brown eyes, the three youths drifted closer, casually but deliberately, until Ivy found herself surrounded—each of them taking up a loose position around her.

She swallowed slowly, feeling suddenly as if she were now in danger. Curious that, since the angry, towering man hadn't imbued her with so much fear as she felt now. Numbers, she realized. She was now encircled by four men—armed with swords of all things! She gulped and slowly turned back around, moving in time with the three younger men, who now came to stand beside the larger, older man.

The tallest of the three youths, a brown-haired kid with a wide jaw and kind eyes, said something now. The brute who'd discovered her first shrugged and said something in the same language before saying in heavily accented English, "Dinna speak our tongue."

"English?" Asked another youth with a wiry frame and clear blue eyes while his gaze impudently roamed over her from head to toe.

"Aye," answered the medieval-looking brute.

Ivy's heart skipped another beat. They said *English* as if that were a very bad thing. The word and the context landed heavy on her, followed by a flicker of alarm. It wasn't just the way the wiry one said it, it was the way all of them looked at her now. Not hostile exactly, but close. Or maybe it was only caution she glimpsed in their gazes. Evidently, *English* was a loaded term around here, not a compliment in any way. She wondered if some old national grudge was still simmering among these people, whoever they were. Something that obviously hadn't made it into the travel guidebooks.

She cleared her throat, lifting her hands slightly in a show of peace. "I'm not... I'm not English," she said clearly. "I'm American."

Their expressions didn't change too much, but she imagined a thread of confusion ran through them now.

"I'm American," she repeated nervously. "Not English." She wanted that to be clear, hoping it would distance her—literally and figuratively—from whatever beef they apparently had with England.

As a prickle of greater unease crawled up her spine, Ivy decided she didn't much care at the moment to have it explained what she'd witnessed moments ago—she'd have to deal with that later, the trauma of it, since it seemed so real. For now, she thought her best plan should be to simply get away.

"Um, look," she said, slowly, enunciating her English, "I got a little turned around—I'm not sure how—but can someone point me toward the Great Trossachs Path?" When she received only four blank stares, Ivy tried again. "Or maybe Loch Katrine?" Nothing. "Okay, can you tell me where the nearest highway or road is?" More silence. Their confusion only seemed to deepen. Even the brute looked baffled, though on him, the expression took a darker, more menacing shape than it did on the others.

"Okay," she said, forcing a smile. "How about just point to the nearest hiking path? Trailhead? Anything paved?"

The men exchanged uncertain glances, and Ivy felt her stomach twist. Either they genuinely had no idea what she was talking about... or they were *very* committed to their weird medieval reenactment.

To fill what now seemed an awkward silence, she cleared her throat and dared to ask, "So I'm not sure what I saw—or maybe I only imagined it," she added, giving a stiff laugh, "but were you...did I see...?" Her words trailed off, and she glanced at the man with the intense brown eyes. Her shoulders dropped slightly. "What *did* I see?" she asked, quieter now, unable to keep the edge of vulnerability from her voice.

The brute didn't answer right away. His gaze didn't soften. "What did ye see?" he asked finally, the words slow and heavy, thick with his accent.

She gave another sharp, humorless laugh. "It *looked* like I saw some kind of... I don't know—fight? Battle? Maybe a reenactment?" She suggested hopefully. Her eyes widened and she laid her hand on her belly as the baby kicked. After a moment, waiting to see if more movement would follow, she continued, "It just seemed so real. The blood. The sounds. The bodies." Her voice faltered. "I mean, that wasn't cosplay. But it wasn't real... was it?"

No one answered. The redhead and the wiry one were both staring at her belly now, their expressions unreadable.

Ivy turned again to the brute. "I—I thought they were dead...all those people on the ground. They *looked* dead."

He didn't blink. "Aye. So they are."

"Dead?" she repeated, the word catching in her throat. "Actually deceased?"

He gave a single, grim nod.

The breath left her in a rush. Her knees softened, the world tilting just slightly as her body sagged.

Incredibly, the brute stepped forward and caught her with one strong hand at her elbow. His grip was solid and steady—hot, even through her jacket—and the unexpectedness of it made her flinch. She jolted back a little, not sure if she were startled more by the contact or the gesture itself.

Her sharp reaction elicited another scowl from the man.

"I'm sorry," she murmured automatically, holding herself perfectly still now. "Thank you. I'm fine, thank you."

It was untimely and ridiculous, but she couldn't help it—she internally dubbed him the Clint Eastwood of Scotland. That narrow-eyed glint he shot her now reminded her so vividly of her childhood evenings with her grandparents, watching old spaghetti westerns where a squint so often replaced words as dialogue.

He stepped back and Ivy straightened herself, closing her eyes briefly to control her mounting anxiety.

"What name do ye go by?"

Ivy opened her eyes and looked at the speaker, the redhead.

"Ivy," she answered mechanically. "Ivy Mitchell."

"And ye say ye're nae English—though ye sound it," said the kid with blue eyes, "but ye bed down with 'em." He gestured meaningfully to her belly.

Ivy gasped. So much had happened just in the last thirty seconds: death acknowledged so coolly, the brute's jarring touch, the dried blood on the hand of the pointing kid, this blatant insinuation that she'd been knocked up by—what? one of the dead men? His *touch*! Oh, right, she'd already mentally logged that.

Slapping her hands on her hips, she said indignantly to the kid with the bloody hand, "I don't *bed down* with anyone, thank you very much. I had a *relationship* with a man—a Scottish man, by the way, not that it's any of your business. And not that he cares about his baby, but I'll have you know—"

She was interrupted by the brute, though what he said was unclear, since he spoke in Gaelic again. In response, the redhead nodded, the blue-eye youth smirked and scoffed vocally, and the wiry kid frowned and jerked his gaze to Ivy's face.

"What? What did you say?" she asked him.

He shook his head as if it were of no importance—though clearly the responses of the youths said the opposite was true—and turned around, dismissing Ivy once more as he walked away.

That is, until the redhead called after him.

"What's to be done with her?"

The question turned him back around, ten feet away, his frown returned. "With her?" He challenged, a bit of heat in the query. "We've wounded to see to, and dead to bury. Stores to sort and count, wagons to strip, blades to clean, and loot to move ere the flies settle thick." His eyes flicked briefly to Ivy. "She's nae my concern."

He'd addressed the first part of his answer to the redhead and—rudely— turned his attention to Ivy to deliver the last bit, his cold tone making it perfectly clear he didn't give a damn what became of her.

Great.

Before he resumed his exit, the brown-haired kid with the kind eyes challenged him.

"We canna just leave her—"

He stopped when the brute's glare intensified, settling on him with enough force to quiet the kid.

"I only need directions," Ivy said quietly, almost pleading now. "That's all I'm asking." She hadn't yet begun to fully process the fact that she'd seen actual dead bodies or figure out what in God's name was going on, but a part of her shuddered at the thought that his answer could have been something far worse. *Put her to the blade,* or whatever terrifying phrase men like him used.

Men like him?

No. Inconceivable. Ivy had never in her life encountered a man like him.

Five minutes in his company had shown her much, all of it setting him apart from any other man she'd ever met.

Not just for the obvious reasons—the sheer size of him, or the sword strapped across his back, or the way his presence seemed to shift the very air around him—but because everything about him felt carved from another world. But not just foreign, not even something old-world, but something deeper than that. There was no softness to him, no trace of hesitation in the way he looked at her. He was commanding without speaking, dangerous without doing a single thing, and his eyes—those sharp, assessing eyes—held not even a flicker of the usual kindness or curiosity Ivy was used to from strangers. He didn't gawk or leer, didn't employ charm or kindness. He studied her the way a general surely studied the enemy, cold and calculating.

And still... beneath all that steel, there was something else. She'd felt it when he'd jumped to her side, when he'd steadied her. Not compassion exactly, but the ghost of something, maybe something he'd tried to bury long ago.

"But ye've yet to ask the way to any place that exists near here," the brute pointed out, his voice like gravel and ice.

Ivy blinked. "What? I—of course I have. You must know where a road is—any main road that'll get me back to Great Trossachs Path or Loch Katrine. Surely that's not too difficult a task, to point me in the right direction."

That did something. His jaw tightened, and without warning he closed the space between them in long, heavy steps. He didn't touch her, didn't raise a hand, but the sheer size of him, the grim set of his mouth, and the storm brewing in his eyes was enough to make Ivy stumble a step back and suck in a sharp breath.

When he spoke, his voice was low but hammer-hard. "Katrine is forty miles from here. Ye mean to walk it, do ye? In yer state?" His gaze dropped briefly—pointedly—to her belly before rising again with unflinching judgment. "I dinna ken ye will. Or can. I said to ye already—had I nae?—to get moving, follow the trail o' yer company. They'll be moving slow, with wounded and broken wagons. If ye make haste, ye should catch them 'fore nightfall. Or nae. Either way, it's nae my concern."

He turned from her then, the conversation—if it could be called that—clearly finished.

Rude! she thought, though she was still holding her breath.

Her lungs expanded again only after he'd fully turned away, his heavy steps already crunching across the summer—dry ground. But it was no use pretending her heart had returned to a normal rhythm. Not after *that*—the nearness of him, the cold fire in his eyes, the way his presence seemed to swallow up all the air between them.

God, he was *intense*. She hadn't meant to notice, but in that brief, electric moment—when he'd loomed in front of her like some furious mountain—she had seen him. *Really* seen him. Up close, his eyes weren't just brown. They were golden and strange, ringed in darker shades that bled into lighter flecks, like whiskey backlit by flame. His lashes were thick and unexpectedly long, almost too pretty for a man like him. His skin, darkened by sun and weather, was rough in places, his stubbled jaw sharp with tension, his cheek marked with what looked like a faint scar just beneath one eye—old, pale, but unmistakable. And somehow, amid the raw terror of being barked at by a very large, very dangerous-looking man, a ridiculous thought crept in: *he smells like smoke and pine and leather.*

What the hell was wrong with her?

She shook her head hard, willing her brain to reboot. She was lost, maybe concussed—she prayed she had a concussion, it would explain *so* much— probably dehydrated, definitely terrified, and she had no business being distracted by the accidental hotness of some medieval dictator with serious attitude problems.

And yet... even as she watched his broad back retreat, muscles shifting beneath the worn fabric of his tunic and leather straps and sword, a small, maddening part of her brain whispered, *Some people don't just enter your life—they crash into you, like omens or storms. And you know it. Instantly.* There was no thunderclap or dramatic swell of music, but something in her gut said: *you'll be remembering this guy.*

Ivy was disturbed by the thought that somehow it didn't feel wrong. Not even a little.

Shaking herself mentally, she blinked and found the three youths staring at her. Before they, too, departed she asked for some guidance. "I was not with those people—that other group. I assume now they're English, your enemy for some archaic reason. But do you..." she paused and winced a bit, "do you think I might be safer with them? Because I...well, because I sound English, anyway?"

"Ye ken ye're nae safe with us?" Asked the redhead, mildly affronted.

"No," she was quick to protest. "No, not at all." She was, after all, not bleeding, not dead. "I didn't mean it like that. I should have said *welcome.* Do you think I'd be more welcomed by them?"

They conferred silently with each other, exchanging speaking glances before examining her—specifically her face and pregnant belly—before the wiry one replied.

"Ye approach a ruined army deep in the wilds, with nae man, and lass," he said, and inclined his chin and eyes, indicating her middle, "there's nae anything to stop them from taking what they'll ken ye're offering."

"Only one reason a woman seeks out a marching army, ye ken," added the wiry one.

Ivy tilted her head, confused—until the meaning hit. Her mouth fell open in a silent *oh*, the implication crawling over her skin like ice water.

Once again, her shoulders sagged under the weight of it all. Tears welled and clung stubbornly to her lashes, blurring the faces before her. Lately, she cried at anything—thank you, pregnancy hormones, or so the internet had warned her. This was different, however. This was earned. She was lost in a place she didn't recognize, with no understanding of how she'd arrived or how to get back. She'd witnessed what appeared to be an actual battle—real weapons, real blood, real corpses. Not actors, not a reenactment, not pretend, she'd just been told. She was alone, dangerously confused, mildly panicked, and beginning to fear that whatever had happened to her was more than bizarre, but possibly unfixable.

"That'll nae be a concern with the MacKinlays, lass. Neither Cap'n nae the laird would stand for it, any abuse of a lass."

It was the brown-haired, kind-eyed kid who spoke, drawing Ivy's watery gaze to him.

"That," she asked hesitantly, hitching her thumb over her shoulder toward the retreating brute, "was the captain?"

The redhead frowned as if she'd just asked whether water was dry. "That was the laird. Alaric MacKinlay, lass. Son of Torcull. Laird to all MacKinlay kin. Mormaer of Braalach."

"Oh." Actually, that made perfect sense. Of course he was in charge. He didn't look like a man who took orders from anyone.

Still, Ivy looked back to the kind-eyed boy, uncertain why he'd said what he did. The laird had made it perfectly clear she wasn't his concern. "I appreciate you saying that about your leaders not tolerating abuse, but I'm afraid it doesn't help me much if he's not—"

"We'll take ye in," he said evenly, as if it were already settled. "See ye as far as the auld Roman road in the Trossachs area. That should carry ye where ye need."

She blinked. "But he just said—"

"He said ye were nae *his* concern," the redhead cut in with a shrug. "Dinna want the chore of ye. But he'll nae stop us taking ye as far as the road, especially in yer condition."

Incredibly, her chest loosened, her spine straightened. Something about their offer—so practical, so unceremoniously kind—emboldened her. Encouraged her.

"Oh," she breathed, then found her voice. "Thank you. I—I promise I won't be any trouble. I can be helpful," she offered, with a burst of inspiration. "I can tally stuff or ...clean weapons. Or carry things and—whatever you need. I can tend horses," she added, a flicker of purpose returning. "I'm a veterinarian. Or will be, officially, once I sit my boards."

They smiled—not mockingly, exactly, but with a kind of quiet amusement, like older brothers indulging a younger sibling's grand but foolish plans.

Ivy didn't care. She didn't want to be left behind, not between one wrecked army and another victorious one, not forty godforsaken miles from anywhere, not alone and pregnant and entirely out of her depth. How the hell had she ended up forty miles from Loch Katrine? Surely the laird had been exaggerating. He must have been.

"C'mon then, lass," said the wiry one. "we dinna need ye to labor, though. Best to keep ye quiet, out of sight."

"I'll be quiet as a church mouse, I promise," she added, hopeful now. "The laird won't even know I'm there."

That made them laugh—cheerful and warm, but clearly unconvinced—and Ivy was left with the impression that little escaped the laird's notice.

Chapter Three

The forest swallowed them whole.

They moved slowly, away from what Ivy now deemed a battlefield, and deeper into the crags and wooded hills beyond. A slow-moving line of Highland warriors, stained with blood and mud, their bodies tired and their faces grim, melted into the shadows like ghosts. She expected victors to be jubilant—or at least relieved—but whatever they'd won back there didn't seem to bring much satisfaction.

Ivy stumbled along behind the walking men, breath ragged, legs screaming with every step after many hours of hiking nonstop. In the last few minutes, her chest had even begun to protest the long march.

The terrain was merciless. Slick moss coated everything. Jagged stones jutted from the ground like broken teeth. Roots rose from the soil like hidden snares. She'd never hiked anything this rugged in her life—not even on her most ambitious trail days. And now she did it six months pregnant, with still no clue where she was or how any of this was real.

Worse, she'd lost her phone—dropped in her blind flight when she'd first stumbled onto the edge of the battle. That was the only reason she'd gone back toward the smoke and carnage at all, the only reason the brute had found her—she'd been hunting for her phone. And God only knew where the rest of her belongings had ended up. At some point in the chaos she'd shed her knapsack too, though she couldn't even remember when. She hadn't realized it was gone until she'd reached for it and found nothing on her shoulders.

She had yet to ask herself—or anyone—the proper, likely questions, about what had happened. She was still coming to grips with the fact that she'd witnessed what truly felt real, that dusty, bloody, incredible battle. More than once, her brain had suggested in different ways that what she'd seen belonged more to another century, a very long-ago century. The absurdity of that had her dismissing such an idea as ludicrous. She certainly wasn't about to ask. She wasn't going to pull aside one of these men—killers, possibly all of them—and casually inquire why they dressed and spoke and acted like they'd fallen out of a history book. Were they... some kind of undiscovered Highland tribe, like those rare groups deep in the Amazon who'd never made contact with the outside world?

It was almost laughable. Except nothing felt funny.

Alaric MacKinlay remained at the front of the column, a looming figure on horseback, his broad back like a wall of stone atop a magnificent black stallion that looked like it belonged in some mythic painting. Every once in a while, the laird rode by, checking on his army she guessed, going from the front to the end of the line, and back to the front again. On none of these occasions did he glance at her.

He hadn't spoken to her again since he'd agreed—grudgingly—to let her come with them. Actually, he hadn't spoken to her then either. When she'd emerged from the woods with the three younger soldiers hours before, it was the redhead who'd spoken, boldly declaring that they'd see to her, that they'd agreed only to take her as far as the Roman road. The laird hadn't objected, but then he didn't need to voice what his face was saying. The look he'd sent in her direction could have soured milk. His entire posture had stiffened with annoyance he hadn't bother to hide.

"We'll take her as far as Caol Glen," he'd muttered after a moment, with an unexpected fierceness, directing his reply to the redhead and not Ivy. "Nae further."

"Aye, laird," agreed the redhead and the wiry one in unison.

The latter turned and winked at her, as if to say, *told you so*, while at the same time Laird MacKinlay scowled once more at Ivy before turning his back to her again.

As promised, she had tried to make herself useful—though how much actual help she offered was up for debate. The clearing—the scene of the battle—showed a hundred men, maybe more, busy with the aftermath still, and her arrival among them caused a ripple that never quite smoothed out. Obviously, being a woman in this male-dominated space turned some heads. And compared to how they were dressed, she imagined that her clothes—lime green jacket and pink summer sweater, her black leggings, and ankle-high beige nubuck hiking boots—must seem very bizarre to them.

The men stared, some openly. Others looked away as if not wanting to be caught gawking, but they all noticed. She heard muttering when she passed, or in some cases awkward silences. Some murmured to their neighbors, eyes flicking toward her and back again, as though trying to work out just what she was and how she had come to be here. Several gave her a wide berth, suspicion etched into their sun-darkened faces. One man had crossed himself.

Still, Ivy had tried to help.

The redhead, who by then had introduced himself as Kendrick, had shoved a worn wooden bucket into her hands and had pointed her toward a stream fifty feet away, charging her with fetching water. On her return, the three-quarters' full bucket had been wrenched from her hands by a MacKinlay man who might have seen her struggling with the load. He'd yanked it gruffly away from her, scowling, muttering something she couldn't understand.

She'd attempted to calm a skittish horse, murmuring soft reassurances as she reached for the animal's halter—but was sharply warned off by a grizzled handler who barked something in Gaelic and pointed her away with a glower, as though she were a dog nosing around where it didn't belong.

It was only after wandering the perimeter of the clearing that Ivy realized a sort of makeshift triage had been established on the far side. Almost a dozen wounded men had been gathered there, some lying flat on cloaks or animal hides, others propped awkwardly against tree trunks or wagon wheels. The sour tang of blood and sweat hung in the air, and muted groans rose like a background hum. One man winced and groaned as a gash in his thigh was stitched. Another was being hoisted carefully into a cart, his face gray and slack, his arm draped over the shoulder of a soldier who looked no older than fifteen. There were no uniforms, no IV bags, no antiseptic gauze—just ripped cloth, carved sticks for splints, and a handful of harried men who looked to be playing the role of doctor or nurse with whatever tools they had. She stood frozen for a long moment, the grim truth of it all sinking in. This wasn't a movie set. There were no cameras, no paramedics waiting just out of frame. These men were hurt. One appeared to have passed on already, his eyes closed and his face colorless.

After being rebuffed twice already, Ivy had hesitated to offer further help. But then her gaze caught that of a wounded man slumped against tree. He sat propped upright, struggling to draw each breath, his face pale beneath a smear of dirt and blood. One arm hung limply at his side, bent at an unnatural angle, the sleeve soaked through with red. In his hand, a leather flask trembled weakly.

Cautiously, Ivy had approached. She'd knelt beside him without a word and gently reached for the flask, her fingers brushing his. His skin was warm—feverish, maybe—and he hadn't let go at first. But she'd kept her grip steady, slowly easing it from his grasp. Then, holding it to his lips, she'd tipped it carefully. He'd stared at her the whole time, his expression caught somewhere between suspicion and disbelief. At last, he drank—sloppily, noisily—never once looking away from her. Even after she lowered the flask and replaced the odd cap, he hadn't said a word.

That was the pattern. Not hostility, not entirely. Just wariness and curiosity.

Presently, as it had been for hours, the mood of those she walked closest to was brittle. No one spoke to her, but she felt their suspicion. No one offered her water or anything to drink, hadn't tried to converse with her, hadn't acknowledged her at all but with guarded glances. Even when she slipped on a patch of loose shale and landed hard on her hands at one point, no one offered any help. She'd bit back a cry, more embarrassed than hurt, and scrambled up again, brushing her palms on her jacket.

Having predicted hours ago that she'd likely develop blisters from this march, Ivy was not surprised when she began to feel evidence of at least one. It started as just a warm sting blooming at the back of her heel, vague and hardly bothersome. Soon enough, however, it grew slick and raw, as if the skin itself were pulling loose with every step. She tried not to limp, not to fall behind, and not to wince or whimper with each step, but she was losing the battle on all three fronts. The steady shuffle of boots and hooves surrounded her while pride kept her upright—pride, and a small fear that if she stopped, they might simply keep walking right by her, continuing without her.

"Ye're droopin' like a frost-bitten fern," came a voice just behind her, a low, amused observation spoken in a Highlander's distinctive lilt.

Ivy managed a weak laugh as she turned. Kendrick, the redhead, rode up beside her, his lanky frame astride a compact, shaggy-coated dun horse. His face, angular and long, was slightly sunburned, and a coppery stubble that she hadn't noticed earlier or that hadn't been there hours ago dusted his jaw.

She opened her mouth to protest, to stubbornly say she was fine, but then he leaned sideways and extended a hand.

"Come, then," he said. "'Tis a guid beast, and ye'll do nae harm ridin' pillion. Should've kent to offer sooner, but I dinna ken the..."

He let that trail off and she wondered if he'd been about to say he didn't think *the laird* would have approved.

Pride fell by the wayside. She was utterly exhausted, depleted. She took Kendrick's hand and let him half-lift her, grateful beyond words. She swung a leg over and settled behind him. The moment she sat, even with the hard jostle of the saddle, a wave of relief rolled through her. She could have wept from sheer gratitude.

"God bless you," she whispered, wrapping her arms around his lean middle, her belly allowing her to keep some distance between them.

"Aye."

The wiry one trotted his gelding up alongside, and the kid with the kind eyes followed close behind. They moved now as a tight knot within the center of the long column, and for the first time all day, Ivy didn't feel utterly alone.

"I know this is Kendrick," she said to the other two, "but I don't know your names."

"Ewan, I am," the wiry one introduced himself.

"Blair," said the youth with the kind eyes.

"Aye, but his wife calls him *The Clod I Married*," Kendrick teased, grinning.

Blisters and fatigue momentarily forgotten, Ivy blinked hard. "*Wife?*" she echoed with a disbelieving snort of laughter. "How old are you?" Her gaze snapped to Blair—lanky, all elbows and knees, and still carrying the awkward grace of a teenage boy trying to grow into a man's frame.

"Ten and eight," Blair answered, bristling slightly, his jaw tightening.

"And two bairns he has as well," Kendrick added.

"Bairns? Kids?" Ivy repeated, her voice climbing with incredulity. "You have *kids?*"

Blair gave a quick, uncomfortable nod.

Kendrick, in front of her, chuckled. "Aye, we're nae sure how he managed that."

Ewan chimed in from the side, "Ye mean to say, how Marion suffered through it."

Blair flushed crimson, clearly wishing the subject would change, and tried to shift the spotlight. "Kendrick's got hisself a wife and a wee bairn, too."

"*What?*" Ivy gaped at Kendrick's back. "Are you serious?"

"Aye," Kendrick said, shrugging, as if he were not a child-groom. "Married last spring."

Ivy stared at them, struck dumb.

These boys—because that's how she saw them—were married, with children? Her mind reeled. Again, she wondered if they were part of some remote, undiscovered Highland tribe. A community so deep in the wilds they'd somehow missed the last few centuries of progress.

"How old are you, Kendrick?" She had to ask.

"Ten and eight," Kendrick replied.

She turned her stunned face to Ewan, who shrugged sheepishly. "Ten and seven, lass."

"Are you married, too?"

"Nay," Ewan replied, cheeks reddening.

"Nae with that face," Kendrick suggested.

"He has a perfectly fine face," Ivy said, made defensive of him for how uncomfortable he looked right now.

"Aye," Kendrick said with a wink. "Fine for scarin' hens off the kirk steps."

Ivy's mind itched with questions. How could they be so young? And married already, and with kids!

"What *year* is it?" she asked, jokingly, then laughed.

"Year?" Ewan asked. "What do ye ask?"

Ivy shrugged. "I just mean—and no offense—but it all sounds like something out of a long-ago century. I feel like I've fallen down a rabbit hole and landed in the fifteenth century."

While she shook her head over the oddness of what they were saying, she caught the exchange of glances between Kendrick and Blair.

"What?" She asked.

Kendrick harrumphed a small laugh. "Ye say *long ago* and then *fifteenth*, which we dinna ken yet—likely willna live to see."

"Dinna make sense, lass," said Blair.

Ivy's mouth hung open while she processed this. *Wait. What?*

A heavy cloud of heat settled in her chest in an instant. It settled there like a lead blanket—thick, pressing, unignorable. She felt it crawl up her throat and lodge behind her tongue, where the next question wouldn't come.

What were they saying? They had to be confused. Or maybe just teasing her. Right?

But nothing in their faces looked playful now. Not even Ewan's.

What were *they saying?* she wondered, her thoughts now racing. *What do they mean they won't live to see the fifteenth century?*

Suddenly, the trees looked taller, the shadows deeper. Ivy glanced between Ewan and Blair, considering the clothing they wore, the way they spoke, the weapons they carried—the battle she'd witnessed!

But no, the very idea was absurd.

Possibly a full minute had passed before Ewan prompted gently, "Lass?"

"Ye've gone all white, lass," Blair commented.

Ivy forced herself to ask again, seriously now, with a strange dread filling her, "What...what year is it?"

Haltingly, Blair answered, "'Tis the ninth year of King Edward's false rule in Scotland."

King Edward? A wave of dizziness overwhelmed her. She tightened her grip on Kendrick's sides.

"What is the *year*?" She asked deliberately. "In numbers."

"Thirteen hundred and five," Kendrick said slowly, as if wondering why he needed to state the obvious.

Ivy blinked. "No," she said, looking from face to face. "Seriously. What year is it?"

They were all staring at her now.

Thirteen hundred and five. She tried to speak, but no sound came.

While it didn't make sense—obviously it made no sense!—it did explain so much. Right?

Still, it was inconceivable.

The forest closed in. The ache in her feet and legs and chest vanished behind the ringing in her ears.

"No," she whispered. "That's not possible." She shook her head, almost vehemently, as much as her waning energy would allow. "No," she whispered again, the word barely escaping her lips.

Her arms, once tight around Blair's waist, slackened. Her spine went soft, her head tilting backward before her vision turned an unnatural gray. A rushing sound filled her ears, like wind through a tunnel. *Thirteen hundred and five.* It couldn't be. Could not be.

She heard Kendrick's voice, which suddenly sounded as if he were very far away. "Lass?"

She slipped sideways from the saddle, her body a loose bundle of limbs. Kendrick reached for her, but she was already sliding.

"Shite!" she heard him curse as he twisted around.

She dropped like a rag doll into the cool bracken of the forest, a hard fall broken only by Kendrick's hand grabbing hers at the last moment.

When next she had a conscious thought, it was of a vicious voice. Loud, harsh, thunderous. It pierced the fog that held her under. She tried to blink, but her lashes felt weighted. Her limbs wouldn't respond. Something warm cradled her head, and somewhere close by, the forest echoed with anger.

"What in the name of Christ is this?"

The roar came from above and slightly behind her, snapping through the air like a whip.

Another voice, panicked and younger: "She just... she collapsed—"

"Collapsed?" That same deep, growling voice again, fury woven through every syllable. "And nae shite! Yer burden, I said to ye, and ye left her to march for all those miles—she's carryin', damn ye!"

She flinched mentally, even if her body couldn't manage it. Her pulse pounded weakly at her temples. *Carrying?* The word echoed somewhere inside her brain, as if she'd forgotten for a moment.

Bootsteps thundered against the forest floor, each one thudding closer. Then... silence.

The air shifted, becoming warmer, closer. And then a callused thumb brushed her temple, sweeping aside the hair clinging damply to her flushed face. A hand touched the side of her head, her cheek.

"She breathes steady," came the muttered observation—rough, low, angry still.

The fog ebbed and light broke through her lashes. Ivy's eyelids fluttered open, sluggish and heavy, blinking against the blur of light and shadow until the shape above her sharpened. A face hovered in close—sharp angles, bronzed skin, and eyes that burned a rich golden brown, flecked with darker notes that should have frightened her, but strangely didn't just now.

Alaric MacKinlay. Son of Torcull. Laird to all MacKinlay kin. Mormaer of Braalach.

She'd known it even before she'd opened her eyes.

As soon as she met his gaze, he averted his. With practical motions, he shifted his weight and began checking her limbs, his touch clinical but never careless. His large hands skimmed over her arms, pressing gently along the length of each bone, apparently seeking any sign of swelling or tenderness. He did the same to her legs, his fingers firm and methodical as he assessed her knees, ankles, and shins.

Ivy held her breath, not from fear exactly, but from the strange intimacy of it. He wasn't caressing her—far from it—but something about the way he handled her made her pulse thud harder. Not once did he pause, hesitate, or glance at her belly.

His palm flattened lightly against her calf and stroked evenly downward, and she flinched—not from pain, but from what seemed a lover's touch. His eyes flicked up to hers then, a question in his sharp gaze, and she shook her head faintly, indicating no pain. He moved on, his fingers grazing over the laces of her boot, turning her ankle just slightly to test the joint. She exhaled sharply, a breath she hadn't realized she was holding.

"Nothing seems amiss," he murmured, half to himself.

Despite everything—the confusion, the humiliation of fainting, the sheer madness of whatever she'd learned that had made her pass out, his way-too-disturbing touch—Ivy found her voice.

"I'm...fine," she whispered, though it was hardly true.

He sat back on his heels, his gaze flicking once more to her face. "Nae blood. Nae broken bones," he said. "Aye, ye'll be sore come nightfall, mayhap, but nae more."

Her brows pulled together faintly as she looked at him, confusion flickering across her face. There was a strange tenderness in his tone, one she hadn't thought him capable of. For a long moment, she didn't blink, just stared—her gaze full of disoriented questions.

Then, as if realizing how closely he'd been studying her, or maybe how gentle he had been, he looked away and stood in one smooth motion.

Hovering just behind him, the boys were strangely quiet until a rough, nervous laugh came from Kendrick, following whatever the laird murmured heatedly to him.

"More likely taken by madness," he suggested, a bit pale under the laird's glower, "with that being her reaction to being told the year."

Ivy, seeing the laird in profile now, six feet above her, watched as his jaw tightened and shifted angrily, as if he didn't appreciate what he deemed Kendrick's excuse, and as if he were holding himself back from really letting the redhead have it.

"It wasn't his fault," Ivy insisted, trying to sit up, realizing for the first time that she'd stopped the entire army, that she had an audience of more than one hundred men.

Alaric MacKinlay was at her side almost immediately when he realized her efforts. He crouched beside her again with a quiet intensity, his large hands steadying her as she pushed herself upright. One arm braced gently behind her back, the other caught her wrist with a careful grip, guiding her movement as if she were breakable.

His touch was unyielding but not unkind, and realizing that she still felt pretty weak-kneed, she appreciated his presence.

"Slow," he muttered gruffly. "Yer head'll still be spinnin'."

It was. The world tilted slightly, her stomach giving a warning twist, but she blinked hard and nodded, grateful for the solid pressure of his hands.

"I can stand," she said after a moment, when she was on her feet, though she wasn't entirely sure. She closed her eyes, hoping the sweeping wave of weakness would pass.

"And I say ye'll crumple like a wind-toppled sapling," was his response.

She stiffened and held back a yip of surprise when Alaric MacKinlay slid an arm beneath Ivy's shoulders, another under her knees, and lifted her as if she weighed nothing. His arms were like bands of iron, warm and strong.

"She'll ride with me now," he said quietly to the three teenagers, who stood close yet. Then, louder: "Kendrick, walk the rest. Ye can reflect on how a bairn near fell because ye'd nae eye for a woman wearied past her end."

"Aye, laird," Kendrick murmured, flushing.

Ivy stirred against him, protesting the punishment. "I told you, it wasn't Kendrick's fault. He had—"

"Hush."

Wide-eyed now, unaccustomed to being hushed so fiercely, Ivy swallowed her guilt over Kendrick's penalty. Guilt gave way to embarrassment, over the special treatment from the laird, which was heightened by the stunned looks on the faces they walked by. Mortified, she stiffened, and insisted, "I can walk."

"Nae," he argued, "ye canna." Alaric made his way to his stallion, barking to no one in particular as he strode, "Fetch me a breacan. And a skin of water."

With an ease that made her blink, he mounted with her still in his arms, shifting her gently into place before settling behind her. A thick woolen plaid blanket was delivered straight-away, with Alaric grunting his thanks. He shifted, maneuvering the blanket around Ivy.

It was awkward at first. Her legs dangled inelegantly to one side and her back touched his chest. She didn't know where to rest her hands—on the saddle horn? On her lap? On him? She was too aware of him: all hard muscle and heat and strength. She couldn't have been more self-conscious if she were sitting with him naked.

But then the stallion shifted, and so did he, adjusting her gently but securely, tucking her a little closer into the curve of his body. She felt his arm, strong as steel, wrap lightly around her middle to keep her steady. The movement was so natural, so instinctive, she didn't realize until it was done that her hands had settled over his arm, her cheek grazing the soft wool of the breacan between her and his chest.

And just like that, the awkwardness melted away.

This was... nice. So much better than riding behind Kendrick, with her sore limbs jostling and her belly pressing forward with every jounce of the horse's gait. Alaric was solid, unshakable, his body a wall of heat at her back and side, and for the first time since she'd stumbled into this madness, she felt secure. Not understood or even safe in the bigger, existential sense, but secure for now.

At a nod from Alaric, the army began to move again. Ivy watched as the long column stretched ahead into the trees, tired men and plodding horses pressing forward into the crags and shadows of the Highlands.

And then—haltingly, quietly—she asked the question again, this time with a greater fear of the answer.

"What... what year is it?"

Alaric didn't glance down at her, didn't probe what surely must seem an odd question. "Thirteen hundred and five," he answered bluntly. His voice was uninterested, unbothered, as though she'd asked the time of day.

Ivy turned her face toward the now-gray horizon, her eyes blurring with tears, her mind whirring with confusion.

Nothing made sense.

She dropped her head and wept.

Chapter Four

"Have ye pain?" he asked. "Were ye injured in the tumble after all?"

She shook her head, and the loose ends of her russet-gold hair brushed against his chest.

"Then why do ye weep?"

A long moment passed. He felt her chest rise with a deep breath, as though she were trying to steady herself. She gave a small shake of her head again, sharper this time.

"It's nothing," she murmured, voice thick. "I'm fine—sorry, I didn't mean to..."

The words trailed away, and the silence stretched between them, filled only by the muffled sound of hooves on damp earth. He let her be, unwilling to press. But then, after a dozen heartbeats had passed, she spoke again.

"Am I hearing this right?" she asked, her voice smaller now. "That only pain or injury is cause for weeping?"

Alaric stilled at the question.

It had been a long while since he'd sat this close to a woman. Longer still since one had spoken to him in tones that weren't hushed, deferent, or guarded. And he couldn't recall the last time he'd been asked such a question—a question, he sensed immediately, with a trap beneath its surface, like a snare hidden beneath leaves. A man might step wrong and not know until the teeth clamped shut around his leg.

So he tread carefully.

"If ye say ye're fine, I'll nae press," he said after a moment, carefully evasive. "But I've learned folk say such things when they're anything but."

She said nothing to this, but did not cry anymore, not that he was aware.

And yet he had to wonder about her odd query, asking the year, and then considered Kendrick's remark—*taken by madness*—when he, apparently had told her the year as well.

Alaric scowled over the top of her head.

They rode in silence for the next few miles.

By the time the MacKinlay captain, Mathar MacCraith, eased his horse alongside, Alaric was nearly certain the woman had fallen asleep. Mathar matched the stallion's pace and leaned slightly, no doubt checking for himself to determine whether she slept or not, his gaze dipping to the face tucked against Alaric's chest.

A quiet sound escaped the woman—something between a sigh and a soft hum—but she did not stir. Her lashes lay fanned over pale cheeks, and her brow was finally smooth, her earlier tension eased in sleep.

When Mathar straightened, he gave Alaric a look that needed no translation, though he spoke anyway, his voice low and urgent in the old tongue.

"She'll not make it another day in the saddle, not in her state."

Alaric's eyes remained fixed on the road ahead, though the tension in his jaw betrayed that he was listening. Of course, Mathar's unflinching indifference, his hard-edged practicality came as no surprise to Alaric.

Mathar continued, as he always did when he thought Alaric too stubborn to hear the captain's wisdom. "Coire Sionna lies ahead. No more than a half-turn east of the river bend. Barely an hour out of our way. Let the sisters see to her. Let *them* see her to the main road, to safer lands."

Alaric protested mildly. "The pass at Caol Glen is more direct than the priory."

Mathar huffed softly and gave a dry snort. "And yet I cannot see you abandoning the lass even then, certainly when the nearest burgh or house is still miles away. Put her into safe hands and be done with it."

When Alaric said nothing, only clamped his lips, Mathar pressed with startling insight.

"I saw how you leapt at her when she fell," he said, his voice quieter, "saw the look in your eyes. She's not Gwen, lad. This lass, whatever her woe, is not yours to save."

Alaric's grip tightened, almost imperceptibly, around the sleeping woman. He'd already reckoned as much. Knew well enough what had stirred him the moment her body had crumpled from the back of the horse, when he'd gone tearing through the ranks like a man possessed. It wasn't Gwen, he knew that, but there was something in the sight of her, lost and fragile, belly full with child, that had struck like a blade between his ribs when he'd witnessed her tumbling off the horse.

For one terrible breath, he'd seen another woman entirely. Though the circumstances were wholly different, worlds apart in context, the memory of it had flashed through his brain.

Just as quickly, the old guilt had resurfaced, not that it was ever far from reach, not that it didn't plague him with maddening frequency.

He'd made the choice once—wife or child—and had lost both. The memory of it never dulled, only lingered, deep and bitter. And maybe that's what had spurred his reaction before his thoughts had caught up—some cursed piece of him still trying to atone for what couldn't be undone. Aye, the lass in his arms wasn't Gwen. But that hadn't stopped his blood from turning to ice when she fell.

Mathar's voice lost its brief gentleness, reminding Alaric of their purpose. "There's vengeance to be had, lad. A reckoning. We're the last thorn in Edward's bloody side, and he kens it. While other men bend the knee and feast under false banners, we bleed in the hills. That was the pact. That was the oath. Do not forget it now. It takes precedence over all else, including things that are none of our business and lost causes—even bonny ones."

Alaric finally exhaled through his nose, slow and steady. "We'll take the eastern fork at the river," he said, his tone clipped. "If the sisters are willing to accept her, then so be it."

Mathar nodded once, satisfied with the answer but scarcely fooled by the evasion.

"Will you never forgive yourself?" he asked after a pause.

It wasn't the first time Mathar had asked him this, it probably wouldn't be the last. Alaric replied as he sometimes had in the past, when he bothered to reply at all. "Would you be able to?"

Mathar didn't respond. He gave a small grunt of understanding, shifting in the saddle and letting the moment settle before he nodded grimly and rode a bit ahead, surely to advise the scouts and the fore-guard of their change of direction.

Alaric shifted slightly, once again adjusting his hold on the sleeping woman, willing his thoughts to silence. One woman wouldn't change the course of war; this small detour wouldn't—couldn't possibly—affect the outcome.

More pertinently, she wasn't Gwen. And this wasn't then, seven years ago.

And still, as his horse picked its path through the darkening wood, and as the army soon faced the dark sky of the east, Alaric couldn't help but feel the press of fate at his back, as if a hand was guiding him down a road he hadn't meant to take.

It was nearly half an hour later, long past the burnished gold of dusk, when he felt her wake. Not with a start or jolt, but a slow stirring. Alaric glanced down, already aware of the way her breath had changed, no longer the deep, even rhythm of sleep, but lighter, more restless.

She blinked and pulled away from his chest, turning and raising her face to him.

The moon had climbed above the trees, casting a cool gleam across the forest floor. He caught only a glimpse of the silver light reflected in her eyes before she faced forward again.

"Yer awake, then," he said quietly. "Do ye ken where ye are?"

"Still riding," she murmured, her voice low and scratchy. She shifted her weight, then stilled again quickly, perhaps remembering her position—cradled against his chest, his arm around her, his hand settled over the swell of her stomach. A sigh was felt more than heard. "And having no more idea where we are now than I did earlier when you...discovered me."

He gave a slow nod. "What's yer name, lass?"

"Ivy. Ivy Mitchell."

A curious name, a plant in English if he recalled correctly. His brows pulled together slightly, but before he might have questioned her about this, she said, "I know yours. Kendrick enlightened me," she clarified. "Right after... after the fight, or actually, after you left me with them—Kendrick, Blair, and Ewan."

She was seated side-saddle and thus her back was not square to his chest. She was angled just enough that a simple glance down revealed a quarter view of her face, an upper view of part of her profile. Her brows were knit. Even in the dark, she was pale. She looked less breakable than she had earlier, but still worn, like a ribbon thinned by wind and weather.

"He called you laird," she said.

"Aye."

She swallowed, then gave a stiff nod, as though unsure what to do with that information. She curled her fingers slightly against the breacan, brushing the thick wool mindlessly.

"So you're... in charge of this army?"

"Aye."

"And your mission is what? Were you chasing those English from earlier? Or did you happen upon them?"

Curious about questions regarding a topic that should be of no interest to a mere woman, Alaric frowned and answered carefully. "We were lucky, came upon tracks, and gave pursuit."

"And you—and your army—killed all those Englishmen? All those dead bodies I saw?"

"Aye."

"Were...were they particularly *bad* or dangerous Englishmen? Or do you simply believe that the only good Englishmen are dead Englishmen?"

"What is it ye're meaning to ken?" He asked, his frown intact.

She drew in a large breath and released it, only a wee bit shakily. "I'm just trying to figure out if there's actually a war going on, or if you're some kind of vigilante or...I don't know, like a rogue knight, who rides around looking for a fight."

His brows pulled closer together in a tight, displeased line. Aye, the name suited her—quiet at first glance, but clinging, persistent. Ivy. Not thorny, no—but she had a way of curling into the cracks of a man's guard before he even noticed.

"We are at war," he reminded her. "A war that's nae likely to end soon."

"With England?"

He glanced down sharply, giving her a sidelong glance as if to be sure she wasn't mocking him. "Aye," he said, stating what should have been known to her, clipped and cool. "With England."

"I thought I read somewhere that in 1305 there was a—" she broke off abruptly and then started again. "Isn't there a truce now?"

He stiffened. "Aye. Some say so."

"And you?"

"I dinna make pacts with men who butcher bairns and murder thousands, trying to seize what doesnae belong to them."

"So if you don't follow the truce, are you part of some rebel army?"

His jaw twitched. "We're nae rebels," he said emphatically. "'Tis our land. We dinna rebel against it. We fight to keep it."

"So you're a patriot," she said, with a strange note in her voice—as if she were weighing the word. "A freedom fighter."

"Call it what ye like," he muttered, bewildered by her questions, her seeming lack of understanding about... anything. Everything.

They rode for another stretch in silence, the wind threading softly through the trees, and she pulled the breacan more tightly around her.

"What were ye doin' out there this afternoon?" he asked when several minutes had passed. "Near the clearing?"

The hesitation was visible. Her breath seemed to catch.

"I don't know," she said at last.

The scowl that had only seconds ago eased, returned. "Ye dinna ken?"

She shook her head faintly. "I mean... well, yes—I don't know. I have no idea how I got there. I was literally just out for a walk, hiking the Great Trossachs Path—Loch Katrine was only a couple of miles away," she said. "That's why I asked if I could be taken back there. I thought if I got back there, there'd be... something. Help. People. A road." She shook her head thoughtfully. "I still have no idea how I got to where you—and the fight—were. You said it was forty miles away. I don't understand how that happened or why Kendrick said it was—"

She stopped herself abruptly, but Alaric asked the question that had been bothering him, which he believed she'd just stopped herself from addressing. "Why did ye need to ask the year?" Alaric's voice was low. "Why did Kendrick's answer cause ye such distress?"

Ivy Mitchell sagged against him, her spine curving into his chest as if the fight had gone out of her. "I... I can't explain it—or rather, you'd never believe me."

"Ye willna even try?"

She gave a short, mirthless laugh. "I don't even know where to start. I haven't made sense of it myself." She exhaled, slow and weary. Her mouth opened and closed but she said no more just then.

He studied the top of her head, the subtle tension still clinging to her frame. "Were ye struck in the head? Fevered? Or insensible for some long stretch—long enough that hearing the year would rattle ye so?"

Her slim shoulders lifted in a faint shrug. "I don't know—no. No, that's not possible. That's... backwards."

"Ye speak in riddles," he said, not unkindly, though the edge in his voice betrayed his mounting frustration. *She* was backwards, he decided. There was something off about Ivy Mitchell, something that scraped against sense. It wasn't only her strange arrival in the midst of a bloodied battlefield, or the garb she wore, or the way she laced her words with unfamiliar cadence—it was this fumbling, shifting refusal—or inability—to explain herself. And Alaric, a man who trusted action over answers, found her vagueness unsettling in a way he couldn't name.

Another few moments of silence passed between them before Ivy tilted her head and face up at him. "But is it really thirteen hundred and five?"

Again with the year, while she refused to answer his questions about it. His rising anger was tempered, however, by the sight of tears once again glistening in her eyes.

"Aye, it is. Same as it was earlier when ye asked Kendrick, when ye asked me," he said, his tone harsh despite the tears.

She lowered her face and turned away from him. "Okay, I'm sorry," she said, sounding weak and small now. "I won't ask again."

Supposing that he should feel like a brute for what she might deem his insensitivity, he nevertheless managed to cling to his annoyance, unable to rouse any sympathy. Aye, she was beautiful. And aye, her condition counseled caution, but he wasn't about to be swayed by either her inadequate words or her weeping.

"Keep yer secrets, Ivy Mitchell," he muttered. "We'll be parting ways soon enough."

Whatever her reaction was or might have been would remain unknown to him, for at that moment, the sound of a swiftly approaching horse reached his ears. The rest of the army was moving at a steady walk, their pace plodding after so many long hours, and what little noise they made was swallowed by the forest.

This new sound was different, urgent, a lone rider, moving fast. One of the scouts, undoubtedly. And scouts only rode like that when something was wrong.

Alaric straightened in the saddle, his body tensing. He felt Ivy shift, too, her spine stiffening as she pushed herself more upright against him.

"What is—?" she began.

"Laird!" came the shout, ringing across the slow-moving line of men.

He kneed the stallion and moved from the middle of the column toward the front. A scout came riding through the trees from further east—Struan, one of the younger scouts, lean and quick, with a keen eye and a stronger sense of urgency than most. His mount was lathered and panting, flanks streaked with sweat, and he hauled the beast to a jarring stop just before them, chest heaving as he leaned low over the saddle horn.

"The priory," he said. "Coire Sionna is empty, my lord. Half-burned. A shell."

"Recently burned?" Alaric asked.

"Seems so, but nae just today," said Struan. "Mayhap yesterday or the day before."

"English?" Mathar questioned, having come to Alaric's side.

Struan shook his head. "Canna say. Too dark to ken."

Alaric nodded and instructed Mathar, "We'll take the cavalry to the priory. Advise the foot soldiers to be vigilant. Keep them along the eastern edge of the wood, off the main road until we've swept the ground proper."

Mathar gave a grim nod.

"Send half a dozen scouts ahead to circle wide and make certain we're nae riding into a trap. I want eyes on the hillocks and the rise behind the ruins. If there's English lurking nearby, I'd have them found before they ken we're here."

"Aye, laird," Mathar obliged.

"And if they find signs of English—fresh prints, dung, campsites—I want word swift. We'll nae linger near smoke-stained stone if it draws carrion." He would not abide near the burnt priory if it risked drawing danger to his men.

Mathar gave another curt nod and turned sharply, already barking orders down the line.

Alaric nudged the stallion into motion, guiding it through the darkening trees with one hand while he braced the other securely around Ivy. He didn't dare a full gallop, not with the woman in his arms. But the pace was hard enough that the trees blurred on either side in their rush. Still, he did something he'd never done before, allowing several riders to outpace him.

He was always the first into battle. The first into the breach. The first into the unknown. But not tonight, not with her pressed to him, warm and vulnerable and entirely unfit for war. He kept to the center of the column, eyes sharp, pulse steady, every muscle poised to react. A thousand choices lay ahead if danger surfaced—and none of them left room for hesitation.

Unbidden, his thoughts turned dark. What if there were some English still nearby? What if they'd torched the place only to return in the night, seeking to finish what they'd begun? Or to use what remained as either their camp or as a launching place?

He cast a glance downward at the small shape in his arms. Despite her round belly, she leaned over the pommel, allowing him to lean into her back, their urgency surely felt by his steed. He considered that she had no armor, no weapon, no notion of survival, he might guess.

What would he do if steel rang through the trees again? If arrows flew or the night erupted with English war cries? He couldn't fight with her in his arms. Couldn't leave her either. He would have to make a choice—and quickly. Dismount, hide her? Find shelter amid stone or shadow? Hope she kept still. Hope she survived the decision.

His jaw clenched as the trees thinned, and the scent of scorched wood began to taint the wind.

The priory came into view all at once—stone bathed in silver moonlight, the outline of its once-proud walls jagged and blackened, like broken teeth in a ruined mouth.

Alaric reined in with those who'd stopped ahead of him.

The skeletal remains of the chapel loomed ahead, its roof gone, the bell tower toppled. Half the compound lay in charred ruin, the other half cloaked in silence. No candlelight. No sign of nuns, or life. Just a softly lifting smoke, winding through the shattered rafters like a ghost reluctant to leave.

Alaric drew the stallion to a halt, his eyes narrowing as he studied the smoldering timbers. The fire hadn't burned hot or recent enough to send up flames, but the warmth still clung to the stones, and thin threads of smoke rose from blackened beams and all the other collapsed wood areas.

It wasn't fresh, he decided soon enough, it just hadn't happened today. A day past, perhaps two, long enough ago for survivors to have fled. But just to be sure, he turned toward the man at his side, Calum. "Take a few men and look inside for bodies. Or survivors," he thought to add, but that hope seemed futile.

In truth, he didn't know yet if the fire had been intentional or even malicious. He only supposed it was, assuming that if not, he might have found nuns and the priory's lay persons lingering—tending the wounded, salvaging what they could, clinging to the remnants of their sanctuary. But there was nothing. No voices in prayer, no rustle of habits, no soft footfalls in the ash, only silence. Even the crackle of a fire had quieted by now.

His eyes raked the yard and fields and dark forest edges around the priory. He discerned no movement, no riders, no threat. But he didn't always trust the quiet.

Behind them, hooves thudded softly as Mathar and the rest of the riders approached. But Alaric kept his gaze ahead, on the ruined priory, the scorched altar visible through the crumbled door.

The world felt cold.

And then a misting rain began to fall.

"Casualties?" Mathar inquired.

Alaric shook his head, peripherally aware of Ivy clasping his hand over her waist now. "Nae yet. The lads are searching."

"Then where are the sisters?"

Alaric's gaze swept the scorched yard again. "Gone before the fire, if they had any sense. Or... taken."

Mathar spat into the mud. "Burning nuns now, are they?"

"They've burned worse," Alaric said flatly. "Churches. Crofts. Children."

Mathar gave a grim nod. "Aye. Nae longer content to fight men with swords, so they make war on the blessed and meek."

A silence followed, broken only by the soft hiss of rain striking charred stone.

"They dinna go quiet," Mathar said at length. "Mistress Barbara would nae have."

No, she wouldn't have, Alaric silently agreed. His father's aunt was as ferocious as he understood Longshanks to be.

They sat and stared for several moments in silence, until Ivy broke it, her voice faint.

"Were you expecting to drop me off here?"

"Aye."

"And now?"

Alaric didn't answer, save to curse quietly under his breath.

Chapter Five

Rain had doused the worst of it.

Though soot still clung in streaks to the stone walls, and the scent of charred wood lingered faintly in the damp air, what had remained of the fire itself had died. Smoke no longer rose from the ruined chapel, and what remained of the convent stood in quiet surrender beneath the fine mist that drifted through the trees.

The part of the convent where Ivy now stood was built entirely of thick, ancient stone, the walls so wide she could sit inside the windowsills. It had likely been the heart of the convent when it was first raised, fortress-like, weathered by time but still strong. The corridors were narrow, the ceilings low, the architecture Romanesque, with rounded arches and vaults of simple elegance. It was colder here, and darker, but solid, utterly untouched by fire.

Outside and elsewhere, however, the damage was obvious.

The central courtyard, once surrounded on all sides, was now open to the night sky. Charred beams lay scattered where wooden cloisters and storage sheds had stood. Roofs were gone. The walls of the refectory and dormitory had been constructed more hastily, clearly added over the years, timber mixed with wattle and daub, practical for expansion, but no match for flame—Ivy wouldn't have known all that, but had overheard Alaric remarking as such to others who'd come inside as well.

It smelled like wet ash and cold stone. Beneath that, she caught faint traces of wax and wool and old lavender, like ghosts of lives once lived here, the kind of scent that clung to old trunks in forgotten attics. Her breath fogged faintly in the rain-damp-ened chill, and she pulled the thick wool blanket tighter around her shoulders. Moments ago, she'd brought up the hood of her jacket to cover her head. Her body ached in strange places—her back, her hips, even her arms, likely from the hard day's ride.

Nearby, Alaric was still speaking with the grizzled older man she'd noticed earlier—who seemed to be of some importance as he was often by the laird's side—and several others in low tones. Ivy edged toward the corridor to listen.

"Was a proper compound once," said the older man, scanning the damage. "Old heart still stands, by some miracle. Rest was additions. Too much timber. Nae enough foresight."

"Too many years of peace," Alaric murmured grimly. "Or fools who thought the English would respect the sanctity of nuns."

The older man, bearing a nasty scar on his face, snorted. "They'll burn anything. I doubt they stopped to ask whether God was watching."

Alaric's gaze swept the surviving structure. "The old wing—she'll hold. Stone's too thick to breech without siege. We can post watches at the halls and entryways, and around the perimeter. It's defensible, for a time."

"Aye," said the older guy, nodding. "Might serve us a few days. Let the lads find their ease, patch their boots—the wound-ed can rest—and we'll send scouts in every direction, dig out the truth of what happened here."

Alaric was still surveying the ruins, kicking aside what looked to be a toppled piece of furniture, a wooden screen, a room divider maybe. "Let us hope there are nae truths buried in the ash."

A movement caught Ivy's eye, low and swift in the corner of the entryway. A small mouse scurried across the uneven stones, pausing near the wall where it sniffed at something unseen. Ivy blinked at it, inexplicably comforted by the sight. Life. Fragile, enduring, searching. She crouched slowly, careful not to startle it, and watched the tiny creature vanish through a crack in the base of the wall. A thread of hay trailed after it like a tail.

A group of men were searching what remained of the all-stone parts of the ancient convent. They lit candles here and there, golden light beginning to fill the space, and shimmering in the narrow corridors that sprang out from this main hall. Ivy had a suspicion that Alaric didn't expect them to find anything, no enemy anyway, or he'd have led the search himself. She wasn't sure why she thought that, how she'd reached that conclusion about him, but sensed she was right. They returned as Ivy was attempting to rise from her squat, a small action she'd not have thought twice about even a month ago. She teetered a bit as she tried to stand and had to put her hand to the ground to steady herself before she pushed upward again. At the same time, a shadow loomed over her and a large hand latched onto her arm, helping her rise.

Mildly startled, she glanced up to find the hand belonged to the laird.

"Oh, thanks."

He did not acknowledge this, but said, "We'll make camp here for the time being, this part is safe. Ye can rest, find a cell abovestairs to—"

"A cell?" she questioned, blinking.

Naturally, he scowled at her interruption, but did clarify, "A chamber, the nuns' quarters."

"Oh, I see."

"Make yerself comfortable, get some sleep."

"What will you be doing?"

"We've got to secure the area and I—" he stopped and shook his head, a bit gruffly. "I'll be gone for a while," he said next, vaguely, as if he didn't like having to describe his plans to her.

"But is some of your army staying here?" she pressed, trying not to sound anxious. Or was he simply dumping her here anyway, as he'd intended before he knew the convent had been burned?

His features tightened, forming yet another deep crease between his brows. "Aye. Ye'll nae be left alone here."

Sensing he'd been mildly offended, she nodded but said no more. If she knew him any better, if she wasn't still a little intimidated by him, she might have challenged, *Well, you were happy to abandon me earlier today, saying I wasn't your concern.*

He left her then, following the others he'd been conferring with outside.

Ivy remained still, face turned toward the open door. Muted voices echoed through the rain-drenched gloom. Alaric's was among them now, low and clipped, issuing orders to his men. She couldn't make out anything as he was speaking his Gaelic again. The sounds blurred together, war-speak in a foreign language, she guessed, but the tone was unmistakable: firm, decisive, utterly in control.

Ivy turned, her gaze sweeping the narrow corridor behind her. She moved in that direction. The space was cold but dry, and she saw that candle sconces had been lit on the walls. Beneath some of those fixtures, wax melted in long crooked lines down the stone. A few doors stood open, revealing rooms that seemed more utilitarian than welcoming, surely not bedrooms. She continued along the corridor, finding a spiral staircase, and climbed to the next level. Here, all the doors were closed. She peeked in a few, discovering that *cell* was certainly an appropriate term, each room small, no bigger than a walk-in closet, with little more than a narrow cot, squat table, and a deep-set window no wider than her forearm. Stark, quiet, spare—a cell indeed, which smelled of musty linen and old stone.

She pressed on. The scent of soot still lingered faintly in the air, but less so here in the ancient wing. Somewhere deeper in the priory, water dripped steadily, tap, tap, tap. She passed another narrow staircase that spiraled upward, its top lost in shadow. Beyond it, the corridor turned, and Ivy paused, caught by the shifting silver light that spilled from a partially open door. She pushed it open farther and stepped inside.

Unlike the bare cells she'd encountered thus far, this one was a large bedchamber and held a carved table and a padded chair near the hearth. A faded tapestry hung on one wall, a Madonna cradling a lamb. Shelves of books lined one corner of the room and a trunk sat beneath the window, its latch a dull silver. The bed frame was carved wood, four posts, the mattress appearing far more plush than those thin ones on the small cots.

Mother Superior's room, she imagined—or whatever they called the head nun in this century.

While the bed looked ten times more inviting than any other one she'd seen yet, she was not at all so presumptuous as to claim this room for herself. She slipped quietly back down the corridor, and continued to open doors, snooping around.

At some point in her quiet wandering, Ivy found what must have been the convent's old garderobe—a narrow stone closet with a built-in bench over a shaft that disappeared into darkness. The smell alone convinced her it was still in use, or had been until very recently. Another chamber, tucked behind a shuttered door, held a porcelain pot discreetly set behind a curtained panel. Ivy hesitated only a moment before stepping inside and closing the door. She might be seven centuries out of place, but some needs were timeless—she was seven months pregnant after all. Possibly only the trauma of the day had kept her mind off her need to pee.

As she made her way back down the corridor, she didn't miss the way the smooth stone walls and worn lintels whispered *authenticity* at every turn. The hallway was dim and cold, but her fingers trailed along the rough stone wall as she walked, finding small comfort in its permanence. Clearly, she could not dismiss this place as a staged set or some elaborate trick of trauma or delusion. Certainly not when the bathroom situation felt convincingly medieval.

Eventually, with little else to do or explore, she decided on a room to use for herself, one of the small cells closer to the first set of stairs she climbed.

Inside, sitting atop the bedside table, was a small squat taper in a metal holder, the wick blackened from previous use. Ivy took possession of the candle and stepped out into the corridor, lighting the wick from the one of the torches in the wall before returning to the room she'd chosen. The flame was weak, barely enough to push back the gloom but she had no intention of sitting or even sleeping in complete darkness.

She closed the door behind her, returned the candle to the table, and rubbed at her arms as she sat down gingerly on the cot. Her mind spun, sluggish and yet scattered, but she was too tired to chase answers. Outside, the rain tapped gently on the roof, a soft rhythm against the silence of stone.

Imagining that it must be near or past midnight by now, Ivy sighed and thought to catch what sleep she might. She didn't undress but did remove her boots and socks before she curled on the cot with the coarse wool blanket tucked beneath her chin, the small window offering a square of inky sky. She thought the rain might have stopped, but that the wind had picked up.

And, as often happened, the moment she laid down her head, her mind began to churn. The ache in her limbs begged for sleep, but her thoughts were relentless.

Somehow—impossible as it seemed—the most unbelievable, dramatic event of the day hadn't yet been fully examined. She hadn't had the space, the silence, the *stillness* until now to let the thought in. Maybe because she didn't believe it. *Couldn't* believe it!

Because how did someone accept that she'd fallen through time?

How did a rational, modern woman—one who had driven stick-shift cars and filled out tax forms and read books about political theory in undergrad—suddenly nod and say, "Yes, that seems reasonable. A hike through the Scottish Highlands ended with me waking up in an actual medieval war zone."

She closed her eyes, trying to slow her breathing, but the images and impressions flooded back—men with swords, horses with iron-plated tack, the press of Alaric's arm across her body as they'd ridden through the dark. Lifeless, bloodied bodies. The scent. The accents. Even the cold, which felt different, deeper. None of it added up unless she believed the only explanation that *made* any sense.

But how could she make sense of the senseless?

She rolled to her other side, ears straining in the silence. Every little sound felt amplified—the tick of water dripping against stone, the wind's breath against the eaves, some distant clang she couldn't identify. A creak in the beams made her sit up slightly, heart kicking. It was nothing, probably the wind. Or maybe one of the soldiers posted nearby. But still, her ears stayed tuned to every faint shuffle, desperate to identify noises to know peace.

Her stomach turned. She pressed her palm to it, feeling the swell of her pregnancy, the undeniable presence of the baby who'd had no choice but to come with her through time. Her mind tumbled over the questions again: Was she delusional? Was this a coma? Some elaborate historical reenactment gone disastrously wrong?

But that didn't explain how real everything felt. The ache in her joints. The smoke in her hair. The very elemental need to pee all day.

She stared at the stone wall, rough and ancient, perhaps older than anything she'd ever touched before. Her fingertips brushed the mortar. It was cool and solid, though little comfort it offered now.

She jerked her head around, toward the door, when another noise startled her, sounding entirely too close to the door to her cell. After a moment, when she heard nothing else, she settled again.

So what did it mean, if this was real, that she'd actually moved through time?

Her chest tightened. She simply had no idea.

If she was really in the first years of the fourteenth century, how was she going to survive? Good Lord, how could she possibly have a baby in the fourteenth century?

Time passed until her brain exhausted itself, and she began to drift off. She didn't know if minutes or hours had passed since she'd laid down when she heard the faint creak of the door.

It opened just a sliver.

Ivy froze on the narrow cot.

A dark silhouette filled the gap, highlighted by those sconces in the corridor, and it took no time at all for her sleepy brain to recognize Alaric MacKinlay. She breathed again. He stood there a moment—silent, impassive. Maybe he was only checking that she was present, perhaps asleep.

"I'm awake," she said softly, pushing herself upright on her elbows.

He paused a moment before the door opened wider, and he stepped inside just two steps.

"Did you find anything?" she asked, voice low. "Anyone?"

"Nae," he said simply, the word as heavy as the stone walls around them. He didn't elaborate.

"I'm sorry." She watched him for a moment. His shoulders were damp with rain. His jaw was tight, the flickering torch behind him casting harsh shadows along the angles of his face. "How far did you go?" she asked, uncertain why she felt so invested in strangers she had never met, nuns she couldn't possibly know and the MacKinlay army, the laird specifically.

"Far enough for tonight. We'll go out again in the morn."

Ivy nodded.

He lingered a second longer, then stepped back into the corridor, murmuring something in Gaelic as he began to pull the door closed behind him.

"Wait," she said, before she could stop herself.

She climbed out of the bed and approached him just as he paused and slowly pushed the door open again. The sharp iciness of the stone floor on her bare feet widened her eyes.

"Where are you going?" she blurted out and then caught herself, and asked a different question, to better get across what she really wanted to know. "Where are you sleeping?"

The question seemed to startle him.

"I just mean—you'll be... close, right?" She was positive she would rest easier, sleep better, if she knew this strong, capable man were close by.

His scowl lessened, and he seemed to understand she was anxious. "Aye." He paused and stared at her. "If ye...need, I can post a sentry just outside yer door."

"Oh, gosh, no. I don't need you to do that, but, um, maybe could you take this room right next door?" She asked, feeling small and weak, but determined to know some peace with his close proximity. Nervously, she pointed to the wall at her left, beyond which her nosing around had already shown her was another small cell like this.

Alaric hesitated, his expression unreadable in the dim light. Then, with a short nod, he said, "Aye. I'll see that it's occupied."

She noticed that he hadn't specifically said he would occupy the room.

He turned slightly, half ready to leave, but then his gaze dropped. His eyes fell to her bare feet, still pale and chilled, and he went suddenly still. And then his entire body jerked back a fraction, as though he'd just spotted a snake curled beside her toes.

"What is—?" His voice faltered, and he pointed abruptly, his brows knotting tightly. "Is that... is that blood?"

Startled, Ivy looked down, following his wide-eyed stare to her red-painted toes.

"Oh! No." She huffed a small laugh, more breath than sound. "No, it's not blood."

He didn't seem convinced. "It glints in the torchlight. Red... shimmerin'. Ye—ye're not wounded?"

"It's not blood," she repeated, gentler this time, lifting one foot between them to show him. "It's nail polish. You know—" She caught herself. "Well, no. You don't know. It's paint. For toes. A cosmetic thing. But not... not war paint or anything."

She could see the confusion in his eyes, the effort it took while he attempted to categorize this strangeness. His gaze returned to her feet, then back to her face, then again to her feet.

Ivy grinned, rather amused by his befuddlement. "It's just a thing some women do," she added. "Paint their toenails. It's pretty," she informed him. She was and always had been a firm believer that unpainted toes were very unattractive.

He made a low sound in his throat—part grunt, part exhale—then slowly nodded, still clearly baffled.

The corner of her mouth lifted again, but her good humor didn't last.

Because his face—that reaction, his bewilderment—was just more proof. Proof she wasn't crazy, and she wasn't merely dreaming. She was far, far from home, hundreds of years from anything familiar.

Her smile fell. The air between them cooled again.

Alaric seemed to catch the shift in her but said nothing. He gave another small nod, this time more to himself than to her.

"I'll be nearby, if ye have a need," he said at last, voice low and sure once again.

Then he was gone, the door closing with a whisper-soft scrape behind him.

***

Light spilled across the rough flagstone floor, bright enough to rouse Ivy from a fitful sleep. She blinked against it, her body heavy, her mouth dry. For a moment she lay still, remembering where she was, the stone cell, the narrow cot, the fourteenth century.

She closed her eyes and sighed, her hand reaching for her belly, concern etching her brow. She had to wait several minutes before she felt her stomach leap. Ivy smiled in relief. A moment later, she laughed softly when her stomach continued to move.

But then the other truth dawned on her and her smile slid away. Nothing had changed. Or rather, she hadn't woken from this dream.

After another few minutes, she sat up. Being seven months pregnant meant that having to pee was a near-constant state of being. She cringed internally at the thought of making use of the garderobe during the day, possibly running into or being walked in on by a MacKinlay soldier.

She thought for a minute before she stood, having made a decision. Though she had no idea how long they'd make use of this place, one thing was certain: men had less need of a chamber pot than a woman—especially a pregnant woman. With that in mind, she tiptoed down the cold corridor to the garderobe she'd used yesterday. The tiny room was dank, drafty, and as unappealing as the night before, but she found a chamber pot tucked along the wall. Hesitating only a moment, she took it up, cringing as she dumped its contents out the glassless window before carrying it gingerly back to her little room.

She'd barely made use of the thing before a firm knock sounded at her door. Ivy startled, shoving the pot beneath the cot, and then took a second to make sure her jacket wasn't accidentally tucked into her leggings before pulling the door open.

Alaric stood there, shoulders squared, though his eyes looked shadowed with fatigue. His nod was curt, more of an acknowledgment than a greeting.

"We'll be out again today," he said without preamble, his deep voice rasping with weariness. "I dinna ken for how long. Kendrick and Blair will remain behind. Ye seek them out if ye have a need."

"Okay. Thank you," Ivy replied, her tone a little brighter than she felt.

He gave another short nod and began to turn away, but she blurted, "Quick question before you go."

He stilled, his head angling slightly back toward her.

"How do I... um, wash my face and brush my teeth? Stuff like that?"

For a moment he actually looked as though he might take the time to explain, but then his mouth closed on whatever thought he had. "Aye," he said at last, "there is a guid reason to seek out either Kendrick or Blair."

Ivy found herself staring, absurdly caught by the shape of his mouth. They weren't polished lips by any stretch; they were roughened from weather and sun, a faint line of dryness at the edges, but they were full, firm, and commanding in a way that made it hard to look away. His upper lip had a stern cut, the kind that seemed to match his every clipped word, while his lower lip was broader, betraying a hint of softness at odds with the rest of him. She realized, with a quick flutter in her chest, that she was watching the way they moved when he drew a breath, and then when he set them tight again, clearly advising their conversation was done.

She blinked, heat rushing to her face, startled by her own wandering focus.

"Oh. Okay. Thanks." She tried to smile, though she imagined it must appear quite thin.

Again he shifted to leave, as if anxious to be gone, but she caught him once more. "Did you not sleep well?"

That made him pause. His brow furrowed, shadowing his already-dark expression.

"You have circles under your eyes," she said quickly, trying not to sound as though she were criticizing him. She gave a little shrug. "You just look like you might've slept poorly."

He seemed perplexed by the question, his mouth opening slightly as if unused to being asked something so ordinary. At last he answered, slow and reluctant. "Aye. I dinna sleep so guid."

Ivy winced, her sympathy unfeigned. "Sorry to hear that." She let her hand rest lightly against her belly. "Not surprisingly, I slept like a baby. And I think the baby did, too. Normally, she wakes me up a lot at night with her kicking, but last night she slept like the babe she is." She smiled brightly at him.

Actually, she'd woken with some concern, wondering if something was amiss, if the trauma of yesterday had somehow harmed her baby. She'd lain rigid in the cot, waiting, listening, praying. And then, as if answering her fear, the baby had stirred quite a bit. Eventually, a flutter came, a rhythmic thump-thump-thump that made her laugh softly. Hiccups. She'd read about them but had never felt them until this morning. Both hands pressed to her stomach, she'd smiled with such relief, joy swelling in her chest despite everything. Whatever else was unraveling around her, her baby was safe.

Alaric's gaze dropped briefly to where her hand rested on her abdomen. "Ye are hoping for a lass?" he asked, the words tentative.

"I had no preference at all, I can honestly say that," Ivy answered, always thrilled to talk about her pregnancy, her baby. A little smile tugged at her lips. "But I know it's a girl—two different ultrasounds said so."

His eyes flicked up sharply, confusion plain.

"Uh, I mean..." She fumbled, realizing too late what she'd said. "Yes. I'm hoping it's a girl."

Another curt nod from the laird and once more, he was gone.

Ivy sighed, realizing she really had to be more careful with her words.

Chapter Six

The convent no longer smelled of smoke so much as men. The burnt essence lingered, yes—charred stone and scorched wood—but the stronger scent was of unwashed bodies, sweat, leather, and blood. The corridor echoed faintly with snores, groans, and the muffled shuffle of boots from below as Ivy made her way along the hall and toward the stairs.

Below, the great hall where she'd seen the mouse skitter across the floor last night, had been transformed. The largest part of the undamaged priory had been claimed for necessity. Pallets of straw lined the floor, filled with men who bore the marks of yesterday's fight. Slashes were bound in rough linen, legs were splinted, and shoulders were swathed in strips of cloth already stained dark. Voices muttered, prayers and curses, punctuated by the occasional raw groan while more than one able-bodied man walked and worked among them.

Taken aback by the sight but knowing she wouldn't have the stomach to be of any use—and while yesterday's wary stares were not forgotten—Ivy kept one hand pressed to her belly, a kind of shield, and shrank against the wall, careful not to draw attention. Some of the men looked up at her anyway—suspicious, hostile, or merely curious—and she ducked her head, suddenly conscious of her modern clothing, of how different she must appear to them.

She moved quickly, weaving past the wounded and the men tending them, until the door gave her blessed daylight.

Outside, the air was crisp, washed clean by the night's rain.

Ivy paused in the doorway, taking in the scene. What she'd glimpsed in darkness last night unfolded starkly before her now. Though the convent's stone chapter house still stood solid, if scorched in places, around it stretched the blackened skeletons of additions and outbuildings, charred beams jutting like broken ribs, collapsed walls reduced to heaps of sodden ash. The ground between was littered with splintered timbers and shattered tiles, a graveyard of what had once been a holy community.

Yet life filled the ruins. Dozens of MacKinlay men moved about, their voices low, their boots crunching over wet stone and ash. Some hauled away charred debris, piling the wreckage at the edge of the yard. Another group of men were propping up a sagging doorway with salvaged timber, as if they might rebuild what appeared to have been the stables. Others swept out blackened debris from corners of the barn where the rain had not reached. Horses stood tethered beneath the dripping trees, their tack being scrubbed and mended, while outside the immediate yard, a few men tended kettles and appeared to have lain out plaid blankets to dry.

Out there near that fire, a few MacKinlay men sat in small groups, eating from wooden bowls. Laughter wafted through the air to Ivy, muted but unmistakable, as though battle and ruin had not managed to strip them entirely of spirit.

She tugged her jacket over her belly and scanned her eyes over the faces of the MacKinlay men, near and far.

She discovered Kendrick first, his shock of red hair easily recognizable. He was well beyond the inner yard, beyond the fire and the drying blankets. His sleeves were rolled back, shoulders bunching with every heavy swing of an axe. Logs split beneath his strokes, sharp cracks echoing into the morning. Without hesitation, Ivy made her way to him.

She ignored every glance thrust at her as she walked but then hesitated when she drew near to Kendrick, who had his back to her. She waited until he had completed a swing of the axe before she spoke. "Um—Kendrick?"

Still, the axe bit clean through another log before he turned, wiping his brow with the back of his arm. His expression softened when he saw her, though it carried a trace of caution.

"Um, hi. Good morning," she said, wearing a self-conscious smile. "Alar—I mean, the laird said I should find you for anything I need and well," she shrugged and flashed a smile at him, "I have needs—a few, anyway."

Kendrick lifted his tunic, using the bottom hem to wipe his face now, scrubbing it over his mouth and jaw, revealing a taut but pasty abdomen in the process.

He grinned when he dropped the shirt, letting it fall back over his hips. "Ne'er met a lass who dinna."

Far different from his laird, Ivy liked that he was genuine, kind, and had this little teasing streak in him.

She lifted her hand, about to tick off her needs, but then thought better of it, imagining it would come across as bossy or pompous. Instead, she joined her hands behind her back. "I'd like to wash my face and brush my teeth, but I'm not sure how to go about doing that, how that might happen. And," she continued, bringing her hands around to smooth them over her rounded belly, "I need to eat something." Before he could answer, she thought she should offer something in return, and said, "Also, I'd like to help." She pivoted a bit, waving her hand across the scene of so much labor around the shell of the priory. "Seems there's plenty of work to be done."

Kendrick eyed her a long moment, then rested both hands atop the axe haft, as it sat on the chopping block log. "Help, is it?"

"Yes. I don't want to just... I can't do *nothing*, can't just sit in that little room all day. It'll drive me insane. And honestly, I'm stronger than I look." She gave a hopeful smile, aware that wasn't saying much in her state. "So, maybe you have some ideas of how or where I can be useful?"

Kendrick leaned his weight on the axe handle, studying her with the squint of a man trying to gauge whether she was serious. "Ye'd help, then," he mused. His gaze swept over the yard as though picking from the dozens of small labors underway. "Och," he said suddenly, turning back to Ivy. "I recall Tàmhas saying he was running low on a few plants and such. Said he was short on what he uses to soothe fever. Chamomile, yarrow, willow bark—anyone of those or all would serve."

Ivy blinked at him. "Right. Plants." She nodded as though she understood, but was forced to confess, "Okay, full disclosure— I wouldn't know any of those plants from any common weed unless it was in a jar and labeled."

Kendrick's brows lifted, then knit together in obvious confusion.

Playfully, trying to make light of her inadequacy, she put her hand to the side of her mouth. "I'd probably end up poisoning half the army."

The corner of his mouth twitched. "Aye, then we canna have ye do that. Ye're bonny, wouldnae look so fine with yer head on a pike."

Ivy's jaw dropped while her eyes widened. "Wow. That escalated quickly. Instant beheading. I'll make note of that."

Kendrick only shrugged, with still only the ghost of a grin tugging at his mouth. "We like to keep our punishments tidy."

Ivy shook her head, laughing despite herself. "Tidy. Right. Nothing says neat and orderly like a severed head on display." She cleared her throat. "All right. Any other ideas of how I might be helpful?"

He thought again, tapping the axe haft. "We can always use more bread, lass. Or oatcakes. Cook took a blade through the gut yesterday, God rest him. Laird hasn't yet assigned who will replace him."

"Oh. Bread?" Ivy echoed weakly. "Like... from scratch?"

Kendrick tilted his head, as though perplexed by her question.

"Oh, um—yeah, no. I don't... bake." She gave a nervous laugh. "I mean, I wouldn't even know where to start." She spun around again, considering the stone priory before facing Kendrick again. "Like, did the kitchen and ovens survive the fire?" She waved her hand, dismissing her own question. "Sorry, it doesn't matter—I have no clue how to make any sort of bread."

This time, he did laugh, just once, low in his chest, before shaking his head. "So nae plants or roots, nae foraging. Nae bread, nae baking. I see. Aye, we have a constant need for water, but I'm loath to have ye hauling buckets. Like as nae, the laird would have my head if he kent I put ye up to that."

While Kendrick stared off blindly, appearing to wrack his brain for any other ideas, Ivy pressed her palms to her hot face, wishing the earth would swallow her. "I'm sorry," she muttered. "You must think I'm completely useless."

"Useless?" He leaned down to grab another log, setting it on the stump. "Nae, lass. Mayhap... misplaced?" The axe came down in a clean, ringing crack. He straightened, knocking the split piece that hadn't fallen off the block into the growing pile.

"Oh, gosh, Kendrick," she all but moaned, "you have no idea."

Kendrick seemed to make nothing of this hint of a confession. "There is one task ye can do that will serve well enough. The laundry. The soiled bandages pile high already, and as a marching and movin' army, we go through 'em quick. It would be helpful if the used ones were washed, dried, and ready to use again."

Relief flooded her. "Laundry, great. That, I can do."

"Good." Kendrick gave her an approving nod, already setting another log in place. He pointed with his free hand toward a copse of trees, where beyond Ivy could see what she hadn't noticed before, the shimmery blue of water. "There's the loch, nice sandy bank it has. All the bandages needing laundering will be in there with Tàmhas," he said, tipping his head toward the stone priory. "Might scrub up yerself there as well—at the loch. There'll be nae fresh water delivered to ye, I ken that."

"Thank you, Kendrick," she said, genuinely pleased with his kindness and patience.

The married father of one—Ivy still couldn't wrap her brain around that; he looked like in her time he might be sitting in an English class, his nose buried in his phone rather than his textbook—Kendrick jerked his chin toward the firepit where a blackened kettle hung over the flames. "Go on, get ye some pottage first. There'll be oatcakes beside the pot. Take what ye can, for it'll be long till the next."

Ivy followed his gaze, her stomach tightening, not just with hunger, but with nerves. Half a dozen men were gathered there, eating from bowls, talking low between mouthfuls. Every one of them wore the same rough plaid, the same scars and wary expressions. She imagined walking straight into their midst, fumbling with the pot, drawing every stare. Her throat went dry.

"Would you maybe... come with me?" she asked softly, hating how small her voice sounded.

Kendrick's brows lifted, and for a moment she thought he might laugh. But he only huffed a breath that was half amusement, half exasperation. "Best ye learn to walk among them, lass."

Before she could protest, he swung the axe into the stump one last time, leaving it quivering there, and gestured for her to follow. Ivy's heart pounded as she trailed him across the muddy yard, past the plaid tartans strewn in neat rows, and into the midst of men who had fought and bled only yesterday. She could feel their eyes, curious, suspicious, measuring.

"Here now," Kendrick said casually as they reached the fire. "This is Ivy. She's to bide wi' us for a time."

The men glanced up. One was young, his freckles stark against pale skin, maybe not much older than David's younger brother, a kid she'd met a handful of times. Another was broad-shouldered and grizzled, his beard streaked with gray. A third was missing two fingers, the stump wrapped in fresh linen. None of them responded to Kendrick's brisk introduction, but their stares pricked her skin.

Unfazed, Kendrick crouched by the kettle. He ladled steaming *pottage*—whatever that was—into a wooden bowl, then reached for a pair of what she guessed were the oatcakes. "Eat this," he instructed, pressing both into her hands.

"Thanks," Ivy murmured, acutely aware of eyes upon her. She glanced around uncertainly. "Um... spoon?"

Kendrick straightened, one brow arched, and without a word mimed lifting the bowl to his mouth. "Or use yer hands."

Her eyes widened. "My... hands?" To eat what looked like a gray, lumpy oatmeal?

"Aye," Kendrick said, utterly unbothered. "Or drink it straight, as a man does. Ye'll get used to it."

The freckled boy smirked, clearly entertained by her horror. The grizzled one grunted and went back to his own bowl. Ivy's face flamed as she lifted the bowl to her lips. The broth was hot and gritty, the oats lumpy, but it filled her empty stomach. She nibbled an oatcake with her free hand, its dry, dusty texture sticking to her teeth.

"Guid lass," Kendrick said, as if she'd passed some unspoken test.

Ivy swallowed and tried to smile, as several watchful expectant gazes were trained on her.

Generally, she tried not to rush her meals, but the minute Kendrick nodded at her, as if to say his work was done, and returned to the axe and the chopping block, Ivy wolfed down the rest of her *breakfast* and smiled politely at those around her before scurrying back to the priory.

The room she'd tried to ignore completely as she'd passed through it earlier was inescapable now, while she waited for the man she believed to be Tàmhas, a medieval army doctor, by her understanding, to finish with a patient.

He was crouched beside a soldier, his thick hands moving with brusque efficiency as he tightened a linen wrap around the man's thigh. His hair was streaked with gray, his jaw shadowed with days of growth, and the deep set of his eyes gave him the look of someone who slept little, if at all.

Ivy hesitated, then forced herself to speak when he rose off his knees. "Um—hi," she said, bounding forward a bit, drawing his attention. "Kendrick said I could help, or, um, be helpful here. He thought maybe I could... launder the used bandages?"

Tàmhas's gaze was sharp, his eyes raking over her in one swift, assessing sweep. "And who are ye?" he asked, the words blunt as a blow.

Heat rushed to her face. "I—my name's Ivy. I'm... with Alaric. He said I could stay here." She instantly regretted the phrasing—'with Alaric' sounded far too personal—and added quickly, "I mean, only for safety. I'm just... here."

One of his brows rose. His glance flicked toward her stomach, then back to her face, but he didn't press. Instead, he jerked his chin toward a corner where a basket sat.

Ivy turned and nearly recoiled.

"There, then," said the doctor. Looking at her again, assessing her it seemed—she might guess she failed whatever test he was silently giving her—he announced shortly, "Might be another basket round here somewhere, some lye as well, but I've nae the time to scrounge for it."

Collecting herself, she smiled her thanks to the doctor and approached the pile, which might actually weigh more than she did. A heap of soiled linen overflowed the wicker, the pile much larger than she'd expected. Some strips were stiff with dried blood, others damp and clotted, tinged with ugly shades of brown and green. The sharp coppery reek stung her nose.

She swallowed hard. "Oh, God," she moaned in earnest now. *I can do this*, she told herself, though even her inner silent voice wavered with doubt. Her stomach knotted with queasiness, and every modern instinct screamed *disease, infection, cross-contamination*. But she straightened her shoulders anyway.

Ivy stared at the mound again. Her skin crawled, but she decided she'd simply scrub herself clean every fifteen minutes or so.

It took her the better part of the day. She'd poked around until she found a stash of lye in a cellar beneath the convent—a cellar that she'd literally stumbled upon with dumb luck—the short barrel of soap not too heavy for her. She made trip after trip to the loch Kendrick had pointed out, hauling smaller loads than she'd first imagined possible. The work was heavy and foul, and by noon—or what she guessed might be the noon hour—she'd stripped off her jacket and her arms were already burning with fatigue from all the scrubbing. Her stomach roiled with each new heap of blood-soaked strips she dumped into the shallow water near the shore. But little by little, the pile diminished. By midafternoon, branches, bushes, and stones all around the loch were draped with drying lengths of linen, pale flags fluttering in the breeze. Ivy knelt at the shore, the sleeves of her pink sweater damp, scrubbing through the last quarter of the rags, her back aching, her hands raw from the lye, nasty stuff that. An hour ago, she'd discarded her boots and socks, though for obvious reasons left her leggings on. She figured she would simply scrub them up last thing and hang them to dry in her cell later, overnight. There'd simply been no way to prevent herself from getting wet, not if she were going to clean the linen thoroughly.

Late in the afternoon, she was sitting on her heels in six inches of water, her legs, leggings, and underwear soaked through. Honestly she didn't mind—she had no other clothes, no other panties, and the ones she was wearing would get somewhat of a cleaning now. At least that's how she looked at it.

Anyway, that's how Alaric found her.

Footsteps in the grass made her look up. Alaric emerged from the trees, his broad frame casting a long shadow, his dark hair unkempt, his plaid streaked with dust. He looked bone-tired, the kind of weariness that went deeper than muscle. Without a word, acknowledging her only by way of a slow inclination of his head, he lowered himself to the bank beside her, though not too close.

He bent, tugged at the ties of his boots, and pulled them free, setting them aside. He released a thin leather strip that might have served the purpose of a garter from just below his knee and rolled down his hose, baring a pair of long, strong feet, lean ankles, and muscled calves, all of which were unsurprisingly pale.

Without a word, he stood again and waded into the water.

Ivy blinked, surprised—she hadn't thought of him as someone who *ever* allowed himself comfort.

He stopped when the water reached his calves, a few yards in front of Ivy, who watched, slightly in awe, the blood-soaked linen in her lap momentarily forgotten.

The laird bent and splashed water onto his face in handfuls, the droplets shining against his short, stubbly beard. Then, as she watched, he scooped a mouthful, gargled, and spat into the reeds.

Ivy stared, half fascinated, half amused. She hadn't realized she was staring until he turned his head, catching her in the act. Their eyes met, and the brown of his reminded her instantly of a long-ago trip to the zoo, when she'd had a staring contest with a leopard from behind a glass wall. She flushed now and looked quickly back to her work, commanding her hands to resume scrubbing, which they obligingly did.

He lingered in the loch water only another moment longer before stepping out, glistening drops sliding down his face and neck. He sat heavily on the bank, stretching his long legs, letting the summer air dry his feet.

She thought he might have simply left after refreshing himself, but something in the way he settled, fairly close to her, made her think he might not mind some conversation.

Ivy scoured her brain for topics, at a loss for anything they might have in common to discuss.

"How was your day?" she asked finally after a long moment. Her cheeks pinkened for how lame and unnatural that sounded.

He turned his face slightly toward her, brows lowered.

"Anything found?" she pressed. "English soldiers... or the nuns who lived here?"

He shook his head once. "Naught. Nae English, nae sisters. The rain had washed any trail we might have followed." His voice was rough, his disappointment obvious.

She bit her lip. "I'm sorry."

He grunted in reply, gaze fixed on the horizon.

Clinging to the logic that since he hadn't risen and walked away, that some part of him was choosing to stay, to engage or be engaged, Ivy asked next, "How long do you think we'll stay here? At the priory, I mean, not the loch."

With his hands set into the sand behind him, he lifted and dropped his shoulders negligently. "I dinna ken. We'll head out again on the morrow for another search, I expect. But if we find naught, there's little reason to bide here."

Eyes on her chore, swishing the scrubbed linen in the water in front of her knees, Ivy then asked, "Do you...have other things you should be doing?"

He watched her thoughtfully while he answered. "Aye, lass. So long as even one English banner flies on Scots soil, there'll always be something I should be doing."

A patriot, through and through, she supposed, something she might have guessed about him even as soon as within hours of meeting him.

Ivy wrung the linen hard, watching the water bead and drip from her hands. She tried to focus only on that, but her brain was screaming inside her, *Tell him! Ask him for help!*

Predictably, her thoughts circled back, again and again, to her inexplicable, improbable predicament.

She bit her lip. *Did* she need to tell him? Maybe not. Maybe she could just keep her head down, keep pretending she belonged here until she figured something out. Yet the thought of one day being left behind by him and his army made her throat tighten. She was scared enough as it was, but alone? Completely alone? She wasn't sure she could handle that. She was going to have a baby. She certainly couldn't do that alone.

Her gaze slid toward him. Alaric sat solid and silent at her side, his arms braced behind him, the sun catching in his golden-brown eyes as he stared across the loch. Strong. Capable. Steady in a way that hadn't ever come easily to her. If anyone could help her make sense of this, surely it was him.

But what if he thought she was insane? What if he told the others? She'd seen how quickly suspicion flared here, had suffered plenty of those stares. If she said the wrong thing—Christ! Was losing her life a possible outcome?

Her stomach fluttered, a sharp, urgent twist. Because of the baby, she really believed she had no other choice but to confide in him.

"I ken it's dead already," he said, startling her out of her tortured reverie.

Ivy snapped her gaze to him. "What?"

He lifted one hand out of the sand and pointed to the linen strip she'd been wringing out. "'Tis dead, lass. Has nae more life in it."

"Oh," she sighed and breathed a laugh. "Right."

Still, her hands twisted, even as she lowered the tightly wound linen to her lap. The words crowded at the back of her throat, wild and impossible, but they wouldn't leave her in peace. She simply had no choice. She had to say them.

"Alaric—um, sir?" she began, her voice catching. "Can I tell you something?"

He fixed his gaze on her, his golden-brown eyes fastening on her with that heavy, unwavering weight that made her insides squirm. "Aye."

She swallowed hard, her mouth suddenly dry. "I'm not... I'm not from here. Not just not from *here* here, like this place, but—" She gave a shaky laugh. "God, this sounds crazy. It *is* crazy. But I don't belong in the year 1305."

His brow furrowed, but he said nothing, waiting.

"I—" She broke off, squeezing the previously brutalized linen, then blurted in a rush, "I come from the future."

For a heartbeat, silence. Then his brows drew together, the lines of his face darkening in confusion.

Silence stretched, heavy and unyielding. Ivy's pulse pounded in her ears.

When he didn't immediately reply, Ivy let out a nervous laugh, and wet her lips, babbling to fill the silence. "You probably think I'm insane. Honestly, I don't know that I haven't lost my marbles. But it's true. I swear. I was hiking in the twenty-first century and—*bam*, I don't know what happened—but suddenly I was here. Well, not *here* here, but—" She gestured helplessly at the loch. "here, in the fourteenth-century."

"Ye come from the future?" He repeated, his voice low and crisp.

"Yes," she whispered. "From centuries ahead. I didn't mean to...to travel through time. I don't even understand how it happened. But I'm not lying to you—seriously, you can't make this up."

His mouth opened, closed. He snarled, like literally snarled. "Ye claim to be a spirit? A seer?"

"What? No. No, no, just—just a woman. A normal person, I swear. Just...me. Only," she went on, shrugging helplessly, "only I was born seven hundred years from now."

His jaw tightened, disbelief hardening into something harsher. "Ye take me for a fool?"

Despite the way her stomach twisted, anxious over his dark and angry reaction, Ivy was quick to refute this. "I'm not toying with you," she said quickly. "I know it sounds insane, but—"

"Mad, aye." His voice quickened, sharp as a blade. "Or wicked. Which is it? Do ye mean to vex me wi' this nonsense, or confess ye're some witch come among us?"

"No!" Her voice cracked with desperation. Tears pooled in her eyes. "I swear to you, I'm telling the truth! I only told you because I'm afraid." She laid her hand and forearm over her stomach. "I'm going to have a baby, and I don't know what to do about that, and I'm scared. I thought—" she stopped talking, made very afraid by the thunder in his expression, the anger that boiled where confusion had been.

He snatched up his boots and rose in one swift movement.

"I'll hear nae more of this," he growled. "Keep yer lies, woman. I'll nae be made sport of."

And with that, he strode away, boots in hand, leaving Ivy staring after him, the summer air suddenly colder for his absence.

Great. What now? she wondered.

Chapter Seven

The young soldier's breathing had grown shallow, his lashes sinking lower with each blink. Ivy sat crossed leg beside his pallet, smoothing a strip of damp, cool linen over his brow. His fever had broken sometime in the last few hours, and now he hovered in that thin place between waking and sleeping.

"You're going to be just fine," she murmured, though she had no way of knowing it. He gave a faint grunt of acknowledgment before drifting off, his lips parting with a small sigh. She set the cloth aside a few minutes later, quietly pleased that he'd managed to find rest.

Yesterday, when she'd returned from the loch with her hands raw from lye and essentially soaked through from the waist down, Tàmhas had been the one to meet her. She'd braced herself for wariness or coolness, but the gruff surgeon had studied the neat stacks of drying and dried bandages and had given her a short nod of approval. He hadn't merely dismissed her, though, but had directed her with a kind of brisk patience, where to lay them, which size strips were best for which wounds. His manner was still clipped, but there was warmth under it now, as though she'd passed some unspoken test.

This morning, he'd greeted her with a nod, which felt rather friendly to Ivy, so that she found herself inquiring if he could use an extra set of hands. If he were surprised by the offer, he didn't let it show, but he was certainly agreeable and soon enough, he was barking out orders at her as if she were simply another grunt in the MacKinlay army—"More water, lass. Bring a fresh cloth. Hold this steady." Not once did he question her presence, and once, when she managed to anticipate what he needed before he asked, she thought she'd caught the faintest glimmer of a smile in his beard.

It wasn't much, but to Ivy, who had felt nothing but alien here, it was something. A foothold, anyway.

When she was certain the young soldier she'd been tending would rest soundly for a while, she rose from his side and shifted to the next pallet, where another man lay awake. He couldn't have been much older than she was — maybe mid-twenties, if that — with a boyish face under the scruff of a few days' beard. His arm was bound in fresh linen, and he looked pale but alert.

She crouched beside him and adjusted the linen around his shoulder, tucking in a loose end.

His eyes lit faintly. "Ye've a gentle touch, lass," he said, his voice hoarse but eager. "Better than Tàmhas, anyway. Hands like an ox, he has."

Ivy smiled. "Tender care is not his job—saving lives is."

The man gave a wheezy laugh, then winced, clutching at his side. "Aye, speak on the right side, lass. Safer, that." His gaze lingered on her face, wide-eyed and far too admiring for someone in his condition.

"I'm Ivy," she offered, realizing she hadn't introduced herself.

"Malcolm," he returned quickly, as though pleased she'd asked. "Malcolm Boyd. Where'd ye come from? I dinna recall ye ever."

Ivy shifted, averting her gaze. "From around the Loch Katrine area," she said, having since decided this was a reasonable and vague answer. "But I was only there the last year. Prior to that, I'm from very far away."

"Nae south? England?"

"No. Much further. West." Several times today, she'd adeptly shifted a man's focus from her to him. She did the same now. "Does it hurt very much?" she asked, nodding toward his arm.

He shrugged, glancing down at it. "Hurts, aye," he admitted, so casually she might have thought pain a familiar companion. Then his mouth curved. "But less when ye speak. Ye've a voice soft as a balm."

Ivy had always considered herself pretty enough, though never beautiful. Still, she'd drawn her fair share of attention from boys and men over the years, and long ago had learned that humor was the gentlest rejection.

She grimaced playfully. "Wow. How long did it take you to come up with that cheesy line?"

The soldier grinned despite the effort it cost him, his gaze lingering far too boldly on her. "Nae a fib, lass."

She gave a weak laugh, dismissive, and pressed her palms to her thighs as if to push herself upright. "Rest now. Talking won't help you heal."

He obeyed, sinking back into his pallet, though his eyes stayed fixed on her even as his lids grew heavy.

Just then, a prickle ran along the back of her neck.

Before the sensation fully registered, a hand closed rough around her arm and she was pulled to her feet with effortless strength. The suddenness of it wrung a short yip from her until she realized it was Alaric, who proceeded to drag her away from the soldier's pallet.

"What are you—?" she gasped, trying to twist free.

He didn't answer.

"Hey!" she protested further, her head spinning as he marched her out of the infirmary.

Malcolm blinked in alarm as she was manhandled out of the room, but of course could not or would not rise. Murmurs rippled through the room, the other men watching.

Ivy's cheeks flamed.

Alaric wrenched her into the corridor.

He spun so suddenly she almost collided with him. The corridor walls closed around them, dim and narrow, his body towering over hers. His eyes were dark, as hard as bronze in the dim light, terrifying in their intensity.

"If ye've any sense at all, woman," he growled, "ye'll ne'er speak the madness again, nae that dangerous drivel ye fed to me yesterday. Nae to me, nae to my men, nae to anyone. Ye ken my reaction was brutal? Ye've nae notion what some men might do upon hearing such witch-talk—that devil's prattle will earn ye a rope, or worse."

Ivy's heart thudded in her chest while tears pricked her eyes, hot and humiliating.

His grip on her arm was rock solid, his voice fierce enough to shake her bones. The fierceness in him was overwhelming, frightening—and yet she bristled at being manhandled like a misbehaving child.

His eyes were fixed on hers, and his lip curled. He gave her arm a small, sharp shake. "Tears willna save ye."

The words landed like a slap. For an instant she was stunned, then fury surged. He thought she was pretending—*pretending to cry*—to win sympathy? She shoved herself up onto her toes, forcing herself closer to his height. She was still several inches short of his chin, but she glared at him all the same.

She yanked her arm free of him, snapping a linen strip she still held in her fist. The motion was meant to be sharp, decisive, but the cloth only floated to the ground in a pathetic drift. She ignored it, standing stiff and defiant.

"I knew it was a gamble telling someone," she hissed, her voice ragged with hurt. "I had some foolish idea you would have reacted differently—maybe with a shred of compassion. I wasn't looking for judgment, or accusation, or even—" Her voice cracked; her chin quivered despite her effort to hold it firm. "I'm lost and scared and simply needed guidance, or... or someone to help me make sense of it. Or Christ—just a way to get hold of a midwife!"

Her hands flew as she spoke, wild and angry, dissecting the air between them. His expression didn't soften. He looked as ferocious as ever, and suddenly Ivy had had enough.

"Actually, you know what? I don't need anything from you after all. I'm sorry I ever said a word. I didn't make it up, but I should have kept it to myself." She spun on her heel, stomping away down the corridor, her heart hammering, glad for once to be the one leaving *him*.

"Where the bluidy hell are ye going?" His voice thundered after her.

"Away from you!" she snapped, tossing the words over her shoulder just as she marched into the hall.

Every head turned. Dozens of eyes followed her progress across the crowded infirmary, men's gazes bouncing between her and Alaric like spectators at a tennis match. She lifted her chin and strode on, her fury carrying her forward.

Behind her, his voice lashed again. "Ye're a fool. Ye'll nae last half an hour by yerself."

"I'll revel in every minute past thirty that I prove you wrong!" she hollered back, her voice breaking but strong enough to carry.

The priory's front door stood open, and she marched through it without slowing, the sudden daylight a blinding relief. She didn't know where she was going, only that she certainly didn't want to be around him. Honestly, she didn't even care that he didn't believe her—she didn't blame him; it was a *lot* to wrap one's brain around—but geez, his very public heavy-handedness, his overblown anger—that caveman act, all snarls and rage—were really too much. Alaric MacKinlay was indeed a brute, a wall of fury and iron who seemed to think barking louder made him right. Maybe it worked on his men, but it wasn't going to fly with her. She might be stranded in his century, barefoot and pregnant for all intents and purposes, and dependent on his grudging protection, but she still had her dignity. And he simply had no right to treat her so harshly.

***

Alaric stood rooted as she stormed across the hall, his chest tight with fury. The men's heads turned with her, whispers pricking the air, and though he could not make out their words, his lip curled with fury all the same.

What manner of game did she play? Why invent such a tale as she had yesterday, so wild and implausible, unless to unsettle him? He had thought her strange from the first, aye—with her odd speech and queer clothing—but still, he had counted her mortal, flesh and blood, no different from any other woman. In truth, her expectant state aside, he had deemed her irrelevant.

Harmless. Yesterday's revelation had struck him like a mace to the skull, so hard he could scarce think past the madness of it.

And yet... she had not looked the liar. Frightened, aye, near undone—but not deceitful. Even now, marching away with her chin high and her eyes bright with anger, she did not wear the face of a woman playing tricks.

But more than her words, more than her wild claims, it was the way his men looked at her today that had set his blood to boil. He was ever, sometimes painfully, honest with himself. And he knew this truth: he could not abide their stares. The hall had fallen still, their eyes following her—some wary, some with the too-familiar hunger of men too long on campaign. And Ivy, in her strange garb that clung indecently to every curve, had today smiled as though she belonged among them. She did not see how perilous that was.

He dragged in a breath, clenching his jaw. Mayhap Mathar was right. Mayhap it was only her condition that made him give a damn about her in the first place. That round belly, that bairn she carried—it softened a man against his will. A man could harden his heart against a woman's tears, but not so easily against the sight of a mother-to-be, lost and alone.

Alaric's thoughts shattered when he saw her drop.

Her silhouette framed in sudden brightness, Ivy's knees buckled just beyond the doorway, folding to the ground with a strangled cry.

Alaric's body moved before his mind did. He sprinted the length of the hall, leaping over startled and incapacitated men, and cleared the doorway, dropping to his knees beside her.

"Ivy?" His voice was harsher than he meant it, sharp with terror. "What?"

She gasped, clutching her belly, her face gone pale. Her mouth formed a circle of horror. "I don't know," she sobbed. "I don't know if she just kicked really hard, or if that pain is something to be alarmed about—"

Tàmhas appeared on her other side, dropping into a squat, calm as ever. "How far along are ye, lass?"

"Thirty-two weeks," she croaked anxiously, eyes swimming with fear.

"Guid way along, then," he murmured, setting his broad hands to her stomach. He pressed lightly here and there, listening with his hands as though the bairn spoke through flesh. After an interminable moment, his stern face broke into a smile. He looked between Alaric and Ivy, his voice gentle. "All is well, lass. Here." He lifted Ivy's hand, set it back to her belly. "Full alive and well, aye?"

Ivy's relief came in a rush, her whole body softening as she smiled, radiant through her tears. Alaric could scarce draw breath for the sight of it. He didn't know how Tàmhas could read the bairn's health with naught but a touch—Tàmhas, who had ne'er once delivered a child, to Alaric's knowing—but none of that mattered. Not when she turned that smile upon him, wide and shining, all fear forgotten now that she knew her child was safe.

"Strong one, this bairn," Tàmhas said, his eyes glinting with a rare humor. He jerked his chin at Alaric. "Feel."

Alaric drew back instinctively.

"Dinna be daft," the surgeon growled, seizing Alaric's hand and shoving it down over Ivy's own.

Heat surged through him at the sudden contact, her small hand beneath his, her warmth seeping into his skin. And then—movement. A solid thump against his palm.

"*Jesu*," he breathed. His eyes flew to Ivy's. "That's the babe?"

"Aye," Tàmhas said with satisfaction. "Sturdy, aye?"

Alaric looked at her then, truly looked, and all the air seemed to leave his lungs. Her eyes glistened, her smile trembled, and for a moment it was only the two of them, bound together by the miracle beneath his hand.

He could not remember the last time he had felt such wonder. Years ago, Gwen had announced to him, with no small amount of sympathy, upon his return, that the bairn was too large to move anymore.

Alaric's eyes widened again, and his lips parted in wonder as her stomach lurched again. The next kick came stronger, a rolling shift beneath his palm. Ivy's breath hitched in a laugh that was half a happy sob. The sound wound through him like a cord, pulling tight. For an instant he forgot everything—the ruin of the priory, the danger of the English, the impossibility of her unholy tale yesterday. There was only the heat of her hand beneath his, the spark of life thudding steady against both of them.

Then, as if scorched, he snatched his hand back.

The wonder drained from him, leaving a hollowness that hurt worse than any blow. What was he doing? What madness had seized him, to share such joy with her? It was absurd—worse than that!. It felt like betrayal. His wife's face rose in his mind, pale and still as the day he'd lost her, and shame slammed hard into his chest.

He curled his hand into a fist. He should not have touched Ivy, should not have allowed himself even a breath of that fleeting intimacy. She was a stranger who spoke of impossible things, a woman who unsettled him at every turn in their too-short acquaintance, and yet—he had felt... joy.

The knowledge burned.

Ivy's smile faltered at his abrupt withdrawal. He was peripherally aware of Tàmhas's questioning frown.

For a heartbeat she looked bewildered, her hand still resting protectively on her belly. Then the brightness in her eyes dimmed, as though she'd remembered herself, remembered him, recalled their harsh exchange of words. Her mouth pressed into a small, resigned line, and she looked down at the hand over her belly.

He could not bear her eyes on him—not when they gave rise to the guilt. Gwen's face haunted him still, pale and fading as he made the choice that saved neither her nor their bairn. That failure lay heavy in his bones, and to feel even a flicker of warmth now, in another woman's gaze, seemed a betrayal. He turned sharply, shoulders rigid, and strode away.

***

The army rode out three days later, leaving the charred priory behind. Nothing more could be done there, it was decided, and no word of the missing nuns had surfaced despite their constant searching. Ivy had managed—through stubborn persuasion of Kendrick and Ewan and no small amount of pleading looks—to secure her own mount. The mare was a rangy bay, not the most elegant horse she'd ever seen, but Ivy was absurdly proud of the independence it offered her.

They followed a narrow, rocky trail northward, scouts reporting that a smaller troop of English had passed through ahead of them. Always just out of reach, the enemy seemed to taunt them with tracks and cold fire pits, as if they were shadows rather than men. Each evening, Alaric's force made camp, only to rise at dawn and press on again, the chase stretching day after day.

Ivy found herself riding often beside Ewan, the young soldier with the easy grin. He never said much about himself, but he had a knack for making her feel less like a burden and more like part of the company. When the trail grew steep and treacherous, he would angle his horse near hers, ready to steady her if need be, though she managed well enough. She suspected he was smitten, though he kept it tucked neatly away.

"You've a knack for riding," Ewan said one afternoon as their horses picked their way along a forested ridge.

Ivy smirked, his tone suggesting he'd have thought she might have been an inept rider. "I'm full of surprises, right?"

His answering grin was boyish, almost shy. "Aye, ye are."

"Actually, I've been riding horses since I was a kid. I was raised on a farm, mostly. My grandfather bought me my first pony and taught me how to ride."

She liked Ewan—his straightforwardness, his eagerness—but she had no heart to give, not while David's rejection was so recent. And honestly, now while Alaric MacKinlay loomed in her thoughts at every turn. It had been nearly a week since that strange, intimate moment in the priory when Alaric's hand had rested against her belly, when he had felt the baby shift. She had almost imagined, in that strange, unguarded moment, that something had softened in him. But then he'd recoiled, and since then he had kept a deliberate distance. He spoke to her only when necessity demanded, his voice cool, his expression guarded. The sharpness of his behavior stung, though she hadn't expected it to—hadn't even realized, until that instant, that she'd been holding on to some fragile, unspoken hope.

Hope for what, exactly, she could not have said. That he might soften toward her? That he might look at her with something other than suspicion and restraint? It was absurd—she scarcely knew him, and what she did know painted him as proud, stubborn, infuriating. And yet, his rejection had revealed something she had not been willing to consider until now: she *had* been intrigued by him, perhaps had even been a little captivated. Perhaps she'd even been waiting for some sign that the connection she felt in his presence was not hers alone. Instead, the way he'd dismissed her—spurned her, really, several times now—had sadly advised that he harbored no similar desire.

It bothered her more than she cared to admit.

At night, Ivy used the plaid, wool blanket—breacan, she'd since learned it was properly called—and slept near the fire with the others, often sandwiched between or around Kendrick, Blair, and Ewan. She found herself strangely comforted by the press of bodies around her, the soft murmur of men snoring; she felt safe and secure. The meals this week had been simple but sustaining, broth thickened with oats, a heel of bread, sometimes dried meat or cheese if the quartermaster doled it out. She ate what she was offered, grateful, though the child within her seemed to grow hungrier by the day.

One evening, when the sky turned purple with dusk, she sat with Ewan at the fire, chewing a strip of salted venison. He leaned close enough for his shoulder to brush hers, his voice pitched low as if sharing a secret.

"Ye're strong, Ivy. Many a lass in yer state would no' walk half so far, much less ride with us."

Ivy smiled faintly at the praise. "Here's hoping I can continue to keep up."

The pace was grueling, but more so for the long hours in the saddle. Most of the time this army trudged in long, weary lines, but mostly the pace was set to a slow walk, in deference to the foot soldiers, she supposed, hardly unsafe for either her pregnancy or the baby. Yet, she worried almost hourly if the jostling might harm the baby, if the strain could bring early labor.

Back home she would never have dreamed of riding at this stage. At this point in her third trimester, she'd imagined herself knee deep in baby books, swollen ankles, doctor appointments, and painting the nursery—and definitely not slogging across the Scottish Highlands on horseback. She'd read warnings about long walks, about heavy lifting, about car rides that lasted too many hours. Yet here she was, bouncing over uneven ground with no doctor to consult, no sterile hospital waiting at the end of the road.

And yet, what choice did she have? There were no Airbnbs, no Ubers, no schooled modern doctors waiting to ease her nerves. This was it—the warm breacan at night, a strip of venison by day, and a horse whose gait she prayed would not shake her child loose.

Often her hand drifted to her belly, part soothing, part bracing, as she begged the baby to stay strong, though she couldn't begin to imagine how things might be any safer by the time it came, how her fear might be lessened so long as she remained lost in time.

Her gaze flicked across the camp to where Alaric sat apart, sharpening his blade in the flicker of firelight. He didn't look up, not once, but she felt the weight of his presence as surely as if he bored holes into her with his stare.

And though she tried to focus on the warmth of the fire, the food in her belly, and the kindness of the boy beside her, and many others over the last week, it was Alaric's distance that made it so that she still didn't feel quite comfortable among these MacKinlays.

Chapter Eight

The road narrowed to little more than a rutted track, threading its way through heather-covered slopes until, quite suddenly, it spilled into a cluster of stone and timber cottages crouched close to the banks of a burn. The late-afternoon sky was the color of pewter, heavy clouds pressing low, and in the gray light the village looked almost painted in shades of ash and earth. She'd smelled it before she saw much of it. Thin curls of peat smoke rose from squat chimneys, stinging her nose with their woodsy tang, mingling with the sour reek of animal dung and the mouthwatering drift of something roasted that sent her stomach growling.

Alaric had taken only a handful of men forward, leaving the rest of the army beyond the ridge. Even so, the sight of men and horses sent chickens scattering across the muddy track. A woman snatched up her toddler, another pulled children behind her skirts, all of them staring wide-eyed as though a storm had come down the slope in human form.

From the top of the ridge, Ivy stared, hardly breathing. This was no tourist site or reconstructed heritage village—there were no neat signs or roped-off displays, no camera flashes, no tidy guides in costume. The cottages leaned crookedly against one another, their thatch patched in places with turf or heather, their small windows dark and glinting like watchful eyes. A handful of stalls slumped beside the lane, half-collapsed frames that gave the impression of a market, albeit one from centuries ago. She could almost hear it—the clamor of voices, the clink of coin, the bleating of penned goats. At first the street had emptied, shutters slamming, voices hushed. But slowly, heads reappeared in door-ways, and a crowd began to gather, curiosity too strong to resist the pull of armed men riding in, Ivy supposed. Or maybe they recognized the plaids draped across so many of the MacKinlays. Not an English troop, they might surmise with relief.

She clutched the reins tighter, her heart battering at the sight. Dumbfounded awe pricked through her curiosity, for here, again, was proof so undeniable it left no room for bargaining. She had fallen backward into history.

Ivy shifted gingerly, grateful for the stop after another long day in the saddle, since every bone in her back and legs protested so many days on horseback. The sight below held her trans-fixed—it was the first true glimpse of civilization she had en-countered since stumbling into this century, and it struck her as both wondrous and unreal.

Though at a considerable distance by the time he reached the town, Ivy had no problem picking out Alaric among his men. There was no mistaking him, the breadth of his frame, the iron-straight set of his back, the quiet authority that clung to him like a mantle. Even at a distance, he seemed larger than life, the axis around which the others turned.

Alaric reined in near the edge of the street, and one of the villagers ventured a hesitant step forward. Though too far to make out words, Ivy saw the wary tilt of the man's head, the way his hands moved in quick, restless gestures. Others soon joined him—one, then two, then more—drawn from doorways and shadowed lanes until a small knot of villagers had gathered be-fore Alaric and his men. The conversation stretched on, too long to be idle chatter. Even from this distance, Ivy sensed its weight in the set of Alaric's shoulders, in the rigid stillness of the men at his back, except for what seemed, even from this distance, to be speaking glances exchanged. When at last Alaric shifted in the saddle, his head bowing sharply as though absorbing a blow, Ivy's stomach clenched. He turned his horse around, the starkness of his movement suggesting he'd just received bad news. His men followed and together they rode back toward the waiting column, leaving behind the silent, watchful cluster of townsfolk.

Alaric and the captain of the MacKinlay army, whom Ivy had since learned was named Mathar, crested the rise, a knot of men riding at their backs. They did not come fast, nor slow, but with a heavy tread, Ivy sensed. From where she sat, she could see the stiffness in Alaric's shoulders, the hard line of his jaw, and made note of the grim silence with that small moving group. A shiver ran through her before she even knew why. Something terrible had happened; she could feel it in the way the air itself seemed to sag beneath the weight of their silence. They reined in at the head of the column, where the foremost soldiers drew close. At first no words carried back, only the low rumble of voices. Mathar's hand sliced the air once. Alaric's head was bent listening as the captain growled out something before Alaric answered with a clipped reply. The soldiers nearest craned to hear, and Ivy felt the ripple of it spread outward—men straightening in their saddles, glances exchanged, whispers passing from rider to rider, carried swiftly on the air, borne from man to man with a terrible weight. Ivy caught fragments only—*Wallace... hanged... butchered in London*—until at last the meaning struck her full.

It was 1305, the specific improbable year having more meaning in this instant. William Wallace was dead.

The name struck her like a stone, familiar from every book she'd ever read on Scottish history, every tourist plaque she'd wandered past in different locales around Scotland, all of her dozen viewings of the movie *Braveheart*. But those had been words in written form, names etched on memorials, cold stone statues, and the American born-Australian Mel Gibson on the screen. Here, the name carried flesh and blood, hope, and now tremendous heartbreak.

Kendrick and Blair had rushed ahead when the laird had returned, but Ewan had remained at her side. He drew in a harsh breath and gave a small shake of his head and spoke gruffly. "Wallace," he muttered. "Dead?"

Ivy's gaze swept the line of men along the ridge. They'd halted as if struck, the column bunching in the lane. Ivy looked around at their faces—the grief was naked, unashamed. Some bowed their heads. Others swore low, violent oaths. One man clenched his fist around his bridle so tight his knuckles blanched white. One man pressed his forehead against his horse's neck, letting out a low, ragged curse. A few stared down toward the town below, but not with the sharp, assessing eyes she had grown used to—these were vacant, dazed, as though they were seeing nothing at all.

It was as if the marrow had been sucked clean from their bones. In an instant, the fierce, unbreakable army she had marched among seemed to hollow, their defiance bleeding out into the cool air. Wallace's death struck them like a blade, not to the body but to the spirit, cutting at the very thing that had kept them riding.

Ivy's heart thumped wildly. She had known this already—of course she had—the betrayal, the brutal execution, every grim detail. And yet, since falling into this century, she had scarcely given it thought. Each day had been consumed with survival, with keeping herself upright in a world that still didn't quite feel real. She hadn't paused to consider the calendar—what had already happened, what was about to happen—until now.

And suddenly, it came rushing back: that this was the season England tightened its grip, that Bruce had not yet seized his crown, that defeat and despair pressed heavier than hope. She had walked herself into the very heart of the chapter she had studied right here in Scotland over the last year, never once having contemplated what it would feel like to be among the people who had followed him, who had fought beside him, who had placed so much faith and hope in him. The sorrow in their eyes was not academic, it was fantastic for the breadth of it.

And suddenly she ached to tell them more. To stand up and cry out: *You will not always be beaten! You will not always bow! The cause does not die with Wallace!* She wanted to tell them that the day would come when Scotland stood free again, that Robert the Bruce himself would lead them to victory at Bannockburn.

The words clawed at her throat, but she bit them back, clenching her fingers around the reins until her nails dug into her palms. Some inner voice warned that she couldn't tell them anything. Sci-fi movies and old novels had warned her about this, about the dangers of meddling. *Butterfly effect*, her mind supplied dimly, though she'd never believed in such things before. And yet now—God, if she spoke, was it possible even the smallest tidbit of information could change everything in ways she could never undo?

She ducked her head, throat thick, staring at her hands on the reins.

She had thought, in these chaotic days, only of survival—of finding food, keeping warm, enduring the endless march with a baby inside her. She had never once paused to imagine *meeting history*. To meet the flesh-and-blood men whose names filled the pages of the books she once read with idle curiosity. Too late now for William Wallace. But Robert Bruce—her heart kicked hard in her chest—he yet lived, was alive in this moment, had yet to assume his greatest role. It was not impossible she might see him with her own eyes.

The thought both thrilled and terrified her.

***

By nightfall the army had made camp on a stretch of open ground beyond the burgh, the glow of the villagers' hearth-fires flickering faintly across the darkening fields. The MacKinlays clustered close to their own fires, voices hushed, the weight of Wallace's death pressing down as heavy as the low-hanging clouds. The men ate in silence, save for the occasional scrape of a blade against a trencher or the muttered shifting of horses.

They had not left the burgh empty-handed. A bargain had been struck—three English horses taken in the last skirmish traded away for provisions the villagers could spare. By the time the column turned out across the fields, pack mules bore sacks of oats and barley, a cask of salted fish, and a stout barrel of ale lashed tight against the jolting of the cart. The gains were meager against the needs of so many men, but even a mouthful more of grain or a draught of ale promised a small reprieve.

Alaric kept himself apart. He sat against a rough-barked oak far removed from the firelight, his back to the main camp and warm fire, an uneaten oatcake in his hand. His men had taken the news hard and while he felt no different, he'd learned to mask it better. Wallace's loss was a wound to Scotland itself, and though Alaric would not let his grief weaken him before the men, it gnawed at him like a dull blade sawing bone.

It had been Wallace himself, a year past, who had shown him how to fight as the outnumbered must fight—not in grand charges, but in sudden strikes from wood and crag. The *war of shadows*, Wallace had called it, the craft of ambush and retreat, harrying the foe until even the mighty English grew weary. Alaric had taken those lessons to heart. They had kept his men alive this past year, kept the flame of resistance flickering though not fully quenched. And now the man who had taught him was gone, cut down not in battle but by English cruelty, leaving the burden of the fight heavier upon every shoulder.

Footsteps whispered against the grass, light and halting. He did not lift his head, though every muscle in him braced. The tread was soft, uncertain, so much so that he guessed who approached—Ivy Mitchell—before she revealed herself, moving around the tree to stand before him.

When at last he raised his gaze, she stood before him tensely, pale in the fire's glow. She wore the same strange garb he had first seen her in more than a week past: the black trews that clung to her limbs, the soft pink tunic, and the odd green cloak that fell to her thighs. He could not fathom how she kept the garments so clean, for she did not appear overly road-worn, though she had marched and ridden the same harsh miles as the rest. The dim firelight drew out the wear in her face, the faint hollowness at the cheeks, the leaner cast to her features since first he'd met her. Her fire-kissed hair tumbled loose about her shoulders, shadowing eyes that seemed too large inside so small and perfect a face.

"I'm sorry," she said softly. "About the death of Wallace. I know he mattered to you. To all of you."

Alaric turned his head slightly, putting his face in full shadow. His voice came out flat, clipped. "Aye. He did."

She lingered, biting at her lip, her fingers curling and uncurling.

"I wish there were something I could say that wouldn't sound empty."

"Then say naught," he returned, with the blunt finality of a man unwilling to share what lay buried deep.

Ivy Mitchell, however, was undeterred. She lowered herself gingerly onto the grass beside him, a hand braced on her knee as she sank. She sat not directly in the shadow of the tree but outward a bit, so that the firelight danced blurry shadows across her face.

"I'm sorry for the way he died as well," she whispered, her voice low but steady. "To have suffered that indignity—half hanging him, drawing and quartering, cutting him open—"

Alaric's head snapped toward her, effectively silencing her. "How could ye ken that?" he demanded, his tone harsher than intended. To his knowledge, no one knew the exact manner of Wallace's end. The townsfolk had said the patriot had been executed, little more than that Wallace had been taken from the Tower of London and had been dragged through the streets to the Elms at Smithfield.

She swallowed thickly at first, her eyes widening as if caught in the act—or a lie. But then she tilted her chin upward and met his stare without flinching. "Because I told you before," she said, a note of defiance threading her voice. "I'm from the future. I've studied the wars, seen movies, and toured all the national heritage sites. I know plenty about how this all turns out—England attacks, Scotland bleeds. Over and over again."

For a heartbeat, he almost believed her. No guile marked her face, no hesitation. She spoke with the certainty of one repeating a truth, not spinning a tale. But then sense returned, cold and heavy. Impossible. Come from the future? From seven hundred years in the future? Implausible. Unreasonable. Madness.

His jaw set hard. "Enough. I've nae stomach just now for such idiocy, lass. Keep yer tales to yerself." He cut the air with a sharp wave of his hand, a gesture of dismissal. "I'll nae be dragged into yer madness."

But she pressed on, quick, almost desperate. "Fine. Forget what I said." She shook her head, and her shoulders drooped a bit. "But...can you just for a moment pretend I'm not strange, not the crazy person you obviously believe I am? Maybe that I'm just a regular um, Scottish woman, who is lost, alone, and needing guidance?" Her voice thinned, the edges worn with fatigue. "Be honest with me, do you think it would be wiser for me to stay here? In this town? They must have a midwife, someone who knows better than I. And..." Though her gaze didn't drop to her belly, her hand smoothed over its curve. "Maybe the baby would be safer here than on the road with an army. What do you think?"

For a moment, he said nothing. Of all the men she might have asked—Kendrick, with his easy smile, or Blair, with his blunt honesty, even Ewan, who seemed so smitten of late—she had come to *him*. It unsettled him, that she looked to him for guidance when he was the least likely to offer comfort. Yet the way her voice wavered, the way her hand pressed protectively to her belly, struck a tender place he'd thought long scarred over.

She had come to him, and with that choice came an unwanted stirring—an instinct to shield, to steady, to be more than the brute he'd portrayed to her thus far.

"Why would ye ask that?" He inquired, stalling while he debated what his response should be.

Her throat bobbed. "Because I'm scared, Alaric. I've never—" She faltered, then shook her head. "I've never done this before, went into labor, delivered a baby. I don't know what to expect, or who might help me. I don't even know if it's safe for me to keep riding, or if I'm hurting the baby every mile we go." Once begun, the words tumbled out unchecked. "But if I stay here... if there's a midwife..." she paused and shrugged. "I'm so frightened for my baby. Forget all my own fear," she said, "being thrust here in this time—if it were just me, I could manage, I could hold my own, I think. But I have the baby to consider, and I just don't...I don't know what to do."

The sound of his name on her lips unsettled him, almost more than her plea. Few ever spoke it—*lad* was used by Mathar and the elder soldiers, *laird* from the rest of his army. *Alaric.* Not *laird,* not *sir,* but his name, said plain and direct. It struck too close, threading past the armor he kept between himself and others. He liked it—far too much, for how it warmed something in him he'd thought long cold. And he did not like that he liked it, not when he had already judged it wiser to keep her at a distance.

His thoughts returned to her question. The thought of leaving her should have eased him. Truly, it would be simpler—let her remain here, out of his charge, out of his sight. She would be among women, perhaps a midwife. She'd be spared the ceaseless march, the rigors of camp life. He thought he should be sorry that he hadn't thought of it.

And yet his chest tightened.

He thought of her bearing the march with stiff determination until weariness dulled her eyes and bent her shoulders. He thought of her small hand pressed to her belly so often, coaxing strength either into the bairn she carried or from it. He thought of how thin she'd grown in just ten days, how fragile she seemed despite the fire in her earlier words. A woman already petite and lean, she was wilting like a bloom cut from its root.

Could she withstand the trial of birth, should it come too soon? Even the strongest women often did not. He knew that too well. To leave her here meant he would not see her fail—if fail she did. He would not bear the guilt of watching another woman slip from his grasp, as Gwen had, her hand gone cold in his.

To turn Ivy over to strangers would unburden him. But the thought curdled.

Could he bear not knowing? Each day, wondering if she yet lived, if her child had come safely into the world, or if she lay in a shallow grave behind some croft?

"Ye canna be left here," he said at last, his voice rough, final. "Nae in this place. 'Tis a market burgh, aye, but one that sees too many strangers riding in and out—merchants from the south, messengers bound for Stirling, even English soldiers when it suits them. Too near to English-held ground, too full of eyes that would notice a woman alone. Ye'd have nae safety in such a place."

She nodded, accepting his answer and reasoning, it seemed, but winced in the next moment, "But I still don't think it's safe for me to keep riding."

"A cart would offer even less comfort, I suppose," he mused.

"I thought the same thing—too much bouncing. At least in the saddle I can control it."

Alaric scowled, thoughtful for a moment before he hit on a solution given their proximity. "I agree the march is nae place for ye, lass. If there is safety for ye, it lies in the home of a man I trust."

"A friend of yours?"

Alaric nodded. "And auld friend, a guid man."

"Okay, *home* suggests some comfort," she considered aloud, brightening dramatically. "That sounds like a better place for me—off the back of a horse, anyway. Oh, but...is it very far from here?"

It wasn't close, not at all, but then it was the closest friendly keep he could think of. "A few more days in the saddle, lass, but nae a difficult path."

"Oh, you would take me there?" she asked.

Alaric understood the question was not unreasonable, given some of his treatment of her, though still it rankled him, that she would believe now, after all this time, that he would simply send her off with naught but a direction.

"Aye."

"Um, will that mess up you and your army?" she asked. "Your mission?"

"We will be delayed, aye, but I'm imagining we might also be resupplied by my friend, enough to keep us marching and fighting for many weeks."

Ivy latched onto this, apparently pleased to know there was some benefit to him. "Okay, that's good then, right? The trip won't be a total waste of time for you and your army."

"Aye, nae a waste of time at all." He would, he knew, rather that she was settled safely.

"All right, if you're sure. Okay," she continued when he nodded. "Thank you. Really, I appreciate this very much."

He nodded again, curtly now, unaccustomed to such heartfelt gratitude.

And Ivy, smiling now, rose awkwardly to her feet, even as she seemed a little more nimble now. She dusted her hands off against each other. "I'll uh—" she pointed vaguely with her forefinger toward the camp behind him. "Thanks again." And with that, she skirted around the tree, returning to the camp, gone from his view.

Alaric drew a deep breath and finally, wearily, rose to his feet. He bit off half the forgotten oatcake and watched Ivy's progress, saw her return to the company of Kendrick, Blair, and Ewan.

His shoulders eased a fraction. With them, she was safe enough. For the most part, his men would guard her without even thinking about it, the way good men watched over their own. However, there were some in the ranks he'd sooner see nowhere near her, men roughened and made mean by so much violence seen and often too much ale. But those three, the lads who'd taken to her, he trusted them as much as he was able to trust anyone.

He'd just swallowed and popped the remaining oatcake into his mouth when Mathar's shadow loomed.

"*Jesu*, tell me I dinna just hear what I ken I did." Mathar's voice was pitched low, edged with accusation. "Ye mean to drag her with us still—and march us *outside* the war?"

Alaric turned, scowling, and finished chewing. "She canna continue at length with us, and she canna be left behind," he confirmed.

Mathar's brows snapped together, his scarred face creasing deep with disbelief. "God's wounds, lad. Have ye lost your sense entirely? Wallace is dead. Too few patriots remain, and those that do will fear the cause is lost. And ye—" he stabbed a hand toward the fire where Ivy sat, her profile soft against the flame—"ye would take us out of the fight for a woman heavy with child?"

Alaric's jaw clenched, but his voice when it came was iron, steady and deep. "I will nae have her birthing a bairn in the dirt, either with us or in some nameless village. She will be seen safely housed, made strong and able for the coming of the babe."

Mathar barked a humorless laugh. "Ye'll nae have—? She is nae a Scot's wife, Alaric—mayhap naught but an English whore for all we ken," the captain hissed. "Why risk so much for her?"

Alaric stepped closer, his voice dropping to a growl. "'Tis nae risk to ride two days to Caeravorn. I think with my conscience, Mathar. And if ye canna stomach my command, ye're free to ride elsewhere."

A tense silence stretched between them. The night noises of the camp seemed to hush—the crackle of fire, the murmur of men who might be eavesdropping on the tense standoff. Mathar's lips pressed thin, but he did not move.

At last, he spat into the dirt. "Stubborn bastard. One unknown woman shouldnae weigh more than Scotland."

"If our cause canna bear the weight of a woman's life," Alaric challenged, "then we're nae better than the English we fight." His gaze was unwavering. "She stays with us, and we'll move to Caeravorn on the morrow. I'll hear nae more on the matter."

Mathar muttered something low and foul under his breath, but he turned away, shoulders rigid, leaving Alaric standing alone.

Only then did Alaric allow himself the smallest exhale. He had made his choice, and though it would cost them time, though it might cost him the loyalty of some men, he could not do otherwise. Better their anger than the torment of abandoning her.

Chapter Nine

Ivy had not slept well. The camp had gone quiet soon enough, men rolling into cloaks and breacans, fires guttering low, but her mind refused to rest. Alaric's words circled back again and again—*Ye canna be left here... I'll see ye safe to a friend's house.* His insistence that she remain with them, that he would go out of his way to see her to a place safe enough for her to give birth had both stunned and relieved her. Honest to God, she had fully expected that he would seize on her suggestion to remain in the town, happy to be rid of her. Instead, he had claimed her fate as part of his own, and that knowledge both steadied and strangely unsettled her.

He'd offered her a friend's home—solid walls, a roof, maybe even women who might not look at her as if she were some mislaid oddity. The thought had warmed her enough to ease some of the cold in her chest, though the warmth did little to calm her restless turning on the hard ground.

By morning, her eyes felt gritty, her limbs heavy. The camp was already stirring by the time she woke, some coughing and wheezing, others hopping to their feet and off into the nearby trees. She slipped away quietly herself, always a bit further than the paths the soldiers took, desiring a bit of privacy to take care of her own needs beyond the camp's edge.

When she returned, she saw a large cluster of men had gathered near the makeshift pen where the horses were kept, bodies crowding together, leaning over the ropes to see whatever had grabbed their attention.

121

As she drew closer, she recognized sounds of distress, not from any man, but from one of the horses. A big red destrier stamped and snorted inside the rope pen, sides heaving, sweat darkening his hide. His ears pinned back, then flicked restlessly, and he swished his tail in agitation before dropping to one knee as if to roll.

"Hold him!" someone barked, and two men rushed in, keeping the animal from thrashing fully to the ground. Other horses were cleared out of the way at the same time. Mathar was there, his scarred face drawn tight, one hand braced against the destrier's neck as he crooned rough words to the beast.

Ivy squeezed through the knot of bodies, earning more than one annoyed glance, until she stood at the rope line. She didn't wait for permission. Ducking beneath, she moved straight to the horse's head, her hands outstretched, steady and unflinching despite the beast's massive size.

"What's happened?" she asked quickly, scanning the animal.

Mathar shot her a look, harsh and incredulous. "He's gone queer since dawn. Wouldna take his feed, and he's tried to go down thrice already."

Her gaze flicked over the destrier's abdomen, the sheen of sweat across his flanks, the way his hooves struck restlessly at the earth. "How's his fecal output been?"

Mathar exchanged baffled looks with several men, one of whom muttered, "What are ye asking?"

Concentrating on the animal still, Ivy answered mechanically. "Dung. Manure. Has he dropped any since morning?"

Understanding dawned. Mathar answered. "Nae that I've seen."

She nodded faintly, already moving, one hand pressing lightly against the horse's barrel, her ear angled toward his side. She listened, frowning, then drew back to lift his lip, checking the gums. "Pale," she murmured under her breath, then louder for the others' sake. "That's not good."

Mathar scowled. "What's nae guid? What are ye about?"

"He's in distress. I'm examining him," she said shortly, the certainty in her tone enough to still further questions. She crouched, watching the horse's restless shifting, the way he stretched his neck and pawed the ground. "It looks like colic. But that's only a symptom. We need to know the cause—spasmodic, maybe, which would mean just trapped gas. That's what we want."

The men blinked at her as if she had spoken in riddles, but her hands never faltered. She laid her palm against the great neck, feeling the frantic pulse there. But how to measure it without any tools or a clock? She looked at Mathar again, meeting his hard gaze with steady eyes.

"Mathar, do you think you can count to one minute—quietly, to yourself—and get real close to an actual minute, without going too far over or under?" she asked.

His brows snapped together. "What sort of fool question is that?"

"Can you do it or not? I want to measure his heart rate," she said firmly.

He hesitated. But, perhaps thrown off by the confidence in her voice, he soon gave a curt nod. "Aye."

"Good." She pressed her fingers tight against the horse's vein. "Give me a sign when you start and stop. One minute exactly," she reminded him. Not wanting to miscount, Ivy hugged the horse's neck gently, putting her ear against his rough coat. She cooed softly to him and then waited for Mathar's cue.

Mathar pointed what looked like a finger-gun at her when he began, his lips moving slightly though he counted without sound. Ivy focused, feeling the hammering beats beneath her touch and her ear, keeping her gaze on the captain, waiting for his signal.

"Sixty-four," she revealed when Mathar pointed at her, indicating his minute was up. She exhaled thoughtfully. "Too high. Maybe not dangerous, maybe elevated for how he was thrashing, but still too high." She said this more to herself, and then met the MacKinlay captain's steady gaze. "He's in trouble. But it's not hopeless. He needs to walk—don't let him roll; rolling could twist his gut—so if we're moving out that's good, He'll need clean water, but only a little at a time. We can reevaluate after an hour or so—you'll know if he's still in distress—but let's pray it's just gas."

She spoke with such surety that even Mathar nodded almost mechanically, and—as she'd noticed he was prone to do—he began barking orders for men to hold the horse, keep him upright and off his belly, while Mathar saddled him.

Ivy turned and scanned the crowd, finding Alaric among the watchers. "Are we heading out soon? If not, Mathar or someone can just walk him around until we're ready."

"Nae need to delay," Alaric said evenly. "We can march anon." His face gave away nothing, but his eyes lingered on her.

More orders were called out and the camp broke with startling speed. Ivy had half-expected a slow scramble of men fumbling with packs and gear, but instead the MacKinlays moved as though they had been preparing since before dawn. Fires were stamped out, weapons slung, lines formed—each man falling into place with practiced ease, the whole army shifting as one, a living, ordered thing.

She noticed something remarkable. As the column began to form, as men shuffled around, some inclined their heads to her, and a few even acknowledged her as they passed, murmuring a quiet "lass"—a simple greeting, she imagined. None had greeted her before. One soldier she didn't recognize—a lean man with a curly beard—appeared at her side, leading the bay gelding she'd been using, saddled and ready. He gave her a brief, respectful dip of his head before pressing the reins into her hand and stepping back without a word.

"Thank you," Ivy muttered, perplexed but strangely heartened.

It unsettled her, in a way, the sudden shift from wary stares to cautious civility. Yet it warmed her, too, loosening the knot in her chest that had plagued her for more than a week. By the time they were half an hour down the road, she noticed another shift in the MacKinlay army. Something was different, almost imperceptible at first—the shoulders of the men not so rigid, their voices no longer hushed with that constant clipped edge of tension. The line of soldiers moved with the same precision as always, but the mood overall seemed lightened, as if the weight of burdens had eased. They seemed chattier, talking more freely, and there were even several instances of laughter. For a brief stretch, one soldier somewhere behind her sang a few verses of a song, his rough voice carried on the crisp air, and others hummed the refrain until it died away into silence again.

Eventually, Ivy leaned toward Ewan, curiosity tugging.

"They're...different today," she said quietly. "Is it my imagination, or is the entire army cheerier today?"

Ewan glanced at her, his own expression lightened. "Aye, and for guid reason, lass. We're nae on the prowl, nae chasing anyone, so we dinna need to be so cautious, dinna need to mind how loud we are. And we're heading north, always cause for joy—on to Caeravorn Keep." His features became more animated. "We'll be removed from the main roads, behind strong walls and well-guarded approaches. A man could breathe there, find rest."

"Rest," Ivy repeated, the word feeling like a luxury.

Ewan nodded. "The laird there—at Caeravorn—greets us as kin. Warm hearths, full tables. The men ken it well. We'll nae find safer shelter this side of Ben Nevis." He looked ahead, toward where Alaric rode at the column's head. "Aye, they've more spring in their step for it. Even the laird and Captain."

***

As was his practice, Alaric rode the length of his army, moving from front to rear and back again, pausing now and then to exchange words with the men still confined to the carts—those not yet fit to walk or ride. Mercifully, their number grew fewer with each passing day; one by one, the wounded deemed themselves strong enough to take to the saddle or the march. On those circuits outside the column, Alaric's gaze strayed more often than he cared to admit toward Ivy.

He'd held his silence this morning when Ivy had worked with Mathar's destrier, though every instinct had urged him to step closer. For a brief moment, as he'd first come upon the scene, he'd had some irrational fear that she was placing a curse on the horse. Watching her inspect the huge beast and listening to her assured analysis, he'd been quickly disabused of that notion. Concern was her only motivation.

The scene lingered with him now as they marched, the rhythm of hooves steady over a broad stretch of grassland. His gaze strayed to her where she rode a few paces ahead as he returned to the vanguard, her hair glinting like burnished copper under the pale sun.

Before he could think better of it, Alaric guided his horse toward hers, closing the gap until they rode abreast. He felt her startle a little, her posture stiffening before she glanced sidelong at him.

"Ye ken horses well," he said, keeping his tone even, almost casual.

A faint flush rose on her cheeks. To his watchful eye, she seemed less guarded today—her shoulders looser, her mouth less pinched, as if the jauntier hum of the army had lightened her mood as well.

She leaned the smallest bit toward him, as if she meant her answer only for his ears.

"In my time, I went to school to be a veterinarian."

The word was unknown to him. His brow furrowed. "And what is that?"

"Oh, it's a kind of healer. But for animals. Horses, cattle, dogs. Not people."

"And ye—a woman—went to university to study such?"

She nodded. "Yes." Again, she lowered her voice and said for his ears alone, "In the future, women go to school as well. The veterinarian program is difficult, years of training. That's why I was—or am—in Scotland. I was studying abroad for a semester.

Well, and that turned out to be more than a year. But anyway, we learned all about anatomy, diseases, treatments—not that I ever expected to use it in the fourteenth century, mind you." She gave a small huff of laughter, quick to fade, though it tugged at something deep in his chest.

Alaric studied her profile, the curve of her cheek, the set of her mouth. She spoke easily, freely, as if indeed she spoke the truth, but Alaric could not fathom either a time or a place where lasses were instructed in the humors of beasts and the tending of their ailments. Madness, the very idea. And yet, he could not wholly dismiss it—not after watching her earlier. Mathar's destrier had improved, just as she'd said he might; simply getting the animal moving had eased the worst of the colic. Not a quarter hour past, Mathar himself had grumbled that the beast was near his usual temper again.

"And in this...future of yers," he pressed, with rare awkwardness, "what else is different? Do all lasses tend beasts? Ride with men? Speak as ye do?"

Her lips parted, then closed again, as if she weighed how much to say. At length she tilted her head toward him, her hazel eyes shining. "Some things are different, yes. Women go to school. They work. Some even lead armies—though not often, and not like you think. But some things..." she paused and shrugged, "...some things are always the same."

Recalling that she claimed to have come from a future seven hundred years away, he kept his expression purposefully neutral and heard himself ask, "What remains the same between now and then?"

She blinked, surprised by the question—mayhap surprised that he engaged her even this much. Certainly, he was surprising himself.

Ivy tilted her head, considering his question. "Um...well," she began slowly, her gaze drifting out over the rolling land as if searching for the right words, "parents still want their children to have a better life than they did." She worried at her lower lip for a moment, then went on. "People still fall in love and do stupid things for it. People still work from dawn to dusk just to feed themselves, behind a plow or behind a desk." Her hands shifted on the reins, thumbs brushing the leather straps. "We still drink ale—we call it beer. Different names, same product essentially. People still wonder where they fit, whether they belong." She paused, her voice softer now. "Hope looks the same, no matter what century you're in." At last her mouth curved, the briefest glint of humor lighting her eyes. "Men still snore. Women still complain about it."

Alaric's brow arched slightly, though he said nothing.

She chuckled under her breath, her eyes lighting. "That reminds me of this boy in my class, back when I was in high school. His name was Patrick O'Connor. Big, broad-shouldered guy, a football player—well, you wouldn't know what football is, but trust me, he was built like one of your soldiers. Every day, like clockwork, he'd fall asleep in Mr. Dawkins's history class. Head on his desk, out cold. And oh my God, the snoring. Like...like someone sawing through logs in the dead of night. It used to drive me nuts."

A few of the soldiers riding just ahead glanced back at her laughter, but Ivy went on, caught up in the memory.

"At first, at the beginning of the year, Mr. Dawkins tried waking him, rapping a ruler on the desk, calling his name. But Patrick never stirred—but man, did he snore loud. We had fun with that all year long. Once, my friend Jess painted his nails pink—I heard he didn't even realize it until like three periods later." She laughed a little louder now. "One time, he snorted so loud, startling himself awake, but so dramatically that he toppled straight out of his chair, hit the floor like a sack of bricks. The whole class burst out laughing. Even Mr. Dawkins laughed, though he tried not to." Ivy's smile lingered. "He was called Sleepy—after one of the seven dwarfs—but honestly, Patrick wasn't fazed at all, not embarrassed by his narcolepsy one bit."

She seemed to catch herself then, and her cheeks brightened with a pink stain. She glanced at Alaric with a now-stiff smile. "You probably didn't understand half of what I just said," she supposed.

Rapping a ruler? Painted nails pink? Seven dwarfs? Narcolepsy? Aye, she was correct—half her words were strange as sorcery. But he had watched her face as she spoke, the way her laughter rose, unguarded and light. He had understood that well enough.

"I ken the core of it," he managed, his tone even.

Mayhap his response was too spare, mayhap unconvincing, that Ivy shrank a little in the saddle next to him. And for reasons not entirely known, Alaric wasn't ready to depart, wanted to hear more from her.

"What of yer parents, then?" he asked. "Do they dwell in this strange world ye left? Would they nae be seeking ye?"

Her brow knitted. "Um, my parents...I don't even know if my mom has or will realize I'm gone. I'm not close with my mom and my father's been out of the picture for...forever. I was clos-

est with my grandparents—I like to think they raised me, really."
Warming to the subject, she continued, "That's where my happiest childhood memories are, on their farm."

Alaric caught the undercurrent of longing and prompted, when she quieted again, "They are gone, I presume, and ye long for them."

Her gaze wasn't on him but somewhere far ahead, past the road, past the ridges that hemmed them in, as if she could see another place altogether. She nodded slowly.

"Oh, God, yes. I miss them every day," she revealed. She tilted her head thoughtfully. "But I guess I should be thankful they're gone now—at this time. They'd be worried sick if they knew I was...lost." Another quiet moment passed before she smiled sweetly, still staring straight ahead, as if warmed by memories. "Every Saturday morning," she said, "my grandmother would fry up eggs and biscuits with gravy thick enough to stand a spoon upright. My grandfather would sit at the table, rattling the newspaper and arguing with the editorials out loud, as if they'd written them just to provoke him. And I—" she laughed softly "—I'd sneak biscuits into this fuzzy purple bag I had—to feed to the horses and cows—as many as I could before Grandma caught me. Sometimes, she'd smack my hand, grumbling about wasting food on a girl who never put any meat on her bones, but I think more often than not, she simply pretended she didn't see."

Her eyes had softened with recollection, her mouth curved in a wistful smile. Alaric found himself listening more intently than he meant to, his hand loose on the reins, his destrier plodding easily beside hers.

"I remember when I was about six or seven," she continued, her voice warm yet, "Gramps let me help bottle-feed a calf once. My arms were barely strong enough to hold him, and it seemed I had to wrestle with him to get him to drink. I was giving him something he needed—wanted—and I didn't understand why he fussed so much. He ended up knocking me flat—milk everywhere, and me dumped in the mud and muck of the barn. Gramps laughed until his pipe slipped from his teeth. I was mad and embarrassed and covered in mud, and Gramps told me it was a baptism—'nobody gets out of raising cattle without being covered head to toe in something,' he said."

The men around them rode silent, but Alaric could see some were listening too, ears tilted back. Her voice carried easy on the air, not boastful, not showy, but full of color.

She shook her head faintly, her smile dimming. "Those were the good weekends. The best, really. But then my mom found husband number four, and that was the end of it. No more weekends at the farm. She wanted me at home, part of her new family. Which—" a shrug, careless on the surface, but her tone thinned with something harder beneath "—wasn't really a family at all. Just another man she tried on, like a pair of shoes. Junior—that was his name. Fitting, since he was a small man in every way that mattered."

Alaric studied her carefully. She spoke quickly now, as if hurrying over the jagged places, smoothing them with dark humor. But he heard the change in her voice, the way the warmth drained when she spoke of her mother, and he understood the contrast without her needing to say it outright.

Again, he wasn't sure he comprehended all the particulars of which she spoke, but he forged out an idea that she'd been a lass dropped between two worlds—one solid, rooted in earth and routine, the other shifting and uncertain, where the only constant was disappointment, mayhap outright unhappiness.

Her grandparents gone, and her mother and father naught but shadows in her life. Alaric's mouth tightened. Whether her tale of coming through time were truth or madness, it mattered little—there would be none searching after her, none to mourn her absence.

As though reaching for the brighter side again, she turned to another memory from her grandparents' farm, recalling an instance of what seemed a fantastic storm, and her fright, but how her grandmother had made it all a game, she said.

He shifted in the saddle, his gaze lingering on her face as she spoke. She liked conversation, that much was plain. Perhaps she always had, but ten days in near silence and suspicion had corked it tight inside her. Now it spilled out in a steady stream, and against all reason, he found himself wanting her to go on.

She carried on, with little instigation, speaking of people and places he could not fathom, names and customs that meant nothing to him, and yet the joy in her voice needed no translation. He found himself listening, not for the strangeness of her tale, but for the music of it. He'd told himself he did not believe her, and yet for these moments, he almost forgot to doubt.

And then, for a stretch they rode in silence, but it was not an awkward one. The road unwound before them, the men's voices drifting in front and behind them.

By the time the sun hung high overhead, Alaric realized their talk had drifted far across many subjects. He could not recall the last time he had listened so long, so willingly, to another's voice. With Ivy, it seemed, he found no weariness in it. Her words came like a stream, and he let them wash over him, surprised by the ease of it. At times, he nearly forgot the men marching around them, the war ahead, the weight that ever pressed on his shoulders.

Chapter Ten

The company pressed on the next morning, the ground soft beneath their mounts, mist rising in slow curls from the damp earth. Alaric rode at the front, eyes ever sweeping the ridgelines and the road ahead.

The thunder of hooves announced the return of his scouts. Struan came first, mud spattered to his thighs, his mount lathered with sweat. He pulled up sharply, directly in front of Alaric.

"Riders ahead, my lord—two miles, maybe less," he informed him. "Royal guard, forty strong. They've a messenger with them, held tight at the center."

Alaric's jaw set. "Which way?"

"East, toward Inversnald."

Alaric's gaze swept the road, his thoughts swift, calculating. A messenger under guard meant intelligence, coin, or orders from Edward himself. None of those could be allowed to pass unchallenged. A ripple of sound went through the men—their interest piqued.

He gave a single nod. "Aye, we'll have them. Form up."

The men straightened as one, steel rasping from scabbards, horses snorting as reins were gathered tight.

Forty armed and armored Englishmen were no challenge and didn't need any particular strategy. The MacKinlays had ambushed parties of this size a dozen times at least, possibly more in the last year. Without either Alaric or Mathar having to call out commands, officers gave orders and men began to break off with their units, understanding what would be expected of them, where and how they should position themselves.

Alaric wheeled his mount down the line until he found her.

Ivy rode pale-faced among an army shifting into different formations, Kendrick, Ewan, and Blair having abandoned her to reach their units. Wearing a wee frantic expression, she met his eyes when he drew up before her.

His voice came low but necessarily firm. "We aim to take on a small band of English," he explained, certain no one else would have enlightened her about what was about to happen.. "Ye'll stay close to me until I tell ye otherwise. When we strike, I'll put ye in the trees. Ye'll nae move until I come for ye. Do ye ken me?"

She gave a stiff nod, knuckles white on her reins.

Alaric's jaw clenched. For a heartbeat he let his eyes linger. The wind had torn strands of her russet-gold hair loose from the plait she'd made, her mouth parted as if she meant to speak. And in that instant he saw her not as his charge but as prey, as any Englishman would see her—soft skin, unguarded beauty, something to be taken. His stomach turned hot at the thought of their hands on her, the ruin they'd make of her if she fell into their keeping.

"Come." He tore his gaze away and drove his horse to the fore, appreciative of Ivy's skill with a horse as she kept close to his flank.

The company surged, hooves hammering the earth as they raced east. The ground dipped ahead, the track funneling into a glen, though Alaric kept his army in the trees, on the crag above.

When he spied dust rising ahead, when the flash of banners and polished helms were visible through the trees, Alaric raised his hand, and riders peeled off to the slopes, archers with bows in hand. They were compelled to wait, of course, to allow the sprinting infantry to catch up.

Alaric angled his steed to the edge of the crag, and the English column came into full view below, neat ranks, armor bright, banners snapping. In their midst, the plumed helm of the messenger bobbed like a prize ripe for the taking.

Retreating a bit, aware that the swiftest of the foot soldiers had begun to arrive, Alaric hauled Ivy's horse from the line and dragged her deeper into the trees.

"Here. Ye'll keep still. If they break this way, go deeper. If nae, remain just here, dinna move. I'll find ye when it's done."

She nodded quickly, wide-eyed, veins in her neck taut.

Satisfied enough, he wheeled away. He glanced over the cliff once more and a moment later gave the signal to the horn-bearer. A sharp blast split the air. Highland war cries erupted, men pouring from the trees and down the steep slope. From the ridge, arrows hissed, finding joints in English mail before the hard charge hit.

Alaric led, drawing his sword when he'd cleared the decline, his destrier plunging straight into the enemy rear. The first stroke cleaved clean through a guard's neck; the second smashed a shield rim into splinters. Englishmen reeled, horses reared, and the neat line crumpled under the weight of the surprise attack.

He bellowed orders above the din, directing his men to press hard at the center. He saw the messenger's guards close ranks and drove straight for them, his sword merciless. One man raised his arm to block—too slow. Alaric's strike shattered through mail and bone, ripping the weapon from the man's grasp.

The man's sword spun loose, jolted high by the force of the blow. For a heartbeat it flashed above them, then came down tip-first. The steel glanced across Alaric's forehead before clattering harmlessly to the mud. Hot pain split across his brow. Blood poured instantly, running into his eye, but Alaric pressed on.

Blood sprayed hot everywhere, the stench of iron thick. The glen rang with screams, with the grunt and clash of men often too close for clean strokes. The messenger spurred hard for the east rise, but Struan and two others cut him off, dragging him down in a tangle of reins. His curses rang high before they stuffed a gag in his mouth.

And then, as suddenly as a storm spent, the field quieted. The last English broke and ran, arrows felling them before they reached the far slope. The ground was churned to muck, bodies strewn among heather and rock, horses stamping nervously.

A shout rose from the men as they circled the fallen messenger, who was dragged back toward his dead guard. His horse was produced, its load cut free. Straps were hacked through, leather torn, until at last a stout little chest was dragged free from where it had been bound behind the saddle. Iron-banded, the lock clung stubbornly. Struan swore, yanked a dagger from his belt, and jammed it hard into the seam. The lock snapped with a crack, and he rattled the box once in triumph before hauling it open. Inside, rolls of parchment lay atop sacks of coin, the wax seals of Edward's chancery pressed deep into each missive. Struan's grin widened as he pulled one free and thrust it toward Alaric.

Alaric broke the seal with his thumb, unrolling it quickly. His eyes flicked over the lines, brow furrowing as he read. He read more as Struan handed them to him, one after another, until his lips thinned.

"Financial writs," he muttered at last, the word edged with disappointment. "Coin owed out—sheriffs, justiciars, garrison commanders. Naught that tells us more than what we already ken." He glanced down at the chest, at the gleam of silver within. "And the coin meant to see it done." Alaric gave one curt nod toward the box. "See it kept. Edward's promises die here. His men will wait on pay that never comes, and men denied their due grow restless and angry."

Mounting again, his sharp glance next found the gagged messenger, the lone survivor, save for those writhing on the ground yet, who might possibly endure as well. "Turn him out. By the time he finds a friendly face in these hills, the silver will be long in our keeping, and Edward's men's faith in their king the poorer for it."

**

Having completely ignored Alaric's command, Ivy pressed herself to the rough trunk of a pine, sap tacky under her fingers. From where she crouched she saw the whole thing, the English caught in the valley as if goldfish in a bowl, with the MacKinlay Highlanders sliding along its rim like the shadow of death.

Her eyes widened when arrows hissed out of the green in a steady stream. Horses screamed, iron rang on iron, and the Highlanders struck the English from several directions. There was no stately crash of lines—just a violent, intimate tangle of men and mounts, so many Highlanders against so few Englishmen.

She never lost sight of Alaric. He fought close, brutal, nothing wasted. Twice she saw him check his swing at the last instant to avoid his own man and turn the blade to a blunt strike; once she saw him hook an English rider's bridle and rip the man clean out of the saddle. He was terrifying and precise and wholly himself in a way that made the breath lock in her throat.

It ended almost as abruptly as it had begun, a swift, one-sided bout.

A horse, riderless, trotted aimlessly until a Highlander caught its head and soothed it. A man on the ground coughed a wet sound and went still. Ivy could find no downed or dead MacKinlay man and breathed a sigh of relief.

It was then she realized how tightly she'd gripped the tree, for how her hands and fingers ached. She made herself unclench them, sap stringing between her fingers.

She watched as they tore booty from a horse, how they rifled through it, rolled scrolls being passed to Alaric for his perusal.

A minute later—unbelievably, possibly not more than ten minutes since the MacKinlays had descended into the valley—Alaric mounted and angled his steed in her direction, as if he would return already. For a mad second she was frozen until she recalled she wasn't where he'd told her to be, and raced back to her mare, left tied to the very tree Alaric had taken her to.

Of course, she wasn't able to vault into the saddle so easily, but she had found her seat, reins in hand, by the time Alaric and the army began to show themselves through the trees.

Alaric broke from the line, riding straight toward her.

Her breath caught. His face was streaked with sweat and grime, but it was the line of red that stole her words—a vivid slash of blood running from his brow, down into his eye and around the outside of it. She flinched, her stomach twisting at the sight.

"You're bleeding," she blurted as he drew near.

He gave her the briefest glance. "A scratch." He waved her forward. "Come."

"Alaric, that is *not* a scratch—it's a hole," she protested anxiously, though followed obediently. "It needs to be stitched."

He cut her off with a shake of his head. "We've nae time for such fuss. It's nae ever safe to remain too long near the fight."

They rode for hours, the road they followed little more than a scar through endless pine. Ivy swayed in her saddle, weary, unable not to worry about Alaric's cut, the blood that had dried dark along his brow and down the side of his eye.

He'd not touched it at all, hadn't even swiped blood away, but seemed completely unbothered by it.

When at last he called a halt, the sun was a smudge of gold behind the trees. Men slid stiffly from their mounts, rubbing at knees and shoulders. Fires were struck, water carried from a nearby stream. Ivy slipped from her horse and nearly crumpled with relief to be on her own legs again.

Alaric stood a little apart, stripping his gauntlets, flexing his blood-stained hand. In the low light the cut on his brow looked worse, swollen and ugly, a crust of dried red pulling at the skin.

Decisively, Ivy drew a sharp breath and strode to the wagon that carried Tàmhas's scant supply of tools. Her hands moved quick, snatching up a clean cloth, a bone needle, and a length of silk thread—the very items she'd seen Tàmhas use back at the convent. Before doubt could creep in, she turned and crossed straight to Alaric.

Back in vet school, she'd practiced sutures on pig skin, having been told it was the closest to human tissue. She'd stitched torn pads on dogs, closed wounds on barn cats, even once helped with a gash along a horse's flank. Muscle was muscle, skin was skin, whether it belonged to a beast or a man. The memory lent her a strange fortitude now—this was familiar work, however strange the circumstances.

"That's getting stitched, whether you want it or not," she said, when he realized her approach, going still.

His brows drew together. "I said to ye—"

"Yeah, I know what you said." She held out the cloth. "Where's your flask? Douse this with water."

Alaric ground out from between clenched teeth, "It dinna need stitching." He spoke slowly, enunciating each word abrasively.

Employing the same harsh tone and annoyed cadence, Ivy gritted through her teeth, "It does need stitching." When he only snarled at her, she shrugged. "You can submit to it now, have it done in under five minutes, or you can stand here and argue with me for much longer, because I won't take no for an answer." To further her cause, she said with frustration, "Alaric, it's still actively bleeding."

For a moment he looked ready to roar at her. Instead, with a muttered curse, he glanced about, found a log, and dropped onto it with a heavy sigh that struck Ivy as more petulant than fearsome. She bit back a grin.

Ivy followed and once more held out the cloth. Without a word, Alaric brought his flask from his hip and uncorked it, tipping it and spilling water over the linen.

"Thank you." She moved directly beside him, her thigh brushing his. "Here, hold this," she said next, giving him the needle and silk before leaning closer to assess the injury. Up close, she could see the line of the cut. A careful inspection showed it was indeed deep. "Luckily, you're hard-headed. Your thick skull likely prevented the blade from going deeper."

Her lips curved at her own jest, though she kept her eyes fixed on the wound.

Alaric jerked his head at that, giving her a hard glare, as if daring her to mock him further.

Ivy ignored it. Calmly, she set her fingers against the rough line of his cheek, firm but gentle, and turned his head back to where she wanted it. "Hold still," she said briskly, angling his face to catch the light.

His jaw flexed beneath her touch, but he didn't move again.

With careful fingers she pressed the cloth to it, wiping away the dried blood. He stiffened under her touch, his jaw working, but he did not move.

"See?" she murmured, her voice steadier than she felt. "Not so terrible."

The log he'd chosen sat high enough that, even seated, Alaric's face was nearly level with hers. She stood close, brushing against him, leaning in to reach the wound. Though she kept her attention on the cut, she didn't need to feel the weight of his stare.

She lost a bit of her resolve, her steadiness. He was too close—the breadth of him filling her vision, the heat of his breath mingling with hers. Her hands faltered, the cloth dragging a little longer than necessary across his temple.

She tried to keep it matter-of-fact, but her fingers lingered, smoothing hair back from his brow. He went still, utterly still, his gaze pinned on her.

Ivy's own breath shortened. She pulled her hand back at last, dropping the cloth onto the log at his side before holding up her hand for the needle and thread. Alaric transferred the implements from his hand to hers without taking his gaze from her face.

A heated blush rose under his unrelenting stare, creeping up her throat to her cheeks. Her fingers fumbled with the thread, trying to slip it into the eye of the bone needle. She clamped her teeth and focused, determined not to let him see how undone she felt.

"All right, here we go," she said when she was ready.

With careful hands she set the needle to his skin, the first prick making her own stomach tighten even as he gave no sign of flinching.

The work was slow—pierce, draw, knot, again. Her breath caught each time she pulled the thread snug through his flesh, each stitch tugging the wound's edges snug, the skin knitting tight beneath her hand.

He stayed silent, save for the long, even rhythm of his breathing, but his eyes never left her face. She tried to ignore it, tried to keep her focus on the line of the wound, though his unblinking stare unsettled her more than the work itself. Her blush deepened until she tied the last knot and asked for his dagger.

His other brow lifted but he did produce the weapon, its weight greater than expected. Ivy handled it awkwardly—it was too big for the task—but she managed to trim the thread and was finally able to step back, releasing the breath she was fully aware she'd been holding.

"There," she murmured, inspecting her work with a mix of pride and satisfaction, the latter borne from having gotten her way for once. "Stitched tight. Easy-peasy."

He nodded rigidly, didn't even raise his hand to inspect her work for himself, and stood from the log.

Ivy sighed. No, she hadn't really expected a spoken *thank you*.

***

The pathway became less friendly as the column wound its way higher into the hills the next day, the horses' hooves ringing sharp against stone. The air had cooled since midday, thin and brisk, carrying the damp tang pine and the scent of imminent rain. Alaric lifted his gaze from the twisting road ahead and saw at last the crown of Caeravorn rising over the crag like a fortress hewn from the mountain itself. Removed from the main roads and guarded by sheer slopes on three sides, Ciaran Kerr's keep was as secure a stronghold as any Alaric had seen.

The approach curled around a dark loch, its still surface mirroring the sinking light, broken only by a line of waterfowl that lifted in startled flight as the riders passed. Beyond the loch, scattered dwellings and barns crouched close together, their thatched roofs tucked low against the wind, which was fierce in these parts. He caught sight of figures pausing in their labors, women herding children out of the road, men straightening from fence-mending to watch the riders climb. The weight of their gazes followed, cautious but not unfriendly, likely having no cause for alarm as they began to recognize the MacKinlay plaids draped over so many men. Caeravorn's folk knew their laird kept his gates well and his allies close. More importantly, few knew of the stronghold's presence, nestled so securely beyond hard-rock beinns, with the Firth of Lorn at its back.

At the last bend, the keep revealed its full might. Its curtain wall was high and thick, the stone dark with age and lichen, and towers jutted at the corners like blunt spears. The gatehouse stood forward on its rock ledge, a choke point no army could breach without paying dearly. Behind it rose the hall itself, a massive block of stone set near to the precipice.

He slowed his horse, letting the column draw closer, his gaze traveling the battlements. Guards stood posted at every vantage, their cloaks snapping in the wind, and braziers burned along the wall walk, signaling readiness even as the day waned, but hardly signifying if the Kerr laird was in residence or not.

There was no need to announce himself, he was known to the Kerr army, had fought beside them often enough. He tipped his head upward, revealing his face, and soon a welcome was called down and the iron portcullis began its slow roll upward while cranks were heaved in the background.

Soon the gate was pulled open, and Alaric raised a hand, drawing the attention of the army behind him.

He turned in his saddle. "Ye ken the order," he called, his voice carrying down the line. "Foot and rank'll find quarter in the village. Post guards and make the camp in the south field, if it be fallow."

A murmur of assent ran through the riders, men peeling off already toward the lochside road that wound down toward the cluster of huts and barns below the keep. They knew the routine well enough; Caeravorn had been their refuge more than once, its villagers hardened to the sight of soldiers bedding down near their crofts.

Alaric shifted his reins as the column began to break apart, men guiding their mounts down toward the village with the ease of long practice. His officers drew in close, waiting for his lead, but his gaze searched the line until it found her—her warm, soft gold hair, slight frame, watching men and horses move all around her.

"Ivy," he called, his voice carrying easily across the din of shifting horses. He lifted a hand, beckoning her forward.

She hesitated only a moment before urging her mare through the press. When she reached him, he gave a curt nod and turned his stallion toward the yawning gate. "With us," he said blandly.

The iron portcullis loomed above, its teeth catching the light of torches within. The bailey opened wide ahead, alive with torchlight and the noise of a garrison at dusk. As he passed beneath the arch, he felt again that old, welcome certainty: within Caeravorn's walls, a man could breathe easier.

The doors to the keep were thrown wide to spill light across the trampled yard. From that glow stepped a tall figure, broad-shouldered but leaner than Alaric, his stride carrying the same self-assured ease that had marked him since boyhood.

Ciaran Kerr.

His green eyes caught the torchlight as he came forward, surprise flickering first across his face before it broke into open pleasure. "Alaric," he said, the name let loose on a laugh. "By God's bones, your timing is perfect. I've only just returned myself, a matter of days ago."

Alaric dismounted and they clasped forearms hard, a thud of leather and flesh between them. Alaric felt the strength in his grip and returned it with a grin that came more easily than he'd thought it might.

"Fortune smiles on us both, then," he answered.

Ciaran released him, turning his easy smile on Mathar, clasping the older man's arm in greeting before nodding to the others who had ridden in close. Only then did Ciaran's gaze slide, just briefly, to the woman who still sat her horse among them. He asked no question, only showed a flicker of curiosity before it was gone.

Alaric turned, letting his expression cool into something more neutral. He moved to her side and reached for the mare's reins, steadying the horse before lifting his hands to Ivy. "Come."

She looked down at him, hesitation plain in her hazel eyes, but leaned into him, placing her hands on his shoulders. He closed his hands under her arms and drew her down, her slight weight—bairn included—no burden as he set her on the ground at his side.

"This is Ivy Mitchell," Alaric said to Ciaran, his voice even, offering no more and no less. Then, to Ivy, he added, "Caeravorn's mormaer and laird of the Kerrs, Ciaran."

"It's very nice to meet you," Ivy said, her voice quiet but steady.

She tipped her face a little, something between a nod and a bow—respectful enough, Alaric supposed, though he doubted she'd done the like before.

"As it is you, lass," Ciaran returned warmly. "Caeravorn welcomes ye."

His green eyes lingered only a moment longer before shifting, first to the swell at Ivy's middle, then to Alaric. No word passed his lips, but the look carried an unspoken question plainly enough.

Alaric held his gaze without flinching, his own expression deliberately neutral. He hadn't given thought to this, that Ciaran, whom he'd not encountered in half a year, might assume the child was his.

Before the silence could stretch, Ciaran gestured them forward and turned toward the hall doors, drawing them inside.

The doors groaned shut behind them, muting the quiet noise of the bailey. Within, Caeravorn's great hall opened wide, its vaulted roof lost in shadow above the glow of torch and hearthfire. Rushes softened the flagstone floor, and long trestle tables lined the chamber, benches shoved back for the evening. At the far end, the hearth blazed, flames casting a restless light on the carved stone mantle. Above it hung the ancient Kerr banner, black and bold, its edges frayed from wind and war.

Ciaran led them across the hall, his stride easy, pausing only to exchange a word with a passing servant who nodded and then bowed before scurrying away.

When they reached the high table, Ciaran gestured to the long benches set before it. "I've asked for food and drink to be made ready," he said, his voice carrying easily through the vaulted space. "You've ridden hard—sit and be welcome."

More servants appeared, hurrying to lay trenchers and pitchers along the board, the smell of roasted fowl and fresh bread drifting up as lids were lifted. Ciaran's green eyes turned briefly to Ivy, who lingered at Alaric's side as though uncertain of her place.

"Have ye need of aught, lass?" Ciaran asked.

Ivy hesitated, her hazel gaze flicking first to Alaric, as though uncertain if she ought to answer without his leave. He gave a short, silent nod, and only then did she turn back to Ciaran.

"A bed, perhaps," she said haltingly. Quickly, nervous now, she added, "If that wouldn't be too much trouble."

"Nae in the least," Ciaran replied at once, a hand flicking toward a waiting servant. "See her to a chamber, and see it made warm." Then, more directly to Ivy, he offered, "I'll have a tray provided anon. Would a bath also be to your liking?"

Her hazel eyes widened, almost childlike in their surprise. "Oh, my God—would it ever!" she blurted, then turned instinctively to Alaric again, as if to share her joy at such an unexpected boon.

Ciaran laughed, the sound easy and unforced. "Then it will be so." He nodded to the hovering servant, a young, dough-faced lass who smiled pleasantly as she approached Ivy.

"Thank you, sir. Thank you so much," Ivy said, genuinely grateful, before she followed the girl away from the table.

Alaric's gaze lingered as she crossed the length of the hall, her slight form dwarfed by the soaring walls and heavy beams overhead. At the far end, just before she vanished through the doorway, she turned back. Her eyes found his across the distance, as though she sought only to make certain he was still there.

Something in his chest tightened, sharp and not entirely unwelcome. He gave another nod and held her gaze until she slipped from sight.

Ciaran drew out a chair at the far side of the high table himself and once all his guests were seated, dropped onto it with the easy grace of a man at home. He reached for the pitcher of ale and filled a cup, handing it to Alaric, and then filled another for himself before passing the pitcher down the table. "It is guid to see ye within these walls again, my friend. Though I confess, I dinna expect it."

Alaric took the cup, settling heavily into the chair at his side, his officers crowding in along the board. "Nae did I. Yet the times make wanderers of us all."

Ciaran's smile faded. "Aye. And now Wallace is gone, the times grow darker still."

The words fell into the hall with the weight of stone, and for a moment no one spoke. The fire popped, throwing sparks up the chimney, and Alaric felt again the ache of loss, though his jaw set hard against it.

Alaric let the silence rest only a heartbeat before he broke it with a slight shrug of his shoulders. "In truth, the lass is what brings us here. She canna abide with us, nae any longer as her time grows near." He took a long swallow of Kerr's fine ale and then turned to his friend. "I was hoping she could abide here, bear the child here."

"So it will be, but God's bluid, man, I'm left to wonder," he said, his tone lighter, though his gaze was sharp as ever. "Who is she? Why is she garbed so strangely? And"—his eyes flicked once more toward where Ivy had departed—"have you fathered a bairn since last we met?"

Alaric's jaw tightened, and his answer came sharper than intended. "We came upon her in the aftermath of a skirmish with the English. Lost, alone. I dinna ken her before then, a fortnight ago." He shrugged, indicating he knew little else. "The child is nae mine," he stated emphatically.

The words hung there a moment, with enough finality that even Ciaran let them be. Yet as Alaric lifted his cup again, the taste of the ale seemed less satisfying than before.

Chapter Eleven

The chamber was larger than Ivy had expected, more than twice the size of that nun's cell she'd been given before. Its thick stone walls caught the glow of a single torch set in an iron sconce. The hearth was cold and dark at first, but the servant girl bustled in without pause, kneeling to coax a flame from kindling laid ready in the grate. Soon the crackle of fire filled the space, smoke curling up through the chimney, warmth spilling into the chill.

The girl was plump-cheeked and round-faced, her brown hair tucked beneath a handkerchief on her head. She spoke softly in words Ivy didn't understand. More Gaelic, Ivy guessed.

"I'm sorry," Ivy said with an awkward smile. "I don't understand."

The girl pointed at Ivy—specifically and separately at her sweater and leggings—murmured something again, and then made some motion over and over again, with her hands that was not—as far as Ivy knew—the universal sign for anything.

Ivy narrowed her eyes studiously and nodded while she tried to guess what the maid was attempting to say. "Okay, my clothes are different? Yes, I'm sure they must seem very strange." Again, the maid brushed her hands together, back and forth. "Are you asking what the material is? The sweater's polyester, I think—though it's seen better days, obviously." Ivy shrugged. "The leggings are jersey—cotton, I guess." As the young girl appeared to become frustrated by Ivy's poor charade skills, Ivy offered her an apologetic grimace.

The girl sighed and stepped forward, reaching out her hands toward the hem of Ivy's sweater. Assuming she wanted to touch it, to feel it—it did look very soft, and it was—Ivy allowed this. But the girl didn't only touch it, she took hold of the hem and began to lift it.

"Whoa, whoa, whoa," Ivy argued with a nervous laugh, pushing away the girl's hands, backing up a step.

The girl tilted her head, completely unruffled by Ivy's resistance. She seemed only to be still considering how to convey something to Ivy. And then she shook her head, offered a few murmured words, holding up her hand, palm forward as if to say *wait*, and then gave a small curtsy before slipping out of the room.

Despite the near-undressing by a complete stranger, Ivy felt lighter of heart and mind than she had in a long time, and jokingly commented to the closed door, "It's going to take more than a soft bed and the promise of a hot meal to get me to drop my drawers, missy."

Alone now, with only the glow of the fire lighting the chamber, Ivy took in her surroundings. The room was nicer than she ever would have imagined for the fourteenth century. Two walls were hung with woven tapestries, their faded colors still rich against the stone. A beautifully embroidered bedspread of dark beige covered what appeared to be a generously stuffed mattress on a four-poster bed. Atop it lay a fur blanket of gray-brown, impossibly thick and large. Ivy sank her fingers into it, her mouth parting in wonder at the plush feel.

A short table stood beside the bed, supporting an ewer and basin, and a tall cupboard filled the space between the two windows. Near the fireplace stood a lone seat—little more than a stool since it was simply a seat without a back—and a small square table, no bigger than a checkerboard.

Drawn by curiosity, Ivy crossed to one of the windows, lifting the latch and pushing the shutters wide. Cool air rushed in, sharp against her face, but her gasp was in reaction to the sight below. The keep sat on a short cliff, its stone walls rising directly above a body of water. The water stretched vast and silver in the twilight, the horizon seeming endless, dissolving into a haze where sea met sky. The window was just high enough that she couldn't look directly down, but thought she heard the sound of small, slow waves rolling in, and wondered if there was a beach down there.

The iron latch of the door scraped, and the door opened again. This time, an older maid entered behind the round-faced girl. Her eyes were sharper, her bearing brisk, and to Ivy's relief she spoke halting English.

"The bath comes," the woman said without preamble.

Ivy nodded quickly. "Great. Thanks."

The older maid gestured toward the plump-cheeked girl. "Evir, she...helps."

"Ohhh," Ivy replied, drawing the sound out in sudden understanding. So that's what the girl had been trying to do earlier. But her relief faltered. Heat rushed to her cheeks as the girl stepped forward, expectant. Ivy balked. Never in her life had she been disrobed by anyone she wasn't dating—or, well, sleeping with. And yet she knew, from all the historical fiction she'd devoured over the years, that this might be normal here. Maids assisted their ladies and visitors, undressed them, bathed them, brushed their hair—normal here, for them, but not for Ivy.

Just then, a young kid carried in a large wooden tub that seemed to be twice the size of him, setting it near the table and chair and fire. With only a darting glance at Ivy, he took off.

Ivy shifted her weight, caught between gratitude and an un-willingness to offend. "That's...kind of you, but I can manage," she said to the maids. When neither seemed to comprehend this, Ivy added, "Thank you, but no help needed." She smiled, hoping they didn't think her rude. "I can manage."

Evir, standing in the shadow of the older woman, looked at the back of the woman's head as if waiting for explanation. The older woman nodded, her lips tight, as if to say, *Fine, do it yourself.*

With a few words to Evir, the older woman departed, just as buckets of steaming water were delivered in the next minute, carried in by another pair of servants.

Evir hovered uncertainly. Only then did Ivy notice what the girl carried. In one arm she held several lengths of rough cloth—toweling of some kind, Ivy supposed, woven and coarse but clean. In the other she balanced a small, pale lump, no bigger than her fist. Ivy blinked. *Soap?* At least, it looked like soap, though she'd never seen medieval soap before. For all she knew it could be a lump of fat or lye or something more sinister.

Evir lifted the cloths as if to show her, then offered the pale cake with an encouraging smile, speaking a few gentle words Ivy didn't understand.

"Thanks," Ivy murmured, reaching out to take them, her mouth quirking despite herself. "I think I get it."

Evir bobbed her head, clearly relieved, and exited the room.

Trip after trip, more water was brought to fill the tub, until it lapped high and a faint mist of steam rose in the flickering light. Ivy clasped her hands together in eager anticipation.

A few minutes later, alone in the room, the door closed by the last departing water-bearer, Ivy finally peeled off clothes she'd been wearing for two weeks straight and slipped into the bath. The heat wrapped her at once, a luxurious embrace that made her groan aloud. She sank deeper until it lapped her shoulders, closing her eyes as if the weight of the past weeks had lifted clean away.

"This," she whispered to the quiet room, "is heaven."

Honestly, she'd tried not to think about it overmuch in the last two weeks, but the truth was she hadn't bathed properly since she'd come to this century. All she'd managed were hurried washes in icy lochs and creeks, crouching behind rocks with numb fingers and an anxious ear for the men nearby. Her mother's voice surfaced then—half amused, half resigned—calling such a thing a "whore's bath." The phrase came back with startling clarity, spoken once long ago as she and her mother had cleaned all the important areas with a washcloth at the kitchen sink when there'd been something wrong with the plumbing in the lone bathroom for more than a week. Ivy smiled at the memory, though it tugged at her heart all the same.

Though she couldn't stretch her legs in the tub, she did let her head fall back. Already she loved this place—the sturdy keep, the warmth of its hearths, the simple promise of a clean bed and a private chamber. For the first time since she had been cast into this strange world, she felt she might truly be safe. This, at least, was endurable—and so much safer for her baby.

She could stay here forever, she thought dramatically, *if* she were forced to remain in this century.

The thought alone was startling enough, but what followed was worse—an addition her mind slipped in, soft as a baby's breath.

But only if Alaric remained as well.

Her eyes flew open, staring at the rafters above. After a moment, she realized this should come as no great shock to her after all. Kendrick, Ewan, and Blair had been fine companions on the march—cheerful, patient, even protective in their own ways—but it had been Alaric's towering presence that had most often set her at ease. Impossibly adrift in time, lost in a distant century, she had every reason to come apart at the seams. Half the time she still felt unhinged, barely keeping herself together. But Alaric's presence—solid, strong, *so freaking capable*—had steadied her more than she'd realized until now. Possibly, he was the sole reason she hadn't lost her mind entirely.

And it wasn't only his steadiness. There was no denying it: he was striking, the kind of man a girl might have conjured up in daydreams. Broad-shouldered and battle-worn, handsome in a way that belonged wholly to this age, he was the sort of figure who could have stepped out of an illuminated manuscript—except he was real, flesh and blood, and here she sat, imagining a forever in this century that included him and his electrifying brown-eyed gaze.

The latch scraped softly a short while later, and Evir slipped back inside, her arms laden with folded cloth. She set the items neatly upon the bed and shyly made motions with her hands as if pulling something over her head.

"Oh, I see," Ivy acknowledged with a fresh surge of joy. A fresh set of clothes. "Thank you, Evir."

When the door closed again, Ivy got to the business of bathing. The faintly scented soap waited on the stool beside the tub. It was gritty, rougher than anything she'd known, but when she lathered it in her hands, a soft fragrance rose. Roses, she thought, or close enough.

She scrubbed every inch of herself, determined to erase two weeks of grime and sweat, and then worked the same soap through her hair. The suds felt too thin, nothing like the careful products she once lined along the edge of her shower, but she nearly groaned with happiness all the same. Her strict routine was gone, her conditioners and rinses possibly lost forever, but for now, her body and hair finally clean, she felt a little more like herself again.

When the water had cooled and her fingers had wrinkled, Ivy finally climbed from the tub. The towels that waited for her were rough cloths, coarse against her skin but absorbent enough. She dried herself briskly, shivering as the air closed in on her bare skin, then turned to the folded garments on the bed after she'd wrapped a second towel around her hair and flipped it over her head.

Two gowns were included in the stack, it seemed. Or maybe a chemise and gown, she decided. One was sleeveless, the other long-sleeved and heavier. Beside them lay a pair of thick woolen tights. Ivy lifted them, incredulous. *In August?* They looked better suited for trudging through snow than for summer. Still, she pulled them on, the wool not as scratchy as she'd expected and undeniably warm, reaching to mid-thigh before she knotted the ties.

She tugged the creamy chemise over her head and smoothed it down. Then she wrestled into the long-sleeved gown, which was rather a dull light brown, and adjusted the low round neckline until the chemise didn't show. It felt bulky, layered, and heavy, but not awful. At least she was covered.

She gave herself a little turn toward the fire, smoothing down the drab brown skirts. It was fine. She'd get used to it, she determined.

A tray arrived as she was combing out her damp hair with her fingers, yet another young girl setting it down on the table near the stool and fire before quickly disappearing. Roasted meat, a hunk of coarse bread already slathered in butter, and a small wedge of cheese were easily identifiable. What looked like a puffed pastry square and had brown gravy oozing out the top, some kind of meat pie, she assumed. But most suspicious—a brown and gray lump that Ivy eyed with deep distrust as she approached.

Still, the full plate of food beckoned her, and she ate slowly, savoring each bite—though that brown lump remained pushed to the edge of the wooden platter.

She'd eaten only the dense, savory bread when a knock sounded at the door.

The door creaked open then, and she startled, having expected yet another servant.

Alaric's head appeared around the jamb, his eyes sweeping the chamber quickly before settling on her.

"Oh, hi," she greeted him, rising to her feet though she didn't know why she did that. "Come on in," she said, twisting her hands with a bit of nervousness then as his brooding gaze raked her from head to toe. Ivy dipped her face and splayed out the skirts a bit. "It's super comfortable but it... feels awkward."

"Ye are well enough?" he asked, his voice low, his gaze lingering briefly on her stomach, which expanded the skirt below the empire seam beneath her breasts.

"Oh, God yes," she said, smiling despite herself. "Honestly, Alaric, I appreciate everything you've done for me over the last two weeks—a lot of it reluctantly, I believe, which makes me appreciate it all the more—but this...? Look at this—the bed, the bath." She smiled brilliantly at him and ran her hands through her wet hair. "My hair is clean," she said with some excitement. Many other parts were blessedly clean as well. "I have this fire, apparently all to myself. This place is incredible."

Before he could respond to that, Ivy gestured to the tray on the table. "Alaric, look at the crowded plate—have you ever seen anything so fabulous? Oh, gosh, did you eat? Do you want some of this?"

"Aye, I've eaten, lass."

She had a niggling suspicion that he was holding back a smile, maybe only a grin, but whatever it was—or might be if he let it be—it amazed her.

She drifted next to the bed, the skirts of her gown floating around her legs, and smoothed her hand over the luxurious pelt. "Look at this fur. Have you ever seen anything so extravagant? But Alaric, is this from a real wolf?" She glanced back at him, half-horrified and half-enchanted.

Alaric's mouth twitched again, still only *almost a smile*. "Aye. Real enough. Likely brought down by your host or his father before him."

Ivy gave a small laugh, still stroking the pelt. "I can't decide if that makes me want to curl up in it, or apologize to the wolf."

He only shook his head, though the glimmer in his eyes betrayed amusement. His gaze flicked to the table then, to the plate she'd abandoned. "Ye've eaten little."

"Oh, I'm getting to it, don't you worry. But come and look at this, Alaric," she requested, crossing the room again. "What's this brown blob? It looks weird and doesn't smell too appetizing."

Alaric sidled up next to her, peering over her shoulder.

"I've heard of haggis," she said, "but hadn't yet worked up the nerve—or the stomach—to try it since I've been in Scotland," she confessed. "This isn't haggis, is it?"

"'Tis pudding—offal and oats boiled in a stomach."

Ivy recoiled. "Oh, Jesus," she gasped, wrinkling her nose. "That's...so much worse."

This time his lips did curve, faint but unmistakable.

Her shoulders sagged a bit in a mock sigh, his amusement at her horror made inconsequential in the face of his unexpected smile. Then she realized he was watching her more closely than before, his fleeting smile fading as quickly as it had come, his thick brows slashing downward.

"Why do ye stare?" he asked.

Ivy shook herself. "Sorry. Nothing. It's just... I don't think I've ever seen you smile, Alaric. It's...nice."

It wasn't merely nice. It was transformative, breathtaking. Strange, though. She had admitted to herself that she was drawn to him, and yet she hadn't specifically thought about his looks, not in a way that measured handsomeness. But—wow!—when he smiled, even just that fleeting curve of his lips, he was super hot.

His gaze dropped, and he shifted as if suddenly restless. "I've been given a chamber just down the hall," he said, his voice rougher than before. "I'll be near if ye have a need."

Sensing an imminent departure, Ivy realized she didn't want him to go. But she nodded all the same. "All right."

He lingered a moment longer, then gave a curt dip of his head and turned for the door. The latch clicked softly behind him, leaving Ivy alone with the warmth of the fire, and the greater warmth still lingering from the memory of his smile.

***

Ivy woke later than she had in weeks. No men snored nearby, no commands were barked out to get the army on the road, no horses snorted and pawed the earth nearby. The silence pressed soft against her ears, decadent in its strangeness. For once, no one was rushing her to mount up, and she harbored no fear that the MacKinlays would move on without her.

The older woman with the careful English appeared not long after Ivy stirred. She carried in a trencher of warm oatcakes and cheese, and when Ivy asked after Alaric, the woman shook her head.

"MacKinlay laird...with Kerr laird. Gone before sun." She set the tray down and straightened, folding her hands over her apron. "He say...you find Mathar, or Ewan, or Kendrick. If need."

Ivy smiled her thanks before the woman slipped back out. Did Alaric ever allow himself to rest? She wondered if he even knew how to simply...be.

She made use of the chamber pot she'd found under the bed yesterday and had her breakfast at the small table by the hearth. Noticing that her own clothes seemed to have disappeared but that her short boots remained, she tugged them on, grateful for their familiarity, even if they looked oddly out of place beneath the brown wool gown that brushed her ankles with each step.

Venturing into the corridor, she paused, uncertain, her hand brushing the cold stone of the wall as she listened. The hall below was quieter than she expected, only a few quiet voices were heard. Ivy walked further and then down the stairs, reaching the cavernous hall. The long trestle tables stood empty, the fire on the hearth burned low, and the air smelled faintly of smoke and grease.

Gathering her courage, Ivy crossed the flagstones and found the great doors at the far end. She pushed one open, blinking against the sudden daylight. The bailey beyond was alive with sound and motion. Blacksmiths hammered at glowing metal while two women—dressed as she imagined peasants would be— seemed to be arguing over a basket, while chickens squawked underfoot.

Unable to understand the language used by the women—and thus unable to eavesdrop—Ivy glanced around, spotting Ewan straightaway. He was crouched near the stables inside the courtyard, a hand steadying the flank of a MacKinlay horse while a Kerr farrier worked the nails into its hoof.

Ivy hesitated only a moment before stepping closer. "Ewan?"

He glanced up, squinting against the sun. "Aye, lass?" His gaze shifted down from her face, the brief surprise shown likely due to her new outfit.

"I was wondering...would it be all right if I walked down to the village?"

He nodded almost immediately, giving his attention again to the horse and its shoe. "So long as ye keep to the road and mind yerself," he said, "there'll be nae harm in it. The folk ken us well enough."

"Thanks."

"Dinna go beyond the village, lass!" Ewan called after her.

Ivy waved her hand over her head as she skipped away, acknowledging his advice.

The path wound down from the gate toward the loch, where cottages and barns huddled close to one another. Thatched roofs sloped low against the wind, peat smoke curling from their chimneys. Some houses appeared to have been built half-buried in the ground, the overhang of their roofs being not more than four feet off the ground.

Ivy slowed, taking it all in. A pair of men appeared to be mending the fence that enclosed one house's back yard. A group of young girls, stooping, gathered bundles of sticks. A short posse of young, wild-haired children raced and stumbled about, chasing a wayward chicken. A dog barked and darted at Ivy's skirts, sniffing almost frantically before racing away again. No one stopped her, but more than one villager looked up, their eyes following her with quiet curiosity.

Once more, she felt as if this couldn't be real, but that she'd simply stepped straight onto a working movie set, about to film from a medieval script. Still, there was nothing picturesque about it—the walls were rough, the barns weathered, the people hardened—but it was alive.

Sadly, she realized that without knowing anyone, and having no one to visit and being unable to speak the language of these people, there wasn't much to see or do. Thus, her desire to immerse herself, so to speak, at Caeravorn, all but deflated inside her.

Still, she meandered about a bit, realizing after a while that she wasn't simply taking in the village. Every deep voice that carried from a doorway or every rumble of wheels along the track pulled her head around, her heart leaping as if she expected to find Alaric. She caught herself scanning the open field beyond the village for his silhouette and straining to catch the sound of hoofbeats, anticipating his return.

What is wrong with me?" she thought, pressing a hand to the small of her back. The answer came swiftly, automatically. That smile he'd shown last night had really fascinated her.

Her other hand drifted unconsciously to her belly, curving firm and round beneath the brown gown as the baby shifted. It wasn't a kick, just a slight adjustment inside the womb.

Just a little more than a month now, Ivy realized.

The thought suddenly turned her mouth dry, Alaric's stunning smile forgotten.

She still agonized sometimes, thinking of what was coming—of the pain, the blood, the risk. True, coming to Caeravorn had relieved much of her worry, but truth was, she was still terrified about giving birth in the fourteenth century.

That thought gave rise to another: she should know the midwife. She should find her before the time came, not stumble into her arms in a panic.

So Ivy began asking, haltingly, of those she passed—a woman stooped over her wash, a man hefting a sack of grain, even a barefoot boy chasing a goat. "Midwife?" she asked, gesturing awkwardly toward her belly. "Do you know...midwife? Where she is?" Each of them blinked at her, some smiling faintly, others shaking their heads, but none offered words she could grasp. Gaelic again, quick and lilting, spilling too fast for her to catch. She thanked them anyway and turned back toward the keep.

Inside the gate, the bailey was quieter than half an hour ago. Ewan was nowhere to be seen, but she did spot Mathar just exiting the stables. Ivy hesitated, then squared her shoulders and crossed to him. "Mathar?"

He looked up, body freezing as if bracing himself.

"I was looking for the midwife, trying to ask around for her without success," she said. "Do you know where I can find her?"

His expression suggested at worst, only that he wondered why she was asking *him*. But then he exhaled heavily through his nose. "Aye. Come on, then. I'll take ye."

She fell in beside him as he didn't hesitate, but made for the gate, his long strides forcing her to quicken her steps.

They walked in silence at first, but she stole glances at his weathered face and searched for something to say.

"Have you been here often?" she asked at last.

"Aye, more than only a time or two." His answer was short, but not unfriendly.

"It's...different than I expected," she said, waving a hand toward the cottages and barns. "Although I guess that's not specifically true, since I don't know what I expected."

That earned her a brief, sideways glance and a "Hmm" but nothing else.

Oh, well. She tried.

When they reached the lower lane, Mathar slowed, catching the arm of an old man passing with a bundle of firewood. The two exchanged quick words in Gaelic, before the man pointed with his chin toward a small house set back from the track, its roof sagging slightly under the weight of thatch.

Mathar gave a short nod and led Ivy on. She clutched her gown, lifting the hem clear of a muddy spot as they crossed to the house.

A woman answered the knock, middle-aged, with sharp eyes that scanned Ivy's face with suspicion before her gaze softened when it fell to Ivy's belly.

Mathar addressed her in Gaelic.

She replied to Mathar in the same unknown language and then said to Ivy, "A bairn soon, aye?"

Relief bloomed in Ivy's chest, and she nodded quickly. "Yes—yes, soon."

Then nothing, only them nodding at each other, until Mathar—with the sound of eyes rolling in his tone, if there were such a thing—said to the woman, "I gather she wanted to meet ye, as she'll be abiding her for a while, until the bairn is born."

The woman smiled with greater understanding than and stepped aside, waving Ivy inside.

Mathar lingered at the threshold, shoulders easing as if some burden had lifted. He cleared his throat. "Ye'll manage back on yer own?"

Ivy turned toward him, touched by the rough courtesy behind the question. "Yes, absolutely. Thank you, Mathar."

He dipped his chin, already stepping back. "Aye then." And with that, he strode away without a backward glance.

Inside, the house smelled of smoke and herbs, as dozens of bundles of dried plants hung from the underside of the thatch. Ivy took note of the blackened walls, where pieces of mortar seemed to have fallen away here and there. Animal pelts covered different spots on the dirt floor and a collection of wooden pots hung directly over the fire in the center of the cottage. The midwife moved with brisk purpose, drawing Ivy toward the hearth where a stool waited.

"Sit, aye?" invited the woman.

Ivy obeyed, lowering herself gingerly onto what seemed a very low and very questionable stool. "You're the midwife?"

The woman nodded and then shuffled off. She was heavyset and walked with a noticeably uneven gait, as if her hips or knees bothered her. "Aye. I help bring the bairns." When she faced Ivy again, she held a larger, more sturdy chair in her meaty hands. She placed that next to Ivy's and sat down.

Relief welled in Ivy again. "Good. I—honestly, I don't know what I'm doing. I've read books, but..." She laughed nervously, gesturing helplessly at herself. "That's not the same thing. And this will be my first time giving birth." *First time ever, either in this century or the one I wish I were still in.*

The midwife gave her a long, steady look, then smiled. "We'll do it together. Ye are strong. Bairn strong." She patted Ivy's hand, then mimed breathing, slow and even. "Calm is most important."

Something in the woman's certainty soothed her frayed nerves. Ivy nodded, repeating the motion of the breath, almost like a student eager to please.

They spoke a little longer, the midwife eventually introducing herself as Ruth. Actually, Ivy had been compelled to ask the woman to repeat her name several times, since she kept hearing *Rut*.

Ruth managed to convey that she'd delivered forty-eight babies, and then pointed to several plants hanging overhead, naming a few Ivy recognized—"mint," "sage"—before slipping into Gaelic, possibly unconsciously. Ivy didn't stop her or ask what she was saying then, she simply nodded, understanding just enough, that the woman had knowledge, confidence, and, most important of all, kindness.

When at last Ivy stepped back onto the lane, she felt much better. She was still hopelessly adrift in time, still terrified of what lay ahead, but now she knew there was someone here, in this century, who could guide her through the ordeal. As much as anything could, it put her at ease.

Chapter Twelve

The loch's water glinted pewter beneath the late morning sun when Ivy finally departed the midwife's cottage. Ivy's attention was caught by two small children toddling around the far bank of the loch. No older than three or four, they wandered dangerously close to the water's edge, their chubby hands full of reeds and stones.

Ivy frowned. Where were their parents? She looked around but saw no one paying them the least attention, saw no one at all at the moment. A chill darted down her spine. What if one of them slipped? The water looked deep not far from shore.

She hesitated, then muttered under her breath, "Well, somebody has to do something."

Gathering her skirts, she marched around the broad curve of the loch, the mud in spots sucking at her hiking boots, until she reached the children, a boy and a girl. They looked up at her with wide brown eyes, wary but not afraid.

"Hi there," Ivy said, smiling. "Let's get you back, okay? Away from the water."

This was greeted with blank stares.

She tried again, gesturing toward the village. "Come on, this way. Back to... Mama?"

Nothing. The boy plopped down in the mud, shoving a stick into the water. The little girl, with her finger in her mouth, stared mutely between him and Ivy.

Ivy pressed on. "Okay, don't do that," she said to the boy, taking his arm, trying to pull him to his feet. "You're way too close. I don't know what you understand, but you can't stay here." Finally, he allowed himself to be brought to his feet, and Ivy collected the pudgy hand of the little girl. "Come on, guys. We're going back."

The little girl began to wail, a high, keening cry. Her brother soon joined, shrieking as if Ivy were dragging them to execution instead of safety. Ivy winced, guilt gnawing, but she pressed forward. "I know, I know, but you're not safe here."

The children's howls carried across the water, and when Ivy glanced up, she saw a man barreling around the far side of the loch, his strides long and swift. Suddenly, it seemed there were several witnesses scattered around the edge of the village and the loch. Ivy felt decidedly conspicuous.

He came at her still, shouting, words sharp as whips. Ivy tried to explain, stumbling through her panic. "They were too close to the water—I was only trying to—"

The man's face was twisted with rage. She kept talking, pleading, not understanding the man's reaction, his rage, but he shouted right over her—again, the indecipherable Gaelic—spittle flying.

Then his hand lashed out.

The blow cracked across her cheek, snapping her head to the side. She reeled and landed hard on her hip, the world ringing as if a bell had been struck inside her skull. Dazed, she blinked up, seeing him looming, fist clenched, hollering down at her.

Shouts erupted from behind. Dozens of figures converged—MacKinlay and Kerr soldiers appearing out of nowhere, villagers rushing from their cottages. Hoofbeats thundered, and in the next breath a destrier skidded to a halt, its rider already leaping down.

Alaric hit the man like a falling tree. They went down in a tangle of fists and curses, Alaric's bellow shaking the air as he drove his knuckles into the man's face again and again. Blood sprayed, the man howled, and still Alaric struck until soldiers seized him from behind, three, and then four men straining to wrench him off.

Stunned, Ivy sat frozen in the mud, her cheek throbbing, her body trembling with shock, as Alaric fought like a madman to get at the man again, his eyes blazing murder.

"Hold him!" someone yelled.

"Christ's bones, he'll kill him—"

The world rang around her—men shouting, grunting, those two toddlers screaming louder now. Soldiers dragged Alaric back, their hands clamped on his arms and shoulders, yet he heaved against them like an enraged bull, eyes fixed only on the man he'd bloodied. Mathar was there, pushing at Alaric's chest.

Alaric surged forward again, breaking free with a wrench of his shoulders that sent one soldier sprawling. He brushed Mathar aside and stalked, not toward his foe this time, but toward her.

Ivy stiffened as he dropped to his knees in the mud, his big hands bracketing her face with startling gentleness. His breath came hard, hot against her cheek, his eyes searing into hers. His touch was restrained, gentle.

"Bluidy hell," His voice was rough, ragged with fury. "Ivy...."

Her lips parted, but no sound came. She could only blink up at him, dazed, heart hammering against her ribs. The bruising sting on her cheek flared where his thumb brushed, feather-light though he tried to be.

Gasps and murmurs rippled through the gathering crowd. Villagers had come, pressing in close, whispering sharply in Gaelic, some with hands to their mouths. The Kerr soldiers stood tense, waiting.

Then a new voice cut through, calm but iron-edged. "Enough!"

Ciaran Kerr strode forward, green eyes blazing as he cast his gaze over the scene—the bloodied man held back by villagers, Alaric crouched in the mud before her, the soldiers caught between restraint and confusion. "Stand down, all of ye."

The murmurs ebbed.

Alaric ignored them all, still bent over her, still searching her face as though he could will the pain from her cheek. His own lip bled, split from the one wild swing the man had landed, a crimson smear against his stubble.

Ivy lifted a trembling hand without thinking, her fingertips brushing his mouth. "You're bleeding," she whispered.

The contact stilled him. His eyes locked on hers, the brown fire of his gaze softening by degrees. For a heartbeat, the shouting, the crowd, even Ciaran's commanding presence faded to nothing. There was only his hand cupping her jaw, her touch against his lip, the storm of rage in him giving way to something else entirely.

Ciaran's voice cut through again. "Drag him to the byre," he commanded, staring daggers at the man who'd smacked Ivy. "Lash him to the great beam and leave him there under guard."

When the man had been escorted away, protesting loudly and struggling against the many hands that dragged him off, Alaric lifted Ivy himself, scooping her up as though she did not actually bear the weight of two. Her cheek brushed the rough wool of his plaid, her body pressed close against the breadth of his chest. Heat radiated from him, steady and solid. He smelled of horse and heather, of smoke and sweat, the scent of a life lived outdoors.

Ivy's breath caught as she curled instinctively against him, the chaos of the last minutes fading beneath the thunder of his heartbeat in her ear. But she was safe now. That was the word her rattled mind kept circling back to—safe—even as her cheek smarted and her body trembled. However terrifying the fury in him a moment ago had been, it was a more powerful fury now shielding her, holding her, carrying her away from danger.

***

Alaric carried her straight through the gates and into the hall, his jaw locked so tightly it near split his teeth. He did not trust his own voice, for if he loosed it now, he'd roar the walls down. He set her gently upon the nearest bench, his mind replaying the moment he'd witnessed her being struck as he, Ciaran, and a handful of others had come upon the loch.

"Cold cloths—quickly!" His shout snapped across the hall, sending the two milling servants scurrying away down the corridor.

Ciaran's boots scraped the flagstones as he approached, his tone maddeningly calm.

"Settle yerself, Alaric. The man's a hothead, aye, but he'll be dealt with. He doesnae strike without cause. What did she do to—"

"I dinna care if she carved up his bollocks, Ciaran!" Alaric roared, spinning toward him. "He struck her. She is heavy wi' child, and he laid a hand on her."

A plum-faced maid returned, anxiously presenting a cool wet square of linen to him, and then hovering near Ivy like a nervous sparrow.

Alaric crouched low, holding the cloth to Ivy's cheek himself. His thumb brushed against her soft skin, the sight of the red and already swelling bruise causing his rage to simmer anew.

"Bluidy hell, I canna trust that Caeravorn is safe for her, can I?" He spat at his old friend when Ciaran came into view beyond Ivy.

"Alaric," Ciaran growled, the tone suggesting Alaric proceed carefully.

Ivy took the cloth from Alaric and kept it pressed to her cheek, her eyes downcast.

Alaric stood straight and rounded on Ciaran. "He bluidy struck her—would've done more had we not arrived!—and I want to ken what's to be done about it!"

"Can I hear what—" Ciaran began.

"There's nae way I can entrust her safety to ye now!" Alaric carried on, his blood only boiling more for Ciaran's irrational calmness.

The maid gave a small squeak and retreated to the shadows.

Ciaran's gaze slid past Alaric's shoulder. Alaric turned as well, to find that Ivy had come to her feet, pale but composed. She lowered the cloth to her side.

"I feel terrible—this was all my fault," she blurted, voice tight with guilt, her gaze on Kerr. "I've caused so much trouble—it's just...where I come from, those kids—those babies—would never be left alone near water, let alone water so deep."

Ciaran folded his hands behind his back, his head canted. "And where is it exactly ye come from, lass?"

Alaric stiffened, every muscle locking. He shot her a warning look, but she only glanced nervously at him before producing an answer.

"I come from around the Loch Katrine area—but I, um, haven't been there lately. Not in...years." Her words tumbled too fast, but before Ciaran could press further, she added quickly, "Laird Kerr, I am genuinely sorry for the trouble. My intent was honest—I thought the children were in danger. The language barrier made it worse than it was. I assume that man was—is—their father? I swear, I'll mind my own business from now on. Alaric, please don't be angry with Laird Kerr. And Laird Kerr, please don't...kick me out of Caeravorn."

"Kick ye out?" Ciaran echoed.

She swallowed. "Make me leave."

"I've nae said that even crossed my mind. This one, however," Ciaran inclined his chin toward Alaric, "seems convinced ye'll nae be safe."

Alaric bristled. "Aye, and with guid cause."

But Ivy turned to him. "Alaric, you can't. If Laird Kerr doesn't mind me staying, I want to be here." She closed the small distance between them, standing close, tipping her face up. Her eyes were wide and imploring. "I talked with the midwife today, Ruth. I feel...so much better about everything now—well, as good as I can, all things considered. Please don't make me leave."

"*Jesu*, Ivy." His voice cracked against the weight of his fury, contrasted against the pleading look in her eyes. "The man struck ye."

"It was a misunderstanding," she insisted softly. "It frightened me, sure, but I don't hold a grudge." She turned, to include Ciaran in her explanation. "He thought I was trying to take his children or something when I was only trying to steer them away from the water's edge. He has every right to protect them."

Alaric growled, pacing a half step away. "He'll hold a grudge now, for being punished for striking ye."

"Punished?" She frowned, looking to Ciaran.

"Aye, lass," Ciaran said smoothly. "Assault it is. Alaric, nae doubt, will demand retribution."

"Oh my God, no," Ivy whispered, horror dawning. "Please, you can't—"

She moved swiftly now, again toward Alaric, setting her small hand upon his arm. The simple touch stole the force from his rage, her palm warm against his sleeve. "I need to fit in here, Alaric," she said quietly. "I need to feel comfortable. I'm anxious enough. I don't want to look over my shoulder, wondering if retaliation is coming."

"Punishment deters others from—"

"Punishing that man will only make *everyone* hate me," she cut in, her voice steady as she met his gaze. "Then I *will* be in danger."

The logic cut deep, though his blood still boiled.

She turned to Ciaran. "Could you arrange for me to speak with him? I want to apologize for frightening him—"

Alaric threw up his hands. "*Jesu,* and will ye fatten a goose for him, too? Polish his boots while ye have him?"

"She's nae wrong," Ciaran said blandly.

Alaric swung a ferocious scowl on his laird. "Mind yer own bluidy business."

Smug as he often was, seeming to enjoy Alaric's rage for some reason—*bluidy bampot!*—Ciaran folded his arms. "My keep, my business. Also—" he paused, a grin tugging at his lips, "my keep, my rules."

"Go to hell," Alaric seethed, heat rising up his neck.

***

Ivy woke to a dull ache in her cheek, the memory of yesterday crowding back before her eyes had even opened. Fingal. That was his name—the father of the children by the loch, the man who had struck her. She winced more at the recollection than the bruise, replaying the strange, tense meeting that had followed, and more embarrassingly, the trouble she'd caused the man.

After no small amount of cajoling on her part, Alaric had finally relented, though he'd grumbled about it at length, and Ciaran had arranged for her to see the man while he was secured in the byre, which Alaric had gruffly explained was one of the communal barns. Ivy had gone in determined, having rehearsed her apology, and yet still stumbling over her words until she was nearly babbling with sincerity. Fingal, however, scarcely seemed to hear a word of it. His angry, watchful eyes never left Alaric, who stood rigidly at her side, sometimes shifting to place his massive frame between them, as though she needed a human shield while the poor man was literally chained to the wall.

"I only meant to help," she had told the man more than once, her voice raw with earnestness. "I thought your children were in danger."

Ciaran translated—without inflection, it seemed.

But if her words reached Fingal, he gave no sign. His gaze had followed Alaric like a cornered beast tracking its hunter, and Ivy had finally realized he wasn't interested in anything she had to say, not with Alaric looming over him so threateningly. Still, she'd done what she'd set out to do. When her apology was done, she insisted the man be released. She wished the entire horrible thing had never happened, and she wanted desperately to put it all behind her.

Now, lying in the soft furs of her borrowed bed, Ivy sighed. Certainly it hadn't been the smoothest peace-making attempt in history, but at least she'd tried.

She went about her morning much as she had the day before—making discreet use of the empty-once-again chamber pot tucked beneath the bed and then sitting at the small table where a tray had been laid. Oat porridge, a heel of bread, and a wedge of something sharp and crumbly that surely must be cheese. Ivy ate in silence, her brain still whirring. She was slightly miffed that her excitement of yesterday—or rather just a general good feeling she had after leaving the midwife, Ruth—had been ruined by her attempts to be helpful, Fingal's loose fists, and Alaric's wild rage.

Ivy couldn't shake the memory of it. It had blazed through him, immediate and absolute. The force of it should have frightened her, but instead it settled deep in her bones, almost warmly. She'd felt safe, of course, so well protected, but something even more than that—as if nothing on earth, or in any time, would be allowed to touch her so long as Alaric MacKinlay drew breath.

It lingered with her. But what did it mean—that a man like him, fierce and guarded, could erupt so violently on her behalf? Could such an instinct be only duty, a warrior's reflex to defend the vulnerable? Or was it something else, something unspoken that she scarcely dared let herself hope for? The question gnawed at her, dangerous in its sweetness. Because if his fury had been more than duty, if it had been born of some deeper place within him...then perhaps her own wayward thoughts about Alaric weren't so foolish. Maybe they weren't even one-sided.

She sighed, having no answers. And though she wasn't exactly eager to face this world today—not after the disaster she'd set in motion yesterday—she knew she couldn't bear to sit in this room all day.

A fresh set of clothes—chemise, gown, and hose—had been delivered at the same time the tray had been brought, and she slipped into them a little easier today before tugging on her short boots. Her own clothes, the leggings, sweater, her underwear and bra, had all been returned, laundered and neatly folded and placed on the end of the bed at some point yesterday, but Ivy decided to keep with the medieval outfit, meaning to not stand out, to not draw too much attention to herself.

Descending the winding stairs, she found the hall quiet, only a few servants moving about with buckets and brooms. She pushed open the heavy door and stepped into the courtyard, almost instantly realizing some commotion at the gate. A small crowd had gathered there, just inside the formidable wall, villagers pressing close with eager faces. Something—or some-one—was clearly the source of the commotion. Ivy was thrilled it wasn't her today.

She noticed Ciaran—and was surprised that Alaric was nowhere around—standing half in shadow at the base of the gatehouse, sleeves rolled, dragging a bundled sheaf of spears out onto the stones. Another man bent to help him stack them against the wall. The Kerr laird looked up when Ivy approached, sweat darkening his temple.

"What's going on?" she asked, glancing from him to the cluster of people at the gate. "Is someone coming?"

He straightened, rubbing his palms together to dust them off before throwing a disinterested glance toward the gate. "Seems the tinker's come to call."

Tinker? Ivy considered thoughtfully while Ciaran returned to his labor. She wasn't overly familiar with the term, but thought she had some recollection that a tinker was a person who traveled from place to place repairing utensils. Surveying the crowd again, she decided maybe they didn't seem so eager, but were more jockeying for position.

Ivy frowned. What? The tinker only mended so many utensils per visit, she wondered, and if you didn't get here early, you might have to wait until his next visit?

Though she was sure he couldn't read her mind, Ciaran more or less answered her question. "The man's a clackit tongue," he said, hefting another bundle of spears against the wall. "And he's nae one for working while his lips wag. Folk dinna care to waste the day hearing his blather, so they crowd early, hoping to be quit of him fast."

"I see," Ivy said with a small smile, amused at the picture Ciaran had painted.

The noise at the gates swelled, then parted like a tide as the cart finally creaked its way through the arch. The mule pulling the rickety cart tossed its head, ears flicking, as the tinker cracked a worn length of leather against its rump and shouted something coarse in Gaelic that made several villagers laugh. His cart rattled and groaned under the weight of his wares—pots clanged, scraps of tin and iron glinted in the sun, bundles of rags and oddments swayed precariously with each jolt of the wheels.

The man himself was as loud as his cart, calling greetings left and right in a rough, cheerful brogue, grinning through a gap-toothed smile. His patched coat flapped behind him, and a hat far too large for his head wobbled with every step as he trudged alongside the mule.

Ivy might have smiled at the comic figure—might even have laughed—but then a shrill cry split the air.

A peasant woman, pressing too close to the cart, suddenly stumbled back, her hand flying to her mouth. She wailed something in Gaelic, her tone suggesting pure horror.

"A body?" Ciaran questioned, possibly repeating what the woman had just shrieked.

The crowd pressed tighter, murmurs rising in alarm. Ivy shoved closer, morbidly curious.

The tinker raised his hands as if to defend himself, babbling loudly, surprisingly in English now, as if under pressure, he reverted to his native language. His voice cracked with exaggerated outrage. "Found her, I did! In the mountains, sprawled like the dead across the heather. Thought her a ghost myself, till I felt her still breathing. I've brought her here for the laird to deal with, same as any honest man would!"

Ivy gasped. He might have mentioned *that* first thing, rather than wasting all that time with greetings, collecting what he might have believed was the villagers' adoration.

Ivy pushed her way to the fore and then was almost shoved into the side of the cart. She went up on her toes, curling her fingers around the wooden board of the wagon, and glanced down, half-expecting to see a decomposing corpse.

Another gasp was wrung from her.

Half-hidden between a jumble of rags and a dented kettle lay the form of a young woman. Crumpled and motionless, yes, but not merely a decayed body, but a woman, flesh and blood, alive it seemed if the heightened color of her cheeks should be trusted. Her head lolled to one side, a tumble of dark blonde hair catching the light as it spread in tangled strands against the rough wood of the cart. Beneath the flush of her cheeks, her skin was so fair it looked almost translucent. Her lips were faintly parted, giving her the fragile air of someone just barely clinging to wakefulness—or worse. Pretty, though, undeniably pretty, even in her disheveled state.

In the next instant, Ivy's breath fled her chest. Her mouth went dry. She clutched at the nearest arm in shock but the woman wearing the sleeve she'd grabbed yanked it free with a snarl at Ivy. Ignoring her, Ivy stared at the sleeping woman in the cart and whispered, "Oh my God," as comprehension dawned.

She stared at the woman's clothes. Not wool, not linen. A blouse of unusual cut, seams too neat, fabric far too fine, dyed a shade of soft yellow Ivy knew had no place in this century. And she was wearing jeans—torn at one knee, but unmistakable.

As Ciaran approached from the open end of the bed of the wagon, Ivy's eyes were locked on the woman's slack face, the rise and fall of her chest that said, yes, she lived.

Then, something drew Ivy's gaze to Ciaran, who hadn't moved in many seconds at the end of the cart, his right hand very near to the woman's left foot—a foot encased in a teal ballet flat, which was caked with mud. He stood very still, his expression unreadable, the line of his jaw cut in stone. His gaze raked across the limp figure once, twice, and then lingered. Color drained from his face as though he had seen not merely a stranger, but something long buried that had come clawing back to life.

Around them, the first stir of shock was already thinning; the clamor of discovery gave way to impatience. Several of the women who had shrieked moments before were already trailing after the tinker, thrusting bent spoons or dented pots in his direction, less concerned about the unconscious woman in the cart than they were with their household utensils. The press of bodies about the wagon eased, allowing Ivy to slip along the wagon's side, until she rounded the corner and stood at Ciaran's side.

Ivy stared at him, startled by the change in him. His hands, so steady a moment before, had curled into fists.

"Do...do you know her?" she asked, her voice barely above a whisper.

His eyes flicked to hers then, wild with some emotion. He looked at her as if he'd forgotten others were about. "Aye," he said, the word breathed slowly. A beat later, almost brokenly, "Nae. Nae, I dinna."

Stricken by his manner and his contrary response, Ivy's mouth hung open.

Ciaran thrust himself into the cart, sweeping aside pots and cloth with brute force until he could gather the woman into his arms. She sagged limply against him, her head lolling against his shoulder, her pale hair spilling from under his arm. For a heartbeat he did not move, only stared down at her with a look that hollowed his face, as though he'd been struck through the ribs. Then, jaw clenched, he turned to descend.

By now several soldiers surrounded the cart, having come from the gatehouse, Ivy presumed. A couple of them, wide-eyed at the sight, stepped forward instinctively, steadying Ciaran as he climbed down from the cart with his burden.

"Summon the healer," Ciaran barked suddenly, his voice hoarse but commanding, shattering the hush. He pushed past the remaining gawkers, carrying the stranger toward the keep with a grim urgency.

Ivy scrambled after him, weaving between villagers and sidestepping a bit of donkey dung as she hurried to keep pace.

Another woman—another time traveler? There could be no other explanation. But why had Ciaran's face gone so pale? He'd been staggered—Ivy would have sworn that he recognized the woman.

At the keep's doors he shouldered his way inside, his tread echoing off the stone floors of the great hall. He did not pause, did not look right or left, but mounted the stairs with grim determination. Ivy's heart hammered as she lumbered along behind him.

He shoved open the chamber door just next to hers, the hinges protesting, and carried the woman inside. Almost reverently, as though afraid she might shatter, he lowered her onto the bed. For a long moment he did nothing else—just stood above her, staring down in a silence heavy with awe, his chest rising and falling as if he'd run miles.

Ivy, a bit breathless from the climb, moved first. She edged closer, sliding around Ciaran toward the head of the bed and bent to touch the stranger's forehead. Her palm met with violent heat. "She's burning up," Ivy murmured.

The woman gave no sign of hearing, her ash-blonde hair spread in a pale halo against the rough-spun pillow.

Again, the Kerr laird stood unmoving, simply staring. Ivy was alarmed, for both the woman and the laird.

Deciding to make him busy, to distract him from whatever tortured him, Ivy touched his arm. "Sir, I can't do the stairs again," she lied, laying her hand over her stomach. "But while we wait for the healer, we need cold water and clean cloths to try and get her fever down."

Her words seemed to jolt him. Ciaran blinked hard, drew in a sharp breath, and shifted his weight as though startled awake from some deep reverie. He tore his gaze from the bed, cleared his throat, and gave a short, brusque nod. "Aye," he muttered, his voice rougher than usual. He moved toward the door with sudden purpose, though a faint flush crept along his neck as if he regretted having been caught so undone. He did not look at Ivy again as he strode out, leaving her with the woman and the silence that followed.

Ivy heaved in a large breath and exhaled, her attention returned to the woman in the bed, wearing clothes from the twenty-first century.

"Who *are* you?" she whispered.

Chapter Thirteen

Ivy sat at the bedside, watching the shallow rise and fall of the woman's chest beneath the woolen blanket. The last hour had been a blur. The healer had come quickly, a hard-eyed woman who wasted no time in grinding leaves and powders into a pungent slurry that she'd thinned with water. With a firm hand, she tipped it between the stranger's lips, muttering under her breath as the poor girl choked and swallowed by reflex. "It will bring down the fever," the healer had promised, before gathering her satchel and vowing to return.

The maids had descended soon after, bustling with their basins of water and linen towels and cloths. They'd clucked and whispered as they peeled away the woman's strange clothing, piece by piece—garments so alien that even the maids' chatter had faltered. When they reached the underthings, Ivy had stepped in sharply, refusing to let them strip her entirely bare. "She wouldn't want that," she'd insisted, her cheeks burning but her voice firm. "No," she said, shaking her head at them.

Instead, they bathed the woman as best they could in cool—but not cold—water, sponging her pale skin and combing tangles from her hair. When at last they'd dressed her in a pale chemise and tucked her beneath a clean sheet, the chamber smelled faintly of herbs and damp linen.

Now Ivy remained, unwilling to leave the stranger alone. Once or twice she stirred, a faint murmur on her lips, but never fully woke.

Ivy sat forward, watchful, nervous. A dozen tangled thoughts warred inside her. She wanted—needed—this woman to live. For her own sake, yes, but mostly for the girl herself, who couldn't be much older than Ivy and who surely had her whole life before her. She deserved more than this, to wither and fade in some drafty keep centuries away from the world that had raised her.

And selfishly, yes, for herself, borne of a desperation to not be the only modern woman in this century. Questions buzzed like bees in her mind: How had she come here? Was it by choice, or had it been done to her the way it had to Ivy? How long had she been trapped in this century? Did she know a way back?

The longing for answers clawed at Ivy's insides. At last, here was proof—solid, undeniable proof—that she wasn't alone in this. Someone else had made the same impossible journey. Someone who might understand what it meant to be ripped from everything familiar, forced to scrape together sanity in a time so far removed from her own.

Ivy reached out, brushing her fingers across the back of the woman's hand, which was—she assessed hopefully—not as heated as it had been an hour ago.

"Please," she whispered, her voice cracking, though whether she spoke to God, fate, or the woman herself, she couldn't be sure. "Please live."

Throughout the day, Ciaran had come and gone, never lingering long. Each time, Ivy gave what little report she had: no, the woman had not spoken and no, she hadn't even opened her eyes. He only nodded, his expression unreadable, before striding out again.

When the door creaked open once more late in the afternoon, Ivy expected Ciaran—but it was Alaric. He stepped inside, his presence filling the chamber, his gaze sweeping from Ivy to the bed and back again. Something inside her lifted at the sight of him, enlivened by the fact that he sought her out.

Without thinking she rose and went to his side, whispering urgently, "Alaric, you have to see this," before taking his large hand and dragging him toward the chest tucked near the wall where the woman's folded jeans and blouse had been laid. She picked them up, squeezing the garments in her excitement, and looked up at him. "Look at these."

"Ye should be resting," he countered firmly, though he did keep his voice low.

"No, listen." She cast a glance over her shoulder to be certain the woman still slept, then lowered her voice even further. "She's like me. From the future."

His jaw flexed, a muscle jumping as he stared down at her. "Ivy," he growled, low, dangerous, "dinna start this nonsense again."

"I'm serious," she hissed, shaking the clothing in her hands as evidence. "I know you think it's all hogwash, but trust me, you guys aren't making riveted jeans in this century. Look at this blouse. Everything she was wearing is straight out of the twenty-first century. Alaric, she's...like me."

Though he did glance down, considering the garments, his lips thinned.

Ivy pressed on. "And what's more, Alaric—I think Ciaran recognized her. He was visibly shaken by the sight of her. He acted like he saw a ghost. And when I asked him if he knew her, he said *aye*, and then *nae*—like, what does that mean?"

She didn't feel as if she were betraying Ciaran—her first allegiance would always be to Alaric, she knew. But when she searched his face, willing him to understand, his expression only hardened further. He looked at her strangely, as if he pitied her, as though he wished she weren't crazy, and that hurt more than outright dismissal.

But the dismissal came as well.

He took one step backward. "It's simply nae possible," he growled, his tone suggesting he wished *she* would believe *that*.

Without another word, he left.

Abandoned in the silence, Ivy's shoulders slumped. She pressed a hand to her eyes, despair creeping in. Would he ever believe her?

***

A gray mist clung tenaciously to the forest floor, curling low around the hooves of their mounts as the hunting party moved in measured silence. The chuffing and sniffing of hounds echoed faintly ahead, trying to catch the scent of either deer or boar.

Ciaran rode stiffly at Alaric's side, nearly unmoving, his bow slung lazily across his lap as if he had no intention of using it, even if the hounds did alert them to prey nearby. Alaric's gaze drifted on and off his friend, recalling Ivy's words of yesterday afternoon, in regard to Ciaran—*visibly shaken*. Alaric chewed on this.

He acted like he saw a ghost, Ivy had said.

Meaning to know if there was any truth to Ivy's suspicion, Alaric maneuvered his steed a wee bit closer to Ciaran and pitched his voice low so the others would not hear. "The lass in yer hall," he said. "The flaxen one found in the tinker's cart. Ye ken her?"

Ciaran did not turn his head, only adjusted the reins with a careful hand. "Nae. I dinna."

It was too smooth. Too quick. Ciaran hadn't turned to Alaric with any hint of surprise, wondering why he might have posed the question.

Alaric studied him. "Strange, then, for a man who claimed nae knowledge to look as though he'd seen a ghost. Ivy said as much."

Ciaran's jaw hardened, a muscle jumping there. "I said I dinna ken her." His tone was flat, but the silence that followed was heavy. He tempered it with, "She... she merely reminded me of someone."

Alaric let the matter hang, though the seed of suspicion dug its roots deeper. Ciaran's manner had been protective, as though he guarded a secret. Ivy had not imagined it, Alaric decided; he too now sensed something amiss, something carefully hidden.

The crack of brush ahead drew their attention; one of the younger men loosed an arrow, and a stag bounded through the trees, wounded but swift. Shouts rose, the chase overtook them, and for a time there was only the thundering pursuit of prey.

By the time the hunters returned to Caeravorn with the carcass across a packhorse, the day had waned into a dim, gold-dappled afternoon. Alaric strode into the hall alongside Ciaran, sweat cooling against his neck, thinking of a quick bath in the loch.

The steward appeared in the hall doorway, face drawn, his cloak dusted as if he'd come at a dead run. The man bowed hurriedly.

"Word from the south, my lairds." His voice carried, steady but tight with strain. "A rider has come—straight from

Strathaven. He bears word of an English host pressing north. The truce keeps them from burning as they march," the steward added, "but there has been blood—a clash near Airdrie the day before last, the entire village burned."

Murmurs rippled among the men who'd followed them inside. Ciaran cursed, and reached for the missive, scanning the contents with a heavily furrowed brow.

"How many?" Alaric demanded of the steward. The man was normally calm, but there was a tightness to his voice that lent weight to his words; if such a rock of a soul looked grim, then every man in the hall knew the tidings were grave indeed.

The steward answered steadily. "Three thousand strong."

"How near?" Alaric asked next.

"Two days' march from here, mayhap less," answered the steward while Ciaran continued to read. "Scouts say their banners stretch near a mile on the road."

Alaric's mind worked swiftly, weighing numbers, routes, the stretch of land between Caeravorn and where the English force might have advanced to since Airdrie. "Three thousand is nae small host," Alaric muttered, brow furrowed.

Ciaran lifted his eyes from the parchment, handing it off to Alaric. "We canna sit idle while Edward's dogs trample our soil."

"Aye." He agreed, scanning the message quickly before saying to Ciaran, and all those around, "They'll be hampered by their own weight, dragging carts and fodder, heavy horses. We ken the hills and passes—we can strike where they are weakest, vanish afore they gather their wits."

Ciaran nodded grimly. "A wolf cannot kill a herd entire, but it can harry the flanks, scatter the stragglers, bleed the beast till it limps."

Alaric nodded. "We canna face them head-on," he said, "but the land itself will be our ally."

"Our men together—near three hundred—we can strike their flanks, harry their scouts, cut their supply lines." Ciaran furthered. "If naught else, we'll learn their intent."

"Aye." Alaric's blood surged hot, the old hunger for battle rising in him. "We ride, then. I willnae be caught sleeping while the lion passes by—the MacKinlays can be ready to march within the hour."

The hall stirred as men caught the sound of steel in his voice, their mood sharpening to match his own.

Ciaran nodded and seemed to calculate his own readiness before advising, "The Kerr army can march today as well, within hours."

Immediately, orders began to fly, men scattering to see to wagons, arms, and provisions. The air grew thick with urgency.

Alaric strode from the dais and the hall, calling sharply for Mathar. The captain appeared from outside the gate and Alaric wasted no time. "The English march north in force," he told him grimly. "Three thousand, mayhap more. We'll nae stop them, but we'll slow their stride. Rouse the men. See every mount watered and shod. We march as soon as all is in readiness."

Mathar bowed and hurried off, shouting for soldiers, armorers, and smiths.

The next hour vanished in a blur. The bailey of Caeravorn was stirred to a mighty din, horses whinnying and armorers, saddlers, and farriers busy attaching heads to spears, shoeing destriers, and outfitting supply wagons. Alaric and Ciaran oversaw it all, walking the yard, calling out commands. The smithy's forge was kindled and not allowed to die so long as there remained a blade to be sharpened. The ruckus was not filled with dread, but was merry; a group of Kerr men even sang in their delight to escape the listless idleness of peace.

But when there were no more orders to give, when preparations sustained without him, Alaric found his steps turning toward the keep, where Ivy likely sat unknowing at the far side of the keep.

Alaric found her where he half-expected—seated once more at the stranger's bedside. Unlike so many sickrooms he'd visited, dark and depressing, the chamber was bright and airy, the door cracked open, the shutters thrown wide. The coarse blanket had been straightened, the pillows fluffed, and Ivy herself sat close, bent forward, her chin propped in her hand, her other hand resting lightly atop the quilt, stroking the back of the woman's hand. There was nothing of death's shadow here; Ivy had somehow made the chamber feel almost hopeful.

She startled when Alaric pushed the creaky door open further, then sagged back with a weary exhale. He saw it then, instantly—the faint shadows under her eyes, the pallor of sleeplessness.

"Ye stayed here the night." His tone was more accusation than question.

Ivy rubbed at her eyes with the heel of her palm. "I didn't want to leave her alone. I didn't want her to *wake* alone."

He stepped nearer, the boards under his boots groaning. "Ye shouldnae be running yerself ragged. Ye've the bairn to consider."

Her lips pressed thin, as if offended by the insinuation that she didn't take care for her babe. "My baby is fine. But if I were in this woman's place, sick and confused and in a world I didn't understand, I wouldn't want to wake up either alone or with strangers hovering over me. I need to be here when she wakes."

Alaric's jaw set, but he did not argue further. A familiar light sparked in her eye—that stubborn spark that no command could quench.

Instead, he got on with the purpose of his visit. "We ride before the sun sets," he said. "Word came—an English host, three thousand strong, pushing north. They dinna march with fire and sword this time, but they've already clashed with one village." He paused, shrugging, while Ivy's mouth fell open. "We have to go," he said simply.

Her hazel eyes locked on his. He did not miss the flicker there—fear.

"Caeravorn will be well guarded," he told her, softly but firmly. "The house guard remains. And I'll leave Kendrick and Ewan with ye. Naught will touch ye here."

Ivy rose to her feet, a wee bit less graceful than she'd been even weeks ago. "I'm not worried about me," she said, her voice tight. "I'm worried about *you*."

The words filled him with a heat he hadn't felt in years, a sharp, heady mix of wonder and something dangerously close to joy. He stared at her, at the truth plain in her face—she *was* concerned for him.

No one had ever said that to him. Not once. Not even Gwen—stoic Gwen, who had stood tall beside him, who had spoken always of honor and the will of God, but never of fear for *him*.

To be worried for Alaric himself—as if he were more than his duty, more than his sword—that was something wholly new. And it tugged, hard, in some place he hadn't even known existed.

He forced in a slow breath, but his voice came rough all the same. "Dinna fear for me, lass, but keep guid energy for the babe—"

"Oh," she gasped. "You won't be... you don't think you'll be back in time for the birth?"

"I canna say," he answered, though her quiet disappointment rattled him more than he cared to let on. He shook himself, as though casting off the poignancy of her words, and straightened to his full height. The commander returned, hard-eyed and unyielding. "While I'm gone, ye'll heed me, Ivy," he said, his voice clipped. "Dinna wander without escort—dinna leave Caeravorn at all, dinna go further than the village. Dinna speak with any soul ye dinna ken. If aught seems amiss, ye go straight to Kendrick or Ewan. Keep to yer chamber at night, bar the door."

Ivy's brows lifted at the litany, but she seemed to bite back a smile. "Yes, sir," she murmured, half-teasing, though her eyes betrayed the sting of worry. "And you—just...be careful, Alaric. Please be safe."

The word lodged between them, soft and disarming. He stilled, his gaze fixed on her as though he meant to brand her into memory. The hue of her hazel eyes, amber and green, shifting with the light, the stubborn tilt of her chin, the faint bruise still shadowing her cheek—he found himself memorizing it all, knowing that ever encountering her again was not promised to him.

He nodded tightly and turned to go, taking two full strides, when something checked him—something fierce and reckless that surged before he could master it. In two strides he was back, his hand closing around her wrist, pulling her hard against him.

The kiss crashed down between them, rough at first, born of all he had bitten back for too long—longing, suspicion, desire. His mouth claimed hers, demanding, desperate, until he felt her soften, until the tremor in her lips answered his own. Then the storm gentled. His hold eased, his mouth lingered, slow and searching, tasting her, learning the feel of her. His teeth teased at her full bottom lip, coaxing her to open for him. She obliged without hesitation, and liquid fire sang through his veins. Alaric framed her face in his hands and took her mouth again, his kiss deepening, his tongue sweeping in slow, possessive strokes.

When at last he tore his lips from hers, they were both unsteady. Ivy's eyes were wide, her breath quick, her fingers curled in the fabric of his tunic.

"I'm pregnant," she whispered, as though it were the only thing her stunned mind could summon.

He blinked, his brow furrowing as he glanced down at her. "And a kiss will harm the babe?"

Her cheeks flamed. "No—oh, God, no. But...why would you kiss me if I'm pregnant?"

His frown deepened, his confusion plain. "I dinna...understand what ye are asking?" His voice was low, roughened, as though he feared she might snatch the moment away with whatever her answer might be.

Her cheeks flushed hotter, and she shook her head. She pushed backward, putting a wee bit of space between them, but still clutched at his tunic. Words tumbled softly, unevenly. "Because I'm carrying another man's child, Alaric. I'm not—" she broke off, searching his face, then pressed on, steady if soft. "I'm not pure—I thought that was something that was important in this century. I didn't think anyone would want me. Not like that."

For a moment his gaze burned into hers, while he weighed something heavy he wasn't sure he could bring himself to say. His hand lingered against her cheek, his rough thumb brushing gently over her skin.

"Ye have curious notions, Ivy Mitchell," he said quietly, the words almost gruff, the response intentionally vague, holding back the truth he wasn't ready to give voice to. Now, as he prepared to depart, was not the time to confess how little her past—or her child—deterred him. Still, he owed her at least part of the truth. "Such a consideration matters less than ye apparently believe." He added one more instruction. "Be safe, Ivy."

And before she could answer, he released her and turned, striding toward the door once more. Despite the difficulty of leaving her, despite the tumult hammering in his chest, a grin tugged at his mouth when her voice reached him in the corridor.

"Seriously? You kiss me now?" She grumbled to herself. "Right before you're leaving?" she demanded, sounding thoroughly exasperated. A second later, her voice dropped, more to herself than to him. "He should've kissed me weeks ago." A huff followed, sharp and indignant. "Medieval men!"

Alaric's grin evolved into a full-blown smile.

***

Ivy slumped back into the chair, her knees wobbling as if they'd carried her across miles instead of only backward a few paces. She pressed both hands over her face, trying to cool the flush that had stolen into her cheeks. Good Lord. Alaric MacKinlay had kissed her. Not a brush, not a slip of impulse easily forgotten—but a real kiss, a glorious one—one that left no doubt he had meant it.

She hadn't seen that coming. Not at all. Of course, if she was honest with herself, she'd imagined it, foolish daydreams tucked away behind closed eyes as she lay awake at night. But this—this had been no dream. He had kissed her.

Kissed her! she mused.

Everything else was forgotten for a moment, while Ivy considered the enormity of this—the thrill of it!

But oh—she was quickly brought back to worrying reality—Alaric was going off to war. The thought pressed into her chest, heavy and unrelenting. She was proud of him—how fearless he was, how steadfast in his duty—but the pride did nothing to soften the sharp edge of fear. What if he didn't come back? What if that kiss had been a beginning and an ending in the same breath?

She thought suddenly of mothers, wives, and sisters from her own century, waving men off to wars across oceans. The grainy black-and-white photographs she'd come across in history books and even on social media had always struck her as poignant, yes, but safely distant. Now she felt the reality of it: the ache of being left behind, the helplessness of not knowing if someone you loved would ever walk through the door again.

And it wasn't only confined to any one century. Even in her time, wars dragged on for years, decades, swallowing up entire generations. She remembered reading about it, about women waiting while their husbands and sons vanished into deserts or jungles, never the same when they returned—if they returned at all. She knew from everything she'd read about the war going on now with England, that it lasted for decades.

The parallels unsettled her. Different century, different weapons, same gnawing fear. Now she understood. Now she knew what it meant to watch a man you cared for shoulder a sword, climb onto a horse, and ride into danger with no promise of coming back.

Ivy's heart twisted again in her chest.

So deep in tormented thought was she—caught between the memory of Alaric's kiss and the dread of his leaving—that at first she almost missed it, the flicker of movement, the bare shift in the bedclothes.

Ivy blinked, refocusing, and her breath caught.

The woman's eyes were open. Wide and startlingly clear, fixed right on her.

For one stunned second Ivy only stared back, frozen in place. Then she jolted upright, nearly upsetting the chair, and stood over the woman, her smile broad. "Oh my God—you're awake!" she exclaimed, the words tumbling out in a rush. She pressed her palm to the woman's forehead, expecting heat, but finding only cool, damp skin. Relief poured through her. "No fever," she informed her, "we've been fighting it for days. You should've seen the awful draughts they made you drink, and I've been at you with cool cloths day and night. The healer's been here three or four times, I can't remember—"

Her voice caught, relief and joy tangling in her throat, half-giddy, half-overwhelmed.

The woman's lips moved, a rasp of sound escaping. "Where...am I?"

Ivy went still. Her stomach dropped. She hadn't rehearsed this part, hadn't even considered this question though she realized she certainly should have. But no, not once had she even thought about how to explain to another lost soul what had happened, or where she'd landed. "Oh, gosh," she stammered, her hands tightening on the blanket. "That's...that's kind of complicated. I don't even know where to begin. But listen—" she leaned closer, earnest, "you're safe. And you're not alone. I promise you that."

The woman's lashes fluttered, her strength already spent. She closed her eyes, her breathing evening out as if sleep had already called her back.

Ivy sank back slowly into the chair, her heart pounding, staring at the pale face against the pillows. She didn't know who this stranger was or what her story might be—but she knew one thing with sudden, unshakable certainty. She wasn't the only one out of place in this century.

Her smile returned, though, as certainty gripped her. The woman, whoever she was, was going to be fine.

Chapter Fourteen

The keep and all of Caeravorn was certainly quieter with the armies gone.

From the open shutters came the steady wash of wind off the water and, faintly, the distant clink of metal from somewhere outside. Ivy sat in the chair she'd hardly left, leaning back to allow her expanding belly space. Idly, while her gaze was held by the blue sky beyond the window, she considered again names for her daughter. She couldn't decide between Lily and Olivia.

A wisp of movement caught in her periphery and Ivy turned her gaze to the bed.

The woman's eyes were open, soft gray, clear now, and once more trained on Ivy.

"You're awake." Ivy leaned in, keeping her voice calm. She'd worried that she might have overwhelmed the woman with her excitement hours ago. "Hi. I'm Ivy."

The woman's lips parted. No sound came out at first. Ivy stood, reached for the waiting cup of water on the bedside table and slid a hand beneath the woman's shoulders, helping to prop her up a bit.

"Just a sip," she said. "You've had a fever for a day and a half."

The woman drank, coughed once, and sank back. Her ash-blonde hair fanned across the pillow.

"How...long?" she whispered.

"Since yesterday afternoon. You've slept most of it." Ivy laid the back of her fingers to the woman's forehead, then her cheek. Cool. Thank God. "No fever now."

The woman's gaze traveled the room, and Ivy grimaced, suspecting plenty of questions would follow.

Her gaze returned to Ivy with a flicker of alarm. "Where am I?"

"Caeravorn Keep," Ivy said. "On the west coast of Scotland. You were found up in the mountain, apparently, and brought here."

"Found," the woman repeated, as if testing the word. "By whom?"

"A traveling tinker." At the nonplussed expression, Ivy explained, "Think...repairman with a cart, with the personality of a used car salesman." The corner of Ivy's mouth tugged. "He did the right thing, though, bringing you here. Do you...remember anything? About what happened—how you ended up in the mountain?"

The woman blinked, her brow pinching. "I... I don't know. It's foggy." She pressed her lips together as if chasing a memory, then shook her head faintly against the pillow.

"That's okay," Ivy said quickly, smoothing the blanket near her shoulder. "Don't push yourself. You've been through a lot."

The woman's eyes drifted, scanning the room once more, the stone walls, the wooden beams above, the glassless window letting in a long, narrow rectangle of pale daylight. Her gaze darted back, uncertain. "My phone?"

"I didn't see a phone with you," Ivy said carefully. "You came with nothing but the clothes on your back. And, um... phones wouldn't work here anyway."

The woman frowned faintly. "No service?"

"Right." Ivy gave a small, gentle nod, choosing her words with care. This wasn't the moment to dump the impossible on someone still pale and weak from fever. Best to wait, see what the woman herself remembered.

"Is there a land line here?" the woman asked.

Ivy winced. "There's not. I'm sorry." After a moment, sensing the woman's increasing anxiety, Ivy thought to distract her. "Obviously, you're from the States. Were you—are you—just vacationing in Scotland? How long have you been here?"

The woman's brow furrowed, as if wading through fog. "Vacation," she said meagerly. "With my husband." A pause, while her brows furrowed. "We were separated—I'd been searching for him for days, but nothing...nothing seemed right. Nothing made sense." Her fingers curled slightly into the blanket. "I can't piece it together." She exhaled sharply, frustration flickering across her face.

Ivy's chest gave a sympathetic squeeze. Oh, God! A husband. Someone waiting, searching, someone she loved. That was a wound Ivy couldn't begin to patch, not with any amount of cool cloths or calming words. And it set their circumstances in such stark relief—this woman, ripped from someone who might even now be desperate to find her; Ivy, who had slipped through time with scarcely a ripple in the world she'd left behind. She'd had no grand delusions about her flaky mother or absent father scouring all of Scotland for her, no frantic family plastering missing posters across cities and towns.

"Don't force it," Ivy said gently, reaching to smooth the blanket at the woman's side. "Memories will come back when you're stronger. Right now, all that matters is you're safe." But curiosity edged through her restraint. "Do you remember where you were last? What you were doing before you were separated from your husband?"

"I can't," said the woman, noticeably frustrated by this.

"Maybe you were hiking near the mountain?" Ivy suggested. "Where you were found?"

She shook her head, having no answer, it seemed.

"Did you notice anything...odd before you were separated?" Ivy persisted. "Like, something felt off, or odd?"

The woman's gray eyes cut to hers, sharp despite their weariness, the question appearing to have unnerved her.

Ivy smiled and waved a dismissive hand. "Sorry, I don't mean to sound like I'm interrogating you. I just... thought it might help you, to talk it through." She reached for the cup again and offered it with both hands, softening her voice. "Here. Another sip. You can rest, and when you feel stronger, we'll talk more."

The suspicion in the woman's gaze lingered, but after a moment she drank, then let her head sink back into the pillow. Her eyes closed, lashes trembling with exhaustion.

Ivy settled quietly in the chair again, chiding herself. Too much, too soon.

When next the woman woke, the room was subtly changed. A fresh rush of cool air drifted in from the open shutters, the sky outside painted with the colors of dusk. A faint fire burned in the hearth, not for warmth so much as to keep the damp at bay. The woman was no longer lying in a fever-sweat but propped carefully against pillows, a long linen chemise softening the starkness of her thin frame.

Ivy had been in and out all day, and returned to find her thus, upright, looking almost expectant. She was relieved now to see a bit of color in her cheeks. She carried with her a tray containing a round of bread, a few slivers of soft and hard cheeses, and a cup of watered ale, having entered the kitchens for the first time to request just this, something gentle for a stomach so long empty.

She smiled at the woman and approached the bed, saying, "Sorry, there's no legs on these trays," as she set the light supper down on the woman's lap.

One of the younger maids popped inside, nodding politely toward the bed though her eyes didn't stray there. She stooped at the hearth, laying in more peat and a few sticks of kindling until the fire caught, then smoothed her apron and slipped out again. Ivy studied the woman in the bed, gauging her reaction. To her mind, Claire seemed... unaffected. Her gaze had followed the maid, but without surprise, no widening eyes or startled flinch at the sight of a girl dressed straight out of a tapestry. Maybe her brain was still sluggish from fever, or maybe she hadn't yet had the strength to grasp what she was seeing.

No sooner had the door closed behind the maid than the healer entered. Her brows rose when she saw Claire upright, but she said nothing, moving instead with purpose across the chamber. She laid the back of her hand against Claire's brow, then gave a satisfied little click of her tongue.

"Aye, the fire's gone from her." A curt nod, then a glance at Ivy. "Keep her drinking, even if she grumbles. She'll be weak as a newborn lamb for a time yet. Nae meat, nae heavy stew. Just this, bread and soft cheese,"

she lectured, pointing to the tray of food. "'Twill serve her better till her strength returns." She paused, glancing between Ivy and Claire for a moment, her sharp gaze seeming to assess them. Finally, she said to Ivy, "Ye've done well, mistress. Few watch as constant as ye have."

Ivy blinked. *Mistress?*

When the healer left, Claire's eyes darted toward Ivy. "Why—who was that?"

"The healer," Ivy said, before adding vaguely, "Kind of the local doctor since we're...pretty far out in the middle or nowhere."

Ivy believed it was helpful for Claire to have seen them, the maid and the healer. Nothing dreamlike about either one of them—the woman would need those little pieces to hold on to later, when Ivy had to explain more.

"Are you a nurse?" the woman asked once the healer had gone.

"Me?" Ivy gave a short laugh and thumped her chest. "Oh, God, no. I'm just a—" The words faltered. *What am I? A farm girl from Indiana. A failed vet student. A pregnant woman stranded in the wrong century. Nothing she could say would make sense.* Finally she managed a wry smile. "I'm just me. Ivy Mitchell."

"I'm Claire, by the way."

Ivy was thrilled with the introduction, and then sorry she'd not thought to even ask the woman's name yet. "Hi, Claire. Nice to meet you." *Sorry for the earthshattering news I'll have to eventually deliver to you.*

The woman studied her, gray eyes curious even in fatigue. "How far along are you?" She asked, gesturing toward Ivy's belly, with half a chunk of bread in her hand.

"Oh, um, almost eight months now," she answered, smiling.

"Your first?"

Ivy nodded and then her heart leapt with alarm. "Do you have children?" *Please say no. Please say no.* She couldn't stomach the idea of the woman being separated by more than seven hundred years from her children.

"No. Not...yet."

"I'm so glad to see you sitting up and eating," Ivy remarked, simply making conversation.

"I didn't realize how hungry I was until I took my first bite."

When she'd eaten as much as she was able, Ivy took the tray from her lap, laying it on the bedside table, forcing the stubby candle and the murky potion that had helped bring down her fever further back on the table.

"Where's the bathroom?" Claire asked then.

Ivy froze. "Right. About that." She cleared her throat. "This place... doesn't exactly have indoor plumbing." Heat crawled up her neck as she reached beneath the bed and tugged out a chamber pot. "Here. I'll step out while you—uh—use it. I'll just be in the hall."

The woman stared at the pot, lips parting, disbelief plain. "You're kidding."

"I wish I were," Ivy muttered, already halfway to the door. "But you'll get used to it. Sort of." *Probably not.* Ivy hadn't yet.

She slipped out and leaned against the corridor wall, giving the woman her privacy. Moments later she heard the scrape of the pot being shifted, and then what sounded like the woman getting back in bed.

When Ivy returned, the woman looked wrung out again, her head tilted back against the pillows.

"Okay. Claire. I think that might be enough for one day, right?" Her lips curved hopefully. Another hour had past, darkness had fallen outside. "I suggest you finish that," she said, pointing to the surely noxious concoction in the cup on the table. "so that your fever doesn't return. And then get some rest. I'll poke my head in, and I'm right next door," she added, pointing to the wall to Claire's left "if you need anything. Don't be afraid to shout if you need me." She smiled again, her brows lifting. "I bet when you wake tomorrow, you'll feel better, and even stronger."

For a fleeting moment, Claire looked uneasy, prompting Ivy to offer, "Or I can stay. If that would make you—"

Claire caught herself. "No, no. Thank you. I'm fine. I can't believe I'm still so tired—I'm sure I'll be able to sleep."

"Everything will be better tomorrow," Ivy predicted. "We'll start to make sense of everything."

***

The next day, Ivy didn't rush. She waited until Claire was sitting up again, the tray emptied, some color returning to her cheeks. No more of the fevered glaze remained in the woman's sharp gray eyes, though a certain guardedness remained.

"I thought you might be ready for some fresh air," Ivy said lightly. She presented the gown she'd bugged Evir to produce, plain and serviceable, the color of river stone. "Your clothes are being laundered. This will do until then. Just something simple to wear over the chemise."

Claire turned until she was sitting on the side of the bed and accepted the gown, her brows drawing together as she smoothed a corner of the fabric between her fingers. "This is... different." She glanced up at Ivy, her gray eyes lifting up the gown she wore. "Is this how everyone dresses around here?"

Ivy nodded.

"Are you in, like, a cult or something?"

Ivy barked out a nervous laugh, never having suspected that Claire's mind would have traveled in that direction. "No, no. Nothing like that." She turned awkwardly, busying herself with moving the tray from the bed to the table. "But yeah, it's a bit old-fashioned, I guess."

With some effort, Claire eased to her feet. Ivy helped her pull the gown over her head, tying the laces at her back with quick, sure hands, then guided her toward the door.

They walked slowly, Ivy steadying her when needed, out of the chamber and down the corridor that spilled them into the great hall. The air was cooler here, so much stone around them, shadows tucked into the high, cavernous beams overhead. A pair of maids swept past with baskets of laundry, their skirts swishing about their ankles, the soft slap of leather soles fading quickly toward the stair.

Beyond the hall the heavy door groaned on its hinges, and they stepped out into the open air. The bailey stretched wide before them, enclosed on all sides by a thick curtain wall, its gray stone mottled with moss and age. Ivy tried to see it through Claire's eyes—the sheer scale of it, the raw, rough permanence that spoke of centuries rather than years, that spoke of an ancient past and not the present as Claire believed in.

The gatehouse loomed to the left, squat and solid, its twin towers framing the heavy oak doors bound with iron. No guards lingered there now, no soldiers clustered with pikes in hand; the yard was hushed, emptied with the armies gone. A restless breeze rustled through, scattering leaves and straw across the packed earth.

Outbuildings lined one side of the yard, their thatched roofs low and weathered—storehouses, the granary, a lean-to where tools lay stacked. To the far end stood the smithy, its wide-mouthed forge cold at the moment. Beside it, the stables crouched long and low, the smell of hay and horse strong even without the bustle of grooms and horses.

It was not grand, not the fairy-tale castle Claire might have imagined if someone had mentioned a medieval castle in real time, but it was formidable, lived-in, heavy with history.

Claire's head turned, her steps halting as she took in the scene. "This is very...picturesque. We're in a castle then?" she deduced. "A historical site?"

"You are at a castle, but no, this isn't merely a historical site—and it's not a reenactment, if that's what you're thinking," Ivy answered, recalling where her brain had gone in those first hours. "It's more of a...working castle." She led her further, out through a side door and onto a narrow path that wound toward the cliffs. The Firth of Lorn spread wide and glittering, the air smelled faintly of brine and resin, and gulls careened overhead against the bright sky. Below, men worked with nets along the shore, their shouts drifting up on the salt wind.

Claire stopped altogether, her brow furrowed as she glanced down, studying the men there, and then all around. "A working castle? Lost in the past?"

Ivy drew a long breath. "It's real—for the actual time period. Every bit of it." She waved Claire away from the edge. "Come this way. I'll explain." She guided her beneath the spreading canopy of a sycamore tree, its trunk gnarled from centuries of wind, its crown arching wide enough to dapple the ground in shifting light. "Claire," she began when they faced each other in the shade, "there's something I have to tell you. Something impossible."

Claire swallowed hard, her eyes flicking between the sea, the keep walls behind them, and Ivy's face. "What?"

Ivy drew in a deep breath and then exhaled. "It's the end of August," Ivy said gently. "The year is thirteen hundred and five."

A silence followed, stretching long and thin, though there was nothing silent about Claire's face. First came a sharp blink, her brows knitting as if she hadn't heard correctly. Then her mouth opened slightly, only to press shut again, the muscle in her jaw twitching. Her eyes flicked away, darting toward the stone wall, then back to Ivy, gray irises widening with disbelief before narrowing, sharp with suspicion. For a heartbeat, Ivy thought she might laugh—her lips even curved that way—but instead the sound that escaped was closer to a scoff, brittle with rising panic.

"I know it's sounds—" Ivy started.

"That isn't possible," Claire finally said. Not angry—just bone-weary certainty.

"I know," Ivy consoled. "I know exactly how it feels to hear that and believe—*know* in your heart—that it's not possible."

"Because it *is* not," Claire insisted. "What are you—why would you say that?" Her face pinched, disappointment shadowing her features, as if the small trust she'd begun to place in Ivy had been carelessly broken.

"I'm sorry," Ivy moaned. "I didn't know how to tell you," she rushed out. "I didn't want you to find out like I did—unexpectedly, on the back of a horse. I passed out. I couldn't handle it."

The woman's eyes narrowed, sharp with challenge. "You're suggesting I traveled through time."

"Yes. Just as I did."

"Obviously, that's not possible."

"I wouldn't have thought so either—until three weeks ago."

"So you've been trapped... here? In another century for three weeks?"

"Yes."

Anger finally surfaced, roughening her voice. "Okay, no. This isn't funny. I don't know what you're trying to do here, but—"

"I'm not making it up—oh, how I wish it weren't true either." Ivy lifted her hands, voice careful. "I was hoping to break it gently—"

"Stop." The woman's eyes shone, not just with disbelief but betrayal. "It's ridiculous. Where is my phone? I had it with me when I was separated from my husband. I want it. I need to—"

"Claire, first I swear to you, you had no phone on you," Ivy assured her. She shrugged helplessly, so very sorry for the distress she'd caused. Her tone was a mix of contrition and pity when she said, "And, you simply can't use a twenty-first century phone in the fourteenth century."

"Stop," Claire pleaded, agitated.

Ivy's shoulders sagged. She nodded slowly. "I know how it sounds. I know it's—"

Claire lurched back a step, palms lifting as though to ward her off. "Enough." The word cut sharp, her voice turned brittle and acidic. "Thanks, but I think I've heard plenty."

She stumbled as she pivoted, muttering a curse, then gathered up the hem of the borrowed gown. Without another glance at Ivy, she fled, the fabric snapping around her legs as she half-ran, half-stumbled across the yard.

Ivy sighed, knowing she would have to try again, either later today or tomorrow.

***

Claire didn't speak to her for two days. Ivy's heart broke a little with the silence, but she understood. If their positions were reversed, she wasn't sure she'd be speaking either.

Still, she made certain Claire was well looked after. For herself, Ivy might never have been bold enough to insert herself into the running of a medieval household; left to her own devices, she would have lingered on the edges, trying not to offend, forever second-guessing what was expected or permitted of her. But it turned out she found it far easier to step forward on behalf of someone else. For Claire's sake, she crossed thresholds she would have never even tiptoed past. She went down into the kitchens, introduced herself to the women bustling there—a few she already knew or recognized—and after the first few nervous times, found them welcoming enough. She asked that meals continue to be carried up, lighter fare at first, so Claire wouldn't be forced to venture outside her room before she was ready.

She also took precautions. It felt uncomfortably like imprisoning Claire at Caeravorn, but Ivy remembered Alaric's strict instructions before he left. The countryside was not safe. So she sought out Kendrick and Ewan, asking them to keep a discreet eye out. If Claire wandered too near the gates, they were to—gently—steer her back. And if things grew heated, they were to summon Ivy at once.

And while she waited for Claire to come to terms with her present reality—as much as she was able—most of Ivy's waking thoughts were miles away—marching with Alaric and his men. She saw him in every still moment: a shadow across her mind as she worried over Claire, as she ate, as she lay sleepless in bed. Again and again she returned to that kiss.

It had startled her, shaken her, undone her in ways she hadn't thought possible. She'd never experienced anything so consuming—not with David, not with anyone. His mouth had taken hers with raw certainty, fierce and tender all at once, and she'd felt herself unravel under the weight of it. It had been less like being kissed and more like being claimed. It had felt as if all the scattered pieces of her had suddenly fallen into place. Nothing before had ever felt half as right.

And yet, he was out there now—somewhere—sword in hand, risking everything for Scotland's freedom.

For hours, her imagination tormented her with grim possibilities: an arrow finding its mark, a blade slipping past his guard, the sound of his voice silenced forever. Fear churned in her stomach until she could hardly eat.

But she forced herself to hold onto something else—hope. To imagine a future, however uncertain. Maybe she hadn't come here by accident. Maybe there was a reason she'd been thrown into this century, into this man's path. Maybe Alaric MacKinlay was meant to be part of her story... and she part of his.

She wouldn't waste that chance, if so.

No—she would not be the woman who merely hoped. If Alaric came back—*when* he came back!—she would tell him. Not with hesitant looks, not with half-swallowed words, but with something plain and sure. She didn't yet know how, or what words could possibly carry all that pressed inside her chest.

She'd have to think of something that was much less embarrassingly sophomoric than, *Do you want to be my boyfriend?*, which was all that she could presently imagine, and which sounded ridiculous in a stone castle in fourteenth-century Scotland, but which did manage briefly to make her smile.

Chapter Fifteen

From the ridge where Alaric sat his horse, the English column stretched like a dull serpent along the lochside track—chain mail and spearpoints, creaking axles, the bawl of driven oxen. Three thousand men, and a tail of wagons so long a man might grow old counting them.

The reek of smoke and iron rode the damp air of the Great Glen. Ciaran edged his destrier upslope until their stirrups brushed. Mist filmed his hair and cloak.

"We canna break that head," he said, frustration evident after three days trailing the enemy. "But a beast that long—aye, it bleeds easy at the tail."

Alaric's gaze never left the road. "Aye, we bleed it, but when? Where?"

A scout scrambled up through the bracken as if on cue, peat and muck as high as his knees. "Laird! There's a choke a half-mile north. The track pinches hard to the water with an old birch stand on the slope and bog to the west. The wagons'll have to slow for a burn crossing—rotten planks and slick stone."

"Guid," Alaric said, drawing Ciaran's gaze. "We make our cut there."

Ciaran nodded and raised his hand, giving a sharp whistle which drew the MacKinlay and Kerr officers close. Mathar, broad-shouldered and steady, bareheaded in the mist, drove his steed up the slope. Mungan, the Kerr captain, lean as a fox and twice as hungry, came in Mathar's wake. Two more Alaric trusted with steel and his life, if need be—Neacal, all scars and scowl, and Petrus, young but quick with a bow—gathered as well.

Alaric spoke low and clean, no words wasted. "'Tis time to move. Mathar, we'll take a unit up among the birches and keep to the roots; the ground will swallow us if we dinna watch. Arrows first, then steel when we spring. We'll break their back at the crossing. Ye want the wagons?" He asked Ciaran, knowing that the first of the fight would happen there.

Ciaran nodded. "Aye, we'll cut the traces, drive the oxen uphill into that gulley; they'll take the carts with them and bog the lot. Nae heroics. Ruadh can hold the far flank and cut down any who try to form a line."

Alaric turned to Neacal and Petrus. "Circle with a dozen, Torches when my horn sounds. Make them ken the shadows have teeth."

"Ye take the rearguard," Ciaran said to Mungan.

They checked girths and leather. Faces were smeared with peat, and steel was wrapped to keep from clinking. Alaric drew his sword a thumb's breadth and settled it again, the familiar weight right in his hand. Below them the English moved with the tired arrogance of men who believed themselves too large and strong, safe from the hill and its wolves.

A flicker of hazel eyes came unbidden to him. Ivy in that chamber at Caeravorn nearly a week ago, her eyes shining and startled after he'd kissed her. *Be safe*, she'd said, small and fierce. He shut it away with a breath and put his heels to his horse.

Dusk sloped down the glen as they took their places. Mist rose off the loch in the distance. The tail of the English column hit the pinch-point—the road squeezing to a slick spine of rock with the burn foaming white over black stone. Wagons squealed and balked. The cattle slowed, hooves slipping. The rearguard formed a lumpish hedge of spears to cover the crossing.

Ciaran raised his arm, fisted his hand, giving the silent signal. The Kerrs and MacKinlays moved into position.

From the birch stand above, a hiss and a thrum, as Mathar's first volley of missiles fell swift and hard. Men shouted; one tumbled backward into the water. Stones came next, the size of a man's skull, loosed from ropes and levered roots, bounding and crashing down. An ox bellowed, struck, staggered sideways; the wagon behind it skidded across the track and jamming the way.

Ciaran and his men erupted from the brush with swords and axes. Two slashes and a heave, and a yoke of oxen bolted, hauling a cart sideways into the bog. Mud sucked, wood groaned, and the cart tipped, spilling sacks of oats like dry sand.

"Now!" Alaric called out and put spurs to his destrier.

They went down the slope at a controlled slide, iron-shod hooves biting. The English shouted and tried to form ranks, but the burn, the jammed cart, the sudden rain of arrows had made a tangle of them. Alaric hit the first man like a hammer, his blade finding the narrow gap where helm met mail at the throat; the man folded as if the bone had gone out of him. The second swung a scythe; Alaric shoved the weapon off course and drove his blade up beneath it.

The thrum of Mathar's second volley reached him, arrows biting into the enemy's side. A horse screamed—another's mount, not his—and then was quiet.

Torches flared in the trees to the north, Neacal and Petrus and their unit ghosting through the dark, fireflies become wolves. A ripple of panic ran the length of the wagons. A call in English went up to form on the standard, but the flag was already in flight, its bearer bolting to save the silk, not the men.

"Dinna waste good steel on unarmored rabble!" Alaric heard Ciaran call out.

Alaric kept his horse moving, never standing to be surrounded, always carving diagonals through soft spots. A lad with a face too smooth for hair beneath the helm tried to hold him, but Alaric's blade checked the lad's heartbeat. The boy's eyes widened. A thrust came for his knee. He cut it aside and felled the boy who held it, then forced his horse through the break in the line.

A horn sounded—three short blasts. The withdrawal. Alaric turned his head, checked the edges. Mathar was already falling back, archers breaking into pairs under the birches. Blair was limping, blood black on his hose but still planting men in the mud as he stepped backward. Someone had set one cart too many alight; flame flared high and hungry, and an iron band snapped off a wheel, coursing through the air, meeting with one of the Kerr men.

"Go! Go!" Alaric roared, and the command cut through the din.

They peeled away in scattered groups, up the slope, back into the hills. An English captain—brave or witless—tried to rally men for a chase; two of Ciaran's infantry raced across the trail and plucked him from his saddle like a goose, and the notion died with him. The forested hillock swallowed the Scots as if it were its job to do so.

They didn't stop running until the hill had them safe. Horses blew hard, men spat blood and wiped mud from their faces. Mathar came at a half-jog, bow over his shoulder, three fletchings snapped. "We've two down that willna rise," he said, breathing steady, grief tucked tight where it belonged. "Four hurt. Ruadh's leg's nicked—nae to the bone, though, thank God." He eyed the glow below. "And the English will sleep cold tonight."

Blair trotted up, hair singed at the ends, grin white in the gloom. "They'll ken our names by dawn," he said. "Did ye see that captain with the boar badge? I've nae heard shrieking like that since—" He caught himself, sobered, and dragged a hand through his hair. "We hit well."

Alaric slid from the saddle and let his sword hang point-down as he listened to the sounds below—the confused bellow of oxen trapped in their own traces, dying men crying out for help for an army that had deserted them.

"Nae well enough to grow drunk on it," Alaric said to Blair.

Alaric wiped his blade on the damp heather and sheathed it. His shoulders eased, just barely, as if the weight never left, only shifted. The men saw only command, the unbending edge that never turned from blood. They cheered him in their rough way, because such nights belonged to them. He gave them a nod; leaders always gave nods when victory, however small, had been won.

Nearby, Ciaran likely did the same.

Inside, the familiar weariness stirred. Not the kind that bent a back, but the kind that sat behind the heart. He had ridden on nights like this more years than he cared to number. He had burned wagons, cut men from saddles, left widows in his wake—he was good at it. Small victories, like this one at the tail but not the entire beast, never truly satisfied. But they kept the greater fight alive.

Alaric wiped his brow, reminding himself that if such skirmishes meant he would live to see his own keep again, perhaps they were victory enough. Perhaps they would carry him back to the woman who, against his better judgment, had begun to thread herself into the spaces a greater weariness used to claim.

"Shift the camp," he said, voice sharp again. "We hold the pine hollow till midnight, then cross the burn and take the high path. Nae fires. Water the horses deep."

Mathar added, "Ruadh, ye ride nae farther than the ash stand; if that leg protests, I'll bind ye to the saddle myself and send ye home."

A few fatigued laughs answered.

"Mungan," Ciaran called, "count what we took."

Mungan had the tally at the ready. "Six carts ruined proper, two teams away into the hills, a crate of crossbow windlasses smashed, and their oats scattered for the birds—though three we claimed as our own."

"Guid." Alaric lifted his chin toward the dark road below. "We'll do the same at the next narrows, when they ken they're safe again." Hopefully, by weeks' end, the English army would be reduced by hundreds, as the Scots kept trimming their tail. By the time the lion reached Urquhart, it would be limping.

"See the men fed," Alaric said, turning away.

He walked to the trees' edge and stood a moment alone, watching the English struggle to knit their column back together far below. Removed from the brief fight, Ivy's face slid into his thoughts once again. And then her voice, exasperated, her mock complaint that he'd waited until the moment of leaving to kiss her. The memory tugged at his lips, curling the corners. He let that small flash of her settle in his chest, a steadier kind of strength than iron or fire before he returned to his men.

***

The sea wind curled around them, sharp with salt from the Firth, snapping at their borrowed wool skirts and tugging loose strands of hair from the braid Ivy had taken to wearing. The sky was pale and restless, clouds sweeping low. Today, the gulls' cries were muffled and carried off by the wind.

Claire had apparently decided she'd had enough of the silence and self-inflicted solitary confinement. She'd appeared at Ivy's chamber door that morning, knocking impatiently just after the maid had delivered a breakfast tray.

"I can't take it anymore," she'd declared, her tone brisk and yet sulky. "I have to get out of here. I tried to go outside yesterday, but some kid told me I couldn't leave."

"That was my idea," Ivy admitted quickly, hands lifted in apology. "Not because I mean to hold you hostage or anything, but because it isn't safe to wander beyond Caeravorn. But..." she'd hesitated, then offered, "would you like to get some air? We can walk the cliffs again. And maybe... we can talk. I know you must still have questions."

Claire's nod had been swift.

They'd strode together through the bailey, Claire's sharp eyes darting about, lighting on the stables with their empty stalls, the cold forge, the shuttered outbuildings, before the two women passed through the side gate and onto the cliff path beyond.

"Why is it so quiet?" Claire asked, her tone edged with criticism. "I mean, if this is supposed to be a real, living, breathing medieval castle?"

"Most of the men have ridden out," Ivy explained. "There's a large English force moving north. The laird here, Ciaran Kerr, and his friend—Alaric—took their men to scout and harry them. Only the house guard stayed behind... and two younger men I trust." She hesitated, then added gently, "You don't have to hold onto all of that right now." A wry thought slipped out before she could stop herself. "Honestly, it would probably be more convincing if the armies were still here. Hard to argue with hundreds of medieval soldiers in one place."

"I still can't believe it." Claire shook her head slowly, gray eyes narrowing at the horizon as if the truth might be written there. "Actually, no—I refuse to believe it. I just haven't figured out your motive yet, for making it up."

"I understand," Ivy murmured. A small, helpless laugh escaped her. "Claire, I still say that to myself sometimes—and it's been nearly a month." She studied the other woman a moment, then asked carefully, "Would it help if I told you what happened to me? How I came to be here?"

Claire's dark expression said she doubted it, but she gave a shrug, her voice still sharp with anger. "I can't stop you."

Ivy pretended Claire *did* want to hear what had happened, and kept her tone level, calm. "Well... I'm from Indiana. I originally came to Scotland to study abroad—I was training to be a vet. Then I met this guy, David, and, well—" she grinned awkwardly and pointed both forefingers at her stomach—"this happened. So I stayed on after the semester. Then David decided he wasn't interested in either me or the baby. My bad. I judged him wrong."

She shrugged and shoved her hands at the skirts, forgetting they had no pockets. Fisting them at her sides, she pressed on. "Anyway, I planned to go home. My flight was booked. I thought I'd take one last easy hike—say goodbye to Scotland, you know? I've gone over it a hundred times, but I still can't pinpoint what happened, or if there were signs. The only thing I remember is the air changing. Like it got heavier. Denser. Then everything around me shifted—suddenly the trail, the trees, all of it... none of it was familiar anymore."

Her throat tightened. She forced herself to keep going. "That was the easy part. The hard part came after. I wandered for hours, trying to find anything recognizable. Instead, I stumbled straight into a battle. Scots against English. Arrows flying, men screaming, blood everywhere." Her voice cracked, but she steadied it. "I didn't understand any of it. I thought maybe it was a reenactment, until I saw a people die. That's when it hit me that whatever had happened—this was real."

Her hazel eyes dropped to the ground, to her skirts brushing along the tall grass in the wind. "And that's when Alaric found me. Sword in hand, face bloody from fighting. I didn't know who he was, only that he terrified me. I was so confused, I thought surely I was dreaming. He looked at me like I'd dropped from the sky, which I guess, in a way, I had. He demanded to know who I was, where I came from. I couldn't even answer him. I was too confused, too scared. And from there..." She trailed off, biting her lip. "From there, it only got stranger. At the same time, it became more real. I found myself traveling with them—the MacKinlays, that is, Alaric's clan. After a while, with things only becoming more confusing, I finally asked what year it was—like who asks that question? Outside of movies, or fiction, who has to ask that question? I passed out when they told me—it didn't make sense, and yet, considering what I'd seen and heard, it was the only thing that *did* make sense."

"But it's impossible," Claire pressed. "You can't just...slip through time like stepping through a doorway."

"And yet here we are."

Ivy angled her toward the wind, guiding them slowly along the cliff path but keeping them well back from the edge. Gulls still circled and screeched overhead, and the sea below hissed against the rocks. "I went through the same thought process you are. I told myself there had to be a logical explanation—that maybe I'd fallen, hit my head, and was in a coma. That I was imagining it all. But no matter how many times I pinched myself, I stayed here. Eventually... you stop fighting what your eyes keep showing you."

Claire shot her a sidelong glance, lips pressed thin. "You don't seem unhinged by it. But I feel like I'm going to be. I feel like I'm losing my mind."

"Honestly?" Ivy exhaled a dry laugh. "I was marching with a medieval army in those first days. Confused, terrified—but survival came first. There wasn't time to break down, not with men and swords and danger everywhere. Sure, it tortured me in the quiet moments, but most of the time I was just trying to get through each day without drawing attention—especially from the laird. Alaric. He scared me half to death in the beginning."

"And now?" Claire prompted, her tone edged with curiosity instead of anger.

Ivy blushed. She felt the heat crawling up her face. "Now... we'll see. But let's just say I haven't prayed in years, and I pray every morning and every night that he comes back safely."

Claire's eyes widened, the sharpness in them easing for the first time all day. "So you walked—or fell—into a historical romance novel?"

Ivy laughed outright, her face still warm. She hadn't thought of it that way, but the words hit their mark. "I guess I did. Or maybe a medieval time-travel fantasy."

Silence stretched between them for a moment, until Claire spoke again.

"But... did you love him?" Claire asked suddenly.

Ivy's head snapped toward her. "Alaric?"

Claire shook her head and clarified, "David, the father."

Ivy hesitated, her throat tightening. "I thought I did," she admitted at last, her voice low. "At one time, maybe I really did. He made me feel like I wasn't invisible, like I mattered. He was my first *real* boyfriend." She let out a breath, realizing the strangeness of it even as she said it. "But since I've been here... I don't think I've thought of him once. Not until now." She showed a wince to Claire, as if to say, *How awful am I?*

Claire gave a short laugh, not at all unkind. "So, you're telling me time travel cured you of a bad boyfriend."

Ivy snorted, the sound caught between a groan and a laugh. "God. When you put it like that..."

Ivy froze mid-step, her hand flying to her stomach. A sharp tightening gripped low in her belly, startling her enough to gasp. "Oh, no. No, no, no," she muttered, her knees locking as though bracing herself against the wind.

Claire stopped short. "What? What is it?"

"I—I don't know." Ivy pressed her palms against the curve of her stomach, eyes wide. "It just... everything clenched for a second." Her voice rose an octave. "Oh God, Claire, what if it's labor? What if it's happening right now? I'm not ready—I haven't read the expectant mother books in months—I thought I'd have time—I wanted Alaric here when the time came—"

Claire reached out and caught her arm firmly. "Relax. Breathe. Did it feel like tightening, or was there pain, like cramps?"

"It didn't hurt," Ivy said, a bit breathless with fright now.

"You're fine. You're not in labor," Claire attempted to assure her.

"How can you say that?" Ivy demanded, her voice pitched high, half whine, half plea. "How do you know? You said you don't even have kids!"

"I don't," Claire said evenly, "but I'm a nurse. A trauma nurse."

Ivy blinked at her, stunned, then sagged with selfish relief. So strong was her reaction to this blessed news, tears misted in her eyes. "Oh, thank God. Oh my God, Claire, you have no idea how happy I am to hear that."

Claire's mouth quirked, then broke into a grin—the first real one Ivy had seen from her since she'd woken. It transformed her face, made her look softer, younger, almost radiant despite the wind whipping her hair across her cheek.

"Those are Braxton-Hicks contractions," Claire said, her tone both confident and a little teasing. "Practice rounds, if you will. Annoying, but harmless. You're not going into labor. Not yet."

Ivy let out a shaky laugh, still clutching her stomach but loosening her grip. "Well, that's just fabulous news."

Claire chuckled, shaking her head and then sobered, as if a thought had come to her. "Maybe," she began, now the breathless one, "if what you say is true, maybe I was—brought here? Sent here?—for a reason."

Ivy stared at her, her mouth falling open, wondering if it might be true.

Chapter Sixteen

The weeks bled together in rain and mud, and blood and steel. The MacKinlay and Kerr armies grew weary of the endless chase, the sustained harrying of the English column along the spine of the Great Glen. They struck where they could—ambushes from the ridges, night raids that cut down stragglers, quick strikes at the tail of the English force on two more occasions. For every man they felled, for every patrol they left broken in the heather, another hundred English marched on. In the end, despite their efforts, the invaders reached Urquhart.

Still, it was not defeat. The enemy moved slower, thinner, bloodied, their numbers reduced and their tempers frayed. But Alaric counted it no victory either. Small gains in a war that never seemed to end. With no other English presence pressing from the south, and with weeks of mud-soaked miles behind them, he and Ciaran at last turned their men to Caeravorn. Alaric gave some thought of returning home himself. He'd not seen Braalach since late winter.

Relief warred with impatience. Alaric found himself restless, near feral, driving his company harder than was wise, his mind fixed on Caeravorn. Not merely the keep, of course, but Ivy. The harrying of the English had served more than only the necessary and obvious purpose, but while they'd engaged the enemy as often as they had, he'd been spared worry over Ivy. But now, with her time so near, concern for her gnawed at him with every mile. He could not, would not, be elsewhere when the babe came—some bone-deep truth told him he must be there.

The march back was no easy matter. Rain had slicked the crags and turned the narrow paths into sucking mire, so that horses stumbled and men muttered beneath their breath. Tempers flared as sodden cloaks and plaids twisted and clung, and boots filled with water. More than once the company was forced to halt while a cart axle snapped in the ruts or a wounded man slid from the litter. A regular cacophony of groans filled the night when they camped, low, broken sounds of men who might never see Caeravorn's walls again. Each dawn they rose stiffer, wearier, trudging on through dripping pines and misted glens until even the strongest looked hollow-eyed.

Twenty-four days after they had departed Caeravorn, the keep came into view at last, its gray towers looming stark and dramatic through the mist. The portcullis rattled upward, the gate groaning wide as a handful of voices called down in welcome. Two score men rode through the arch with Ciaran at their head, the bulk of the armies already scattered in and around the village. Alaric was bone-weary, every muscle aching, yet strung taut with expectation.

And then his heart near stopped.

Ivy—heavily burdened with child now, her dark hair braided back in a careless plait, her skirts hitched higher than modesty would allow—stood in the bailey, struggling with a basket of firewood slung against her hip. Of all the cursed things!

No comfort was it that her troubled hazel eyes searched the riders anxiously—perhaps for him—for she looked pale and strained, a vision that struck him harder than any English blade might have.

Lost amid a throng of riders, Alaric was off his horse in a heartbeat, boots striking the stones, unseen yet by the one pair of eyes he sought. "Ivy!" His roar cracked across the bailey like a whip. He strode just as sharply, while horses and men seemed to part before him as if a hand had come down to move them. Then she found him. Across the swirl of men and horses, their gazes locked—hers wide with surprise, his fierce with alarm. In that instant her expression shifted, softening as relief chased the worry from her face, as if the long weeks apart had fallen away in a breath.

"Are ye daft? D'ye ken the weight of that basket?" He asked as he closed the distance between them. "What in God's name are ye doing?"

She startled, smiling while her eyes filled with tears. The basket slipped against her hip and she set it down. "Oh, for heaven's sake, Alaric. You don't have to yell. Your face already booms like thunder."

He stopped dead, glowering, and she had the audacity to laugh at him. A bright, exasperating laugh that cut straight through to him, like sunlight through the clouds.

Around them, men dismounted, servants bustled out from the keep, all of Caeravorn stirring at their laird's return. Mathar, brushing road dust from his hair, cast a sidelong glance as he passed them, muttering, just loud enough for Alaric and Ivy to hear, "God help us, look at the eyes they're making at each other." No other would ever dare to speak to him with such insolence.

Alaric ignored him. His gaze never left Ivy.

She met it unflinching, as if she'd been waiting all these weeks to see him—mayhap she'd watched for him to come over the rise, mayhap had counted the days, offered prayers for him alone. He'd imagined this, just this, seeing her again, had thought he'd have hauled her into his arms—the very idea seemed both natural and necessary, to make known what had been whispering in him for weeks then had become a roar he could no longer silence while he'd been parted from her.

Instead, he found himself saying, almost casually, "I kent I should be here when the babe was born."

Her lips parted, and then slowly curved, not in mirth but in something softer, joyous. Her eyes held his, hazel warmed with a light he had not seen before, as though those simple words had reached some quiet, frightened corner of her she had kept hidden. Relief and joy mingled there, unspoken but unmistakable, her face transformed.

"Alaric," she breathed.

Her smile and tears broke in the same instant, and she flung herself against his chest, arms tight about his neck. Alaric crushed her to him, heedless of the eyes upon them, and kissed her hard. The weeks apart, the weight of battle, the sheer relief of finding her alive and well—all of it poured into that kiss, fierce and hungry, until at last it slowed, softened, deepened.

When he drew back, breath still rough, his thumb lingered against her cheek.

"Dinna lift heavy things, Ivy," he said, the words low, almost pleading.

Her lashes fluttered, her tears giving way to a quiet, knowing smile. "Okay, Alaric."

***

Ivy leaned into Alaric's arm as they crossed the bailey, her cheeks and lips still warm from his kiss, her steps quickened by the strength of his stride. She tried to look composed—they'd just put on a rather shameless display in front of his men—but she couldn't quite stop smiling.

Claire had come outside and stood waiting near the keep's door, pressed almost against the stone as though she meant to vanish into it. It struck Ivy as odd. Claire was not timid by nature—if anything, she carried herself with more assurance than Ivy ever had. Yet now her hands twisted restlessly in her skirts, a faint crease marked her brow, and she seemed intent on making herself smaller, less seen. Perhaps it was only the change of company, Ivy thought; the keep had been quiet with most of the men gone, and the sudden return of armored soldiers and the noise of horses might have unsettled her. Or perhaps, Ivy realized, her eyes widening, to Claire it was more jarring proof of what she had not yet managed to fully accept—that they were not in some elaborate dream or cruel trick, but truly here, in the fourteenth century.

Ciaran approached the keep at the same time as Alaric and Ivy did, coming from a different angle, tall and commanding. Even wearied by the march as Alaric appeared, his dark hair damp with mist, Ciaran's stride was steady as he headed toward the keep. He paused, though, mid-step, as his eyes fell on Claire. Something unreadable flickered across his face.

Ivy's eyes flickered between Claire and Ciaran, half a dozen feet apart, curiosity piqued despite herself. Something about the way Ciaran stood so still, his expression taut but veiled, brought to mind that first moment weeks ago when he had seen Claire unconscious in the wagon—how his face had sharpened then, too, in a way that had unsettled Ivy enough to remember it. Now, seeing them face to face, Ivy thought Claire's reaction mirrored his own.

Ivy opened her mouth to speak, meaning to bridge the inexplicable awkwardness with an introduction, but she never got the chance.

Claire's gaze had locked on Ciaran, wide and unblinking. She took a quick breath of what seemed utter astonishment. Her lips parted, breath catching, and in a voice hushed and dazed, she whispered, "I've been waiting for you."

Ciaran froze, every line of him tightening; his shoulders squared, his jaw clenched, and his eyes narrowed with sudden intensity. He did not speak, but the tautness in his stance and the sharp focus in his gaze unsettled Ivy. Even Alaric seemed to stiffen at her side, as if he, too, was disturbed by Ciaran's reaction.

Ivy looked from one to the other, startled by the strangeness of it, before she gently ventured, "Claire?"

Claire blinked, as though roused from a dream, and flushed to the roots of her hair. "You must be the laird," she said quickly, her voice thin. "I've been waiting to meet you, to thank you for allowing me refuge in your home."

The silence pressed on, the faintest edge of unease prickling over Ivy's skin. Claire's flush lingered, and Ciaran's gaze had not left her, nor had he moved.

Ivy disengaged from Alaric and stepped forward, meaning to dispel the awkwardness. "Ah—Ciaran," she began, her voice catching before she steadied it. "This is Claire. She... she came with the tinker, if you recall, and has improved greatly...as you can see." Her hand gestured faintly, as though that might smooth the moment, though it hardly did. She pressed on. "Claire, this is Ciaran Kerr, laird of Caeravorn."

Claire dipped her head in acknowledgement, her composure returning with almost deliberate care. "My lord," she murmured, the words even enough, though her color still burned high.

Ciaran inclined his head in return—too sharp, too curt, Ivy determined—his gaze lingering on her longer than politeness required before he brushed past her and stepped inside.

Ivy exchanged a questioning glance with Alaric before they fell in step behind Ciaran. At the door, Alaric paused and extended a hand, a silent courtesy that implied Claire should enter ahead of them. Distractedly, Ivy introduced them as well, each of them murmuring likewise distracted greetings before Ivy moved, slipping her arm through Claire's, steering her gently forward, the two of them stepping together into the keep's shadowed hall with Alaric following.

**

The day had unfolded in a rush of noise and motion, the keep stirring to life with such force that the quiet of the last month was quickly forgotten. The return of a laird and his men after a month away was no quiet matter. The laughter of men glad to be home echoed through the hall. Servants hurried to and fro with buckets of water and armloads of linens. Smoke thickened from the kitchens, the smell of roasted meat and fresh bread filling the keep.

Ciaran had scarcely crossed the threshold before duty called him away again. A laird's absence apparently left matters to fester, and no sooner had he greeted his household than word came from the village. An accusation of thievery had boiled over to shouting, and one man had drawn steel. He went at once, grim-faced, and Alaric—still weary but unwilling to idle under another man's roof—went with him, sending Ivy an apologetic grimace.

Ivy and Claire, in the last month of peacefulness about the keep, had become friendlier with the household staff and had offered themselves in the kitchens, extra hands for labor.

The men of Caeravorn dined early, shortly after midday, the household staff having worked tirelessly over the preceding few hours. Trenchers of venison, dense rounds of oat bread, and pigeon pies were laid out. Casks of ale and wine were carried up from the cellars, and the hall rang with voices. Soldiers sat shoulder to shoulder at the tables, eating hungrily, their faces ruddy from the march and brightened by relief. The scrape of knives, the rise and fall of laughter, the deep voices rolling beneath the beams was almost overwhelming to Ivy, who had grown used to the hush of a half-empty keep, and hadn't before witnessed a meal partaken in the hall. She thought Claire, too, looked startled by the press of bodies, though like Ivy, she tried to mask it.

When the meal was done, Ciaran excused himself again, summoned by his factor to hear accounts left waiting these many weeks. Alaric trailed after, lending an ear as matters of tenants, tithes, and border-watch were sorted—that had been his brief explanation to Ivy as he'd excused himself. Ivy suspected he'd gone along same as he had earlier, to be less a burdensome guest and more a useful friend.

When the hall had cleared, and after Ivy and Claire had once more made themselves useful with the clean-up, Ivy suggested they return to Claire's chamber for a little while.

"I need to put my feet up," she said. But then, rather struck by inspiration, she ducked back into the kitchens and begged a favor of the servants who would have an early day since supper had already been served.

She rejoined Claire a moment later and they climbed the stairs settling in Claire's airy chamber, Ivy flopping on her back on the foot of the soft bed, her feet on the floor, while Claire paused to gaze out the window.

"We should have returned outdoors," Claire said. "Before the rain returns."

Ivy had learned that about Claire—she loved being outside, loved most of all being near the water.

Her eyes closed, Ivy grinned. "You'd have to help me up. If we did, that is, but we can't now, because I just bugged Evir and the kid, Pàdair, to start boiling water and set up two tubs in here so that we could have baths."

She sat up then, not without difficulty, just as Claire turned from the window.

"A bath? Now, in the middle of the day? With everything going on—oh, I think I might know why." With mock severity, she asked, "Why, Ivy Mitchell, have you something planned for your reunion with the strapping Alaric MacKinlay?" Her grinned widened. "Something that makes you want to be fresh as a daisy? I saw that kiss—wow."

Ivy rolled her lips inward as heat blossomed in her cheeks. "I might be." Anxiously, she pulled her hands from behind her and rubbed them up and down her thighs. "That's all right, isn't it?" Ivy bit her lip, words tumbling awkwardly. "How far can I—we—what I mean, is, you know, how... far can a woman go with a man when she's this far along? Without harming the babe? Is it... dangerous?"

Claire blinked, then burst out laughing, not unkindly but bright, surprised. "Oh, Ivy. Honestly? As long as things are healthy—and they seem to be—you can do it right up until the baby comes. You're fine."

Ivy stared, half-scandalized, half-thrilled. "Truly?"

"Truly," Claire said, still grinning. "If anything, it might even help when you're ready to deliver. Nature's funny that way."

Ivy covered her face with her hands, laughing through her fingers. "Oh heavens. How embarrassing." She lowered her hands, blowing out a thoughtful breath. "Not that I'm even sure—I mean, I don't know if Alaric..." she broke off, her cheeks growing warm again.

"Oh, trust me, Ivy," Claire teased, leaning against the tapestry beside the window. "I wasn't born yesterday—actually, it was seven hundred years from now—" she paused while they both laughed at her quip. "And I never met Alaric MacKinlay before today, but that man wants you. Badly. I saw the way he looked at you—shit, the way he consumed you with that kiss." She grinned again and slanted her head. "Well done, you little twenty-first century minx."

Another round of laughter followed. She got the biggest kick out of Claire sometimes.

When the laughter faded, Claire looked thoughtful, reflective.

Ivy ventured, "Are you thinking about your husband now?" Ivy had asked this question several times over the last month.

Claire straightened and forced a small smile. Then she grimaced, admitting, "Actually, no."

Ivy wondered aloud, quietly, "Are you...thinking about Ciaran Kerr?"

The question definitely startled Claire, but Ivy couldn't tell if it were genuine surprise or guilt that colored her cheeks now. "What? No." Claire answered, folding her arms across her chest.

Carefully, Ivy pressed on, "Claire...earlier. In the bailey. When you saw Ciaran. You looked—" she searched for the right word "—I don't know, surprised, but almost as if you recognized him." She didn't mention that Ciaran had twice now had the same reaction, didn't ask if Claire had noticed it as well in the Caeravorn laird.

Claire made a little face and shook her head dismissively. "He reminded me of someone, that's all." She shrugged it off, though her fingers plucked restlessly at her skirt. Then, with a wry grin she added, "Besides, it's not like I *know* anyone in this century."

Ivy gave a soft laugh, though she tucked the moment away. Perhaps it was better not to press.

Their baths arrived shortly thereafter, and they watched and waited while the wooden tubs were filled, again and again, with steaming buckets of water. When the last of the servants departed, Ivy closed the door and set the latch.

Funny, how she'd been so opposed to stripping in front of the medieval household women but wasn't in front of Claire. With Claire, it felt like being back in the high school locker room, and at least she didn't have to worry about Evir or any other staring in horror at her modern bra and panties.

"Actually, this is a perfect idea," Claire allowed. "A leisurely afternoon bath." She sent a teasing glance at Ivy, her gray eyes dancing. "So you can clean your *virginia*."

Ivy sputtered a laugh. "My what?"

Claire's smile was very pretty, so relaxed now. "I have this elderly aunt—Aunt Pat, though we call her Pitty Pat. Remember that ditsy character from *Gone with the Wind*? Anyway, Pitty Pat has this wonderfully entertaining habit of misusing words. So, your lady bits, if you will," Claire said, smirking cheekily at Ivy as they continued undressing, "is your *virginia*. She's got a million of them. My cousin once had to get a testicle shot—*tetanus* shot, we figured out. And she once said to me—I swear to god—that this guy, some friend of her son, was *arranged* in court."

Arranged! *Arraigned*. Ivy nearly doubled over, laughter bursting out of her until her eyes watered. "Oh, my God—I want to meet her." She wiped at her face, still gasping. "No, even better—remember those word-of-the-day calendars? I want *you* to deliver me a daily Pitty Pat-ism. Just one a day, every day."

Claire slunk down into the tub a moment after Ivy had. "Consider it done."

Ivy sighed, her smile serene as she let her head fall back. She honestly couldn't remember the last time she'd laughed so hard—full-bodied and delighted. It felt foreign and familiar all at once, as though some piece of herself she'd long forgotten had come tumbling back.

Chapter Seventeen

Ivy had fallen asleep, waiting for Alaric to return from whatever had taken him out of doors in the evening. Tired and restless at the same time, she'd lain on the bed, only comfortable on her side these days, and had waited. Having fallen asleep, she was woken when a soft kiss touched her lips.

Her eyes fluttered open, and she found him bent over her, his dark hair hanging over his face a bit, the hard planes of his face softened by shadows and weariness. Ivy reached up her hand, laying her palm against his cheek. Another kiss followed, lingering this time, then another, until the tenderness gave way to something hungrier. His mouth deepened over hers, and Ivy sighed into it, her fingers curling into his tunic, clinging to him, drawing him down to her.

The kiss built, heated, until her heart raced and her body ached with the simple need of him. But then he pulled back, his breath ragged. "Rest, lass," he murmured. "Ye need your strength."

Ivy gave a plaintive little whine at the sound of his retreat, tugging lightly at his tunic. "Don't go. Please. Just—lie down with me."

For a moment, he hesitated. And then he gave in, shucking his boots, and stretching out beside her on the bed. She nestled into him at once, her cheek against his chest, his arm coming around her as if he'd done this a thousand times before.

God, he felt good!

For a time, both were content with silence.

Ivy lay quiet for a time, her fingers idly tracing patterns across his chest. Then, softly, "How old are you, Alaric?"

His chest rumbled with a faint chuckle. "Past thirty summers."

"What of your family?"

He answered in what felt like a mechanical or auto-response. "My father is gone, taken the first year of the war. My mother died of fever ere I ever kent her. I've nae memory of her face."

Her heart squeezed. She lifted her head a little, searching his expression, but he kept his eyes on the rafters above. "No brothers or sisters?" she asked quietly.

"Aye, by my father's second wife. They fled south after his passing, down to England, to her kin. I've heard naught of them since."

Ivy swallowed, her fingers stilling against him, recalling how young Kendrick and Blair were, and already wed.. "And...have you ever been married?"

A long silence. His jaw worked, his gaze fixed on the flames. Finally, low and reluctant, he said, "Aye. I was wed."

Her breath caught. "And—your wife?" His answer, whatever it might be, would break her heart. Either he was still wed, had lied to her—a lie of omission—or he'd buried his wife.

For a moment he didn't answer, his jaw tightening, his gaze set hard. At last, he said simply, "She's gone."

Ivy frowned, unsatisfied. "Gone...away? Or...?"

"It was some years ago," he muttered, still not looking at her. "It dinna matter now."

"It does matter—she was your wife," Ivy said softly, her voice gentle, coaxing. "Was she sick? Did she...did she die in the war, too?"

"Nae." The single word was clipped, reluctant. At length he added, "She and our babe died...in the birthing."

"Oh." Ivy's throat tightened, a pang cutting through her chest. She looked at him, her heart heavy, imagining what it must have been to lose them both. The silence between them thickened, carrying the weight of his grief until it seemed almost to press down on her. "Alaric, I'm so sorry."

"Aye," was all he said.

Possibly he mistook her sympathy, or suspected Ivy of having other emotions, for how she'd gone still in his arms, because his voice came rough but steady, quick to soothe. "Many births end well, Ivy. Plenty of mothers and bairns live, hale and strong."

"Oh, I know that," she concurred. "I just... I feel so bad for you."

"'Twas a long time ago," he murmured.

"Okay, but I'm sure that doesn't make it any easier."

He'd gone just as still as Ivy, and she sensed the wound was still raw, despite how he tried to downplay it. But she knew Alaric—she felt she understood a lot about him, his character—and sensed he didn't want to or wasn't ready to share more with her now. She let it rest and, wanting to ease the heaviness, she tried to make light of her own dread. "I am very nervous, Alaric, about giving birth, that is," she confessed, a small laugh slipping out. "I've only ever fainted twice in my life. Once, when I first met you—when Kendrick said what year it was. And the only other time, ironically—or prophetically, we might find out—was back in high school, when they made us watch the film on childbirth. It was a very graphic film—oh, that probably means nothing to you, film. Um, imagine...a play, but not live. Picture images and sound—like a memory maybe—caught and held on a flat surface so you can watch again and again. That's a film. Anyway, we were showed a film about childbirth in school, all the details up close, and I fainted dead away. Hit the floor."

At that, the corner of his mouth twitched. "Ye woke both times, did ye nae?"

"Well, yes—obviously, but that's not the point."

"It is, though." His tone was gruff, certain. "Ye are strong enough, Ivy. Faint if ye must, but then ye'll get on with it."

She stared at him, stricken, startled—and then burst out laughing. "Oh, okay. Sure, it's probably that easy." The laughter died almost as quickly as it came, replaced by a tremor in her voice as a thought struck her. "But...Alaric, if something happened to me, and the baby lived—what would become of her?"

At that, his gaze snapped to hers, sharp and unwavering. "What nonsense is this?" he demanded. "If ye dinna...survive, I'll take your babe. My child or nae, I would see the child raised well."

Ivy blinked at him, stunned by the bluntness, then felt the sting of tears well in her eyes. Not from fear this time, but from the fierce, unshakable certainty in his voice. He was a good man, she knew.

And maybe Alaric was as distressed as Ivy by such talk and didn't want to discuss it anymore. He turned toward her, positioning himself over her, rolling her onto her back. He kissed her then, slow at first, then more fiercely, hungrier, until her fingers curled in the linen at his shoulders. When at last his lips trailed to her throat, her pulse fluttered wildly beneath his mouth, she whispered with delight, "Alaric..."

He drew her closer, one hand splaying over the swell of her belly, and broke away with a groan. His forehead pressed to hers, his breath harsh. "I want ye, Ivy. God help me, I do. But I'll nae risk it, nae cause ye or the bae harm."

Hot color rose to her cheeks, but she forced herself to speak, knowing what she wanted, "It's fine, Alaric, not dangerous at all to the baby."

He drew his lips wide in a grimace, reluctant still.

Ivy understood almost immediately—this wasn't rejection, but fear. The same fear born of loss that still lived in him. Her heart softened, even as need coiled low in her belly.

"It's all right," she whispered, her hand sliding up to his jaw. "I understand. But you can still kiss me, Alaric."

"Aye," he agreed, the word rough.

His mouth found hers at once, the kiss slow at first, then deepening with a heat that stole her breath. His hand cradled her face, his thumb brushing her cheek. When she sighed into him, he answered with a low sound from deep in his chest, his restraint already fraying. His hands moved over her with deliberate care, undressing her, exploring, until she gasped his name again, her body arching beneath his touch. Every movement was purposeful, measured, as though he feared to take or even give too much, yet couldn't deny himself entirely.

Alaric gave to her freely, his every kiss and caress meant for her alone. His own hunger he kept leashed, held back with ruthless restraint.

Ivy's hands were no less searching. She slid them over the breadth of his shoulders, down the hard planes of his back, marveling at the strength coiled there. She compelled him to remove his tunic, and her fingers traced the ridges of old scars, lingered on the curve of muscle, tugged him closer still. She wanted to feel all of him, wanted to be touched everywhere by him.

With his hands and fingers, he teased her and tortured her, and when at last she shuddered in his arms, her vision blurry and heart hammering, he gathered her close, his lips brushing her temple. "Ye have so much passion, lass," he murmured, his voice raw. "And ye are mine, Ivy, from this day forward—mayhap from the moment I laid eyes on ye."

The words sank into her like warmth seeping through her very bones. He wasn't only restraining himself for the babe, he was binding himself to her, claiming her in a way that made her heart soar. He feared for her, yes, but beneath that fear was something she had yearned for all her life: to be chosen, wholly and without condition. She'd not experienced that, not anything even close outside her grandparents' love.

Her hand slid up his chest, resting over the steady beat of his heart. "I am yours," she whispered, her voice trembling but sure.

***

The next morning found Ivy and Claire once more walking the cliff path beyond the keep. The wind swept up from the sea, tugging at Ivy and Claire's skirts. Below, the gray waves slapped at the rocks in a steady rhythm, almost lulling despite the wildness of it.

"I don't need any details," Claire said, "but am I to imagine that silly grin you've been wearing means Alaric at least got to second base?"

Ivy squawked with laughter at the corny, vintage expression. "What are you—sixty?"

"Hah! Don't deflect." Claire dropped into a mock-stern, manly voice. "Just answer the question!"

Ivy blinked at her, half-sure it was a movie quote, though she couldn't place which one.

"Well, if you must know—"

"And as you're probably bursting to tell me," Claire cut in, grinning.

"That, too," Ivy admitted. Her smile softened. "We had the most wonderful time, Claire—really talked, and that was before—" She stopped abruptly, bending, one hand clutching her middle.

Claire was at her side in an instant. "Ivy?"

Ivy blew out a shaky breath. "I think—oh God—oh, boy."

Claire's eyes lit, not with alarm but delight. "You're going to be a mother soon." She slipped an arm through Ivy's, steadying her as they turned back toward the keep.

Ivy gave a weak laugh, half-whine, half-disbelief. "I need to tell Alaric." She pressed a hand harder against her belly, shuffling her weight. Her frantic gaze found Claire. "She's early—almost a week early."

"And still everything is going to be just fine," Claire said with a confidence that soothed Ivy, then she spun abruptly toward the bailey and bellowed, "Alaric! Someone fetch Alaric!"

Ivy gasped, scandalized. "Claire!"

"What?" Claire shot back, not the least bit apologetic. "I wasn't about to leave you here and go running after him. He could be anywhere."

Ivy groaned, shaking her head as they continued on. "I just imagined we'd send someone once we actually reached the hall."

"Oh, yeah. I suppose we could have done that."

By the time they reached the gates, Ivy was lumbering and holding her back for the pain there.

And then suddenly, Alaric appeared, sprinting from the yard with his men—as if Claire's wild call had actually reached him.

"Ivy." His voice was hoarse, ragged, as he reached her side and took her hand. "Are ye—? Is it—?"

She nodded, swallowing at the same time, trying to smile to assuage the stricken look on his face.

"Aye." His voice was a rasp, his face gone pale. In an instant he had her in his arms, lifting her as though she weighed nothing. "Clear the way!" he barked over his shoulder just as the great doors opened before them, his shout carrying across the bailey. "Send for the midwife!"

Claire hurried after, piggybacking on Alaric's orders, saying to the cluster of servants just inside the doors, "And hot water—clean cloths, plenty of both!"

Alaric carried Ivy up the stairs, his arms iron bands around her, his breath harsh in her ear. "I've got ye, lass. I've got ye."

Claire skipped up the stairs after them, her skirts in her hands.

Inside Ivy's chamber, Alaric eased her onto the bed where just last night, he had indeed gone further than second base.

"No, wait," Claire said quickly, shaking her head. "Hold her up a moment, so I can untie her laces."

Alaric perched on the side of the bed at once, drawing Ivy forward until they were face to face. His big hand spread over her back, steadying her as Claire's nimble fingers worked at the laces of her gown.

A contraction seized Ivy then, sharp and consuming. She tried to hold back a cry, mostly succeeding, her hands fisting in Alaric's tunic. His other hand rose to cup her cheek, his thumb brushing across her damp skin.

"Everything will be fine," he said, his voice low but certain.

She leaned into him, forehead pressed hard against his, drawing strength from the heat of his breath and the solidity of him, holding fast until the pain ebbed and released her at last.

Ivy turned her face up to Alaric but spoke to Claire. "It's starting too fast. What if—"

"Nope, it's fine," Claire assured her. "You can lay her down now," she said to Alaric, before assuring Ivy further, "I haven't timed it yet, but they are not too quick, seem right on time."

Just as he lowered Ivy, Alaric turned his sharp gaze to Claire, hope in his tortured gaze. "Ye are a midwife? Ye have birthed bairns?"

"I have," Claire said confidently. "And I've met Ruth, the midwife, and between her and me, Ivy is in good hands, I promise you." When Alaric looked as if he needed more convincing, Claire added, her tone tender, "She's young and strong, and I have every confidence she will sail right through this."

The door opened again, Evir arriving with a stack of clean linens.

Claire received them. "Thank you, Evir, and would you see Laird MacKinlay to the hall—maybe find him something stronger than ale."

Alaric bristled, coming to his feet. "I'll nae leave her."

The midwife bustled in just then, Ruth's sleeves already rolled up and her face set in brisk lines of command. She clucked at Alaric as though he were simply a wayward boy underfoot. "Out wi' ye, laird. 'Tis nae place for men."

Alaric looked helplessly at Ivy.

She reached for and squeezed his hand, forcing a smile she did not entirely feel. "It's all right. I promise. I can do this." Her voice came out steady, stronger than she'd imagined.

The midwife planted herself firmly near the door, her hand on the latch. "Ye will go now. Else I cannae do my work. I'll send for ye when it's done."

For a heartbeat Ivy thought he would argue, but his grip only tightened painfully on her hand before he bent, pressed a kiss to her temple, and whispered, "I'll be just below."

Then he was gone, the door closing behind him, and Ivy found herself breathing differently—less afraid of distressing him.

Claire shifted to Ivy's side, smoothing her hair back from her damp brow. "I'm right here," she murmured. "I know you're entering unknown territory, Ivy, but everything is going to be fine. In a few hours, you'll be holding your daughter."

Claire and Ivy had discussed the birth more than a week ago, Claire insisting she didn't want to interfere with the midwife—but that if she saw something she didn't like, if she thought for one minute that the midwife didn't know what she was doing, she would step in. "I will toss her ass out," she'd said.

Claire and Evir then proceeded to undress Ivy, removing everything but her chemise, which was bunched around her waist. When they were done, Ivy let her head fall back against the pillows, sighing, bracing herself for the next contraction.

This was happening. At last, the moment she had dreaded and longed for was here.

After the first hour, the pains came steady and hard. At first, they were only tightening bands across her belly, sharp enough to catch her breath but not enough to steal it entirely. For a while, the midwife sat idly—Claire assured Ivy there wasn't anything she could do at the moment, anyway—but did bustled about here and there, stripping Ivy's bed to clean linens after Ivy's water had broken a few hours in, laying cloths at the foot, setting water to steam in the hearth and herbs to steep.

"Walk, if ye can," the woman ordered at one point. "It'll bring the bairn quicker."

Claire slipped an arm around Ivy's waist, helping her pace the chamber. Ivy's knees wobbled with each contraction, but she obeyed, pacing between the bed and the hearth, her free hand pressed hard to the small of her back. Claire kept her tone bright, almost merry. "You're really doing it, Ivy. You're going to meet your baby before the sun goes down, I bet."

Since her water had broken, the pains had grown sharper, radiating down her thighs, leaving her breathless. Ivy leaned on Claire's shoulder, whimpering despite herself. "I can't—"

"You can," Claire whispered back. "Every woman since Eve has. And so will you."

***

Alaric paced as well, stomping the length of the hall like a caged beast, the rushes scattered by his boots as he turned back and forth until a clear line of flagstones was visible. His hands flexed and clenched, useless things when the only work they longed for was barred from him. Above his head, muffled through timber and stone, came the faintest sounds—women's voices, hurried footsteps, and every so often a cry that made his stomach knot until he thought he might retch.

Ciaran sat at the high table, sipping on ale. "Ye'll drive yerself mad like that," he said at last. "Come outside. Let us ride. Or set the men to drills—anything to take yer mind from it."

Alaric whirled on him, breath ragged. "Ride? Drill?" His voice cracked, nearly incoherent. "I canna leave her, not when she's..." He broke off, swallowing hard, running a hand through his hair. "I need to be here. If she calls for me—I need to be here."

Something softened in Ciaran's face then, the guarded look slipping a fraction. He knew. He happened to have been at Braalach when Gwen....

He'd seen it before, the helplessness of waiting, the terror of what might be lost in a single moment.

Alaric dragged in a breath, forcing himself still, though every muscle vibrated with tension. He lowered onto the bench, elbows braced on his knees, staring into the rushes. "She's strong," he muttered, more to himself than to Ciaran. "Stronger than she might believe of herself even. She'll see it through."

Above them, another cry carried faintly down, and Alaric's head snapped up, jaw tightening. His hands closed into fists again. "I'll wait," he said fiercely. "I'll wait here, until they bring her through it."

***

Another pain tore through Ivy, so strong she nearly sobbed with it. Claire leaned close, clutching her hand, her voice brisk but teasing. "Breathe now, Ivy—deep, steady. Don't tense up, you'll strain your *abdominables*."

Despite herself, Ivy barked a laugh through the pain, nearly choking on it. "Abdominables? Really? A Pitty Pat-ism now?"

Claire grinned, brushing damp hair from Ivy's brow. Straight-faced, she instructed, "Don't argue with Pitty Pat—she's practically a medical authority."

The contraction ebbed, leaving Ivy trembling but smiling faintly, the sharp edge of fear and pain blunted for a moment.

"Please, Claire, run down and tell Alaric everything is fine, progressing as expected," Ivy begged, exhausted. "Lie if you have to."

"I wouldn't have to lie," Claire assured her, "but I know my head would roll if I left your side. I'll give that message to Evir to convey when next she pops her head in."

The midwife came then, checking her progress with brisk efficiency, her roughened hands surprisingly gentle. "Another while yet," she muttered. "The bairn's slow, but she's coming."

The afternoon wore on. Servants padded in and out with hot water, with cloths, with herbs. The air grew thick with steam and the sharp bite of crushed rosemary. Ivy gripped Claire's hand through each wave, knuckles white. Between, she slumped back, hair plastered to her cheeks, lips silently murmuring her baby's name—she'd decided on Lily.

At one point the midwife urged her to squat, propped by Claire and another maid. Ivy obeyed, trembling, until her legs gave way. She collapsed back onto the bed, sobbing. "I can't—"

Claire stood beside her, brushing damp hair from her face. "Yes, you can. You already are. And when it's over, you'll hold Lily in your arms."

The words struck through Ivy's fog of pain: *Lily.* Her daughter. The hope steadied her.

By late afternoon the pains grew fierce, tearing through her body with an urgency that left her hoarse from her grunting cries. Claire held cool cloths to her brow, whispering nonsense comforts. The midwife's voice cut through it all, steady, commanding: "Now push, lass. With all ye've got."

Ivy bore down, groaned deeply, and thought she would break apart. Again. Again. The world narrowed to fire and blood and the rasp of her own breath. She was certain she would die. And then—

Heat, the pressure gone, relief.

A thin cry split the chamber. High, wailing, indignant.

The sound pierced Ivy like sunlight breaking storm clouds. She sagged back, spent, tears streaming as the midwife lifted a slick, squirming bundle and set her onto Ivy's chest. "A lass," the woman announced with satisfaction. "Strong lungs, too."

Ivy stared down at the tiny, red-faced creature, her daughter, her heart breaking open. Claire laughed softly, tears in her own eyes, leaning close. "She's perfect, Ivy. You did it."

***

The chamber had quieted after the storm of labor. The midwife moved briskly about, tidying cloths and murmuring instructions to the maid, while Claire perched right beside Ivy, their shoulders touching.

Ivy was exhausted but couldn't even think about resting now, not with her cleaned and swaddled daughter bundled warm against her chest.

"She's perfect, right?" She asked Claire. "You counted her toes? Her fingers?"

"Everything," Claire confirmed. "Your little mini-me is precious, Ivy."

"Thank you, Claire," Ivy said softly, leaning her head against her friend's. "Thank you for being here."

The door creaked, and Alaric stepped inside, Claire having given the all-clear to Evir a minute ago, when Ruth had finished stitching Ivy and she'd been changed into a fresh gown, just as Claire had laid the babe in her mother's arms.

For a heartbeat he did not move, only stood on the threshold, as though unsure if he should enter. His face was pale—paler than Ivy's, she suspected.

"Here," Claire offered, vacating the spot next to Ivy.

He crossed the room slowly, almost reverently, until he reached her bedside. His gaze was first for Ivy, trained on her as to ascertain for himself that she was all right.

Ivy smiled brilliantly at him. "Hi."

"Ivy," he breathed, sinking down to his knees, which put him nearly eye to eye with Ivy. His hand came to the one stretched extended to him, rough thumb brushing over her knuckles, and then he bent and kissed her. Not hurried, not desperate—just full of joy and release, as though that kiss was the first breath he'd taken in hours.

"This is Lily," she said to him, beaming with pride and love.

He leaned close, gaze fixed on the tiny features, the scrunched pink face, the damp wisps of dark hair. His breath caught audibly. His eyes shimmered with wonder, with tears he did not bother to hide.

"She's... she's flawless," he whispered, voice rough. His great hand hovered, hesitant, before brushing one careful finger against the baby's small fist. Lily twitched in response, curling her hand around his finger, and he let out a broken laugh. "God help me, Ivy, she's nae my own bluid, yet I've never been prouder in all my days."

Ivy's throat tightened, tears slipping down her temples. "But can she be, Alaric? Can she be yours? Ours?"

He nodded fiercely, too choked up to speak.

Claire added her two cents from the background. "She might as well, already has him twisted around her fingers."

Chapter Eighteen

The keep was quiet but for the thin wail echoing up the stairwell. Alaric paused at the foot of the stairs, listening, and then bounded up them, not wanting the babe to wake her mother. It had taken immense powers of persuasion—his, Claire's, the midwife's—to finally get Ivy to take some rest during the day.

He eased the door open with care, mindful of the spot halfway where it always creaked. Slipping through before it could give him away, he caught himself wondering why he bothered. If Ivy hadn't stirred at the child's strident wail, she certainly wouldn't wake for the faint groan of a door hinge.

He crossed the room and looked down at the squirming, red-faced bundle, her fists flailing as though she meant to fight her way out of her swaddling and cradle.

"Whisht now, lass," he muttered, though his voice held no real conviction. He cast a glance toward the bed where Ivy lay in heavy sleep, finally surrendered after days of stubborn refusal.

Awkwardly, gingerly, he lifted the infant from her cradle. Lily was warm and impossibly small against the size of his hands, her cries rising like a war horn. He held her stiff-armed at first, away from him, unsure what part of her was most fragile. "God's wounds, ye've a voice on ye," he muttered, wincing at the pitch.

He carried her down the stairs, boots thudding softly on the worn stone. The noise came with him, piercing as any blade. By the time he stepped into the hall, his ears rang with it.

Claire was just coming from the corridor, carrying a piece of wadded linen in her hand. Alaric caught the quick twitch at the corner of her mouth, likely amused by how awkwardly he held the bairn. He had some idea of how he must look. One would think Ivy had birthed ten bairns with how at ease she instantly was with her babe in her arms.

"Dinna laugh," he warned darkly, though he had the sense that made it harder for her to obey.

She bit the inside of her cheek, eyes dancing. "I wasn't going to," she said far too innocently. Then, with a nod toward Lily, "I was just on my way up with something that might help. She doesn't need to feed for another hour at least. A rag dipped in sugar water—works like a charm. Though we don't want to make a habit of it, it's not good for her teeth."

"Her teeth?" Alaric questioned, alarmed. *The bairn had teeth already?*

"When they come," Claire clarified, another grin bit back.

Alaric frowned, shifting the babe who screeched all the louder for it. "Should we nae hire a wet nurse, then? To spare Ivy this—"

"No." Claire cut him off without hesitation, shaking her head. "Ivy will never go for that. I guarantee you."

He lifted a brow, unwilling to yield so quickly. "It's a common enough thing. Why nae?"

"We don't do that in our—" She stopped, caught herself, cleared her throat. "We don't do that, not if we can help it. Ivy has plenty of milk and would sooner keep her close."

Alaric narrowed his eyes at her slip, having some suspicion—he didn't know why—that she'd been about to say *we don't do that in our time*. Lily let out another shrill squall that near made him wince. Claire gestured to a bench.

"Sit," she said firmly.

Grimacing, Alaric obeyed, lowering himself to the bench. Claire guided his hands, showing him how to tuck the babe into the crook of his arm, her tiny head supported against the inside of his elbow and his forearm. He stiffened at the intimacy of it, between him and the babe, but when Lily settled a little, blinking up at him, his breath caught.

"There," Claire murmured, twisting the linen cloth lightly and producing a thumb-size end, pressing it gently to the baby's lips. Lily latched at once, her cries softening into greedy little snuffles.

The silence that followed was profound. Alaric blinked down at the child, stunned, as if he'd just witnessed a miracle. The corners of his mouth twitched, then curved into an astonished grin.

"By Christ," he whispered, awe in his voice. "It worked."

Claire's smile was gentle now, no longer hidden. "Told you." She moved to stand directly in front of Alaric. "And babies like soft, swaying motion—constant sometimes." Claire rocked her hips, lifting her arms to pretend she was holding a bairn as well, showing Alaric the pace and rhythm, side to side.

Alaric rose slowly to his feet carefully. He squared his shoulders and glanced at Claire, studying the easy sway of her hips. With a grunt, he shifted his stance and tried to imitate her rhythm, rocking side to side.

It was clumsy at first, he knew, not smooth at all, but he was moving. And the babe still wasn't crying again.

Claire—damn her—seemed again to be trying not to laugh.

However, she advised straight-faced, "Sometimes, that's all she'll need to calm her."

Alaric nodded, and continued the motion. He was still marveling at the quiet—at how swiftly she had gone from red-faced fury to peaceful suckling—when the door to the hall opened.

Ciaran stepped in, pausing mid-stride. His gaze caught on the tableau, and for the briefest instant his expression shifted, though Alaric could not read what flickered there.

Beside him, Claire made a soft, incoherent sound and in the next heartbeat she ducked her head and all but fled, her skirts snapping behind her as she hurried away.

Still swaying, Alaric frowned after her, then turned his stare on Ciaran as he crossed the hall. "What the bluidy hell is wrong with ye, man?" He asked, keeping his voice low, continuing to bounce and sway. "Why do ye snarl with yer gaze at her? What has she done to earn yer contempt?"

Ciaran's jaw tightened. For a moment he seemed inclined to brush it off, but then he exhaled hard, annoyance roughening his voice. "She wears the face of a woman I held once—near Dunbar, in the first weeks of the war."

Alaric's brows drew together.

Ciaran's gaze fixed on the calmed babe. "The lass at Dunbar perished." His shrug was sharp, defensive. "This one reminds me of her, that's all. It's...disquieting." His expression eased, fractionally, and he seemed to realize just now Alaric's steady movement. "What the bluidy hell are ye doing?"

"Hush," Alaric scolded. "She likes the swinging. I want Ivy to rest. The babe's kept her up most the night for days now."

Ciaran, possibly not understanding—or truly caring—nodded curtly and strode away.

***

The weeks that followed slipped by in a gentler rhythm than Ivy could have imagined, the sharpest edges of fear dulled by small mercies. Lily thrived, her tiny fists no longer clenched so tight, her cries, needs, and schedule beginning to be understood.

Ivy herself healed well, as expected, according to Claire. Though she had fought the idea of rest while Lily was awake, she began to understand she simply couldn't function well with too little sleep. She'd begun to nap during the day to make up for hours of sleep lost overnight, easier to do with Claire near at hand. Claire proved tireless, taking care of both Ivy and Lily, minding Ivy's stitches, and becoming familiar enough with the household that she was easily able to make her—or Ivy's—needs known. She became, without fanfare, complaint, or any needed coaxing, Ivy's right hand.

Alaric now shared Ivy's bedchamber and bed. It had begun almost by accident. A week or so after Lily's birth, Alaric had come only to say goodnight, lingering for a while as Ivy rocked the baby. He had stretched out fully clothed sideways on the bed, telling of his day after listening to Ivy speak of hers. He'd remained then, listening to Ivy hum to Lily as she paced before the hearth, until sleep had stolen over him just as it had Lily. After Ivy had placed a sleeping Lily in the cradle, she'd removed Alaric's boots and nudged him awake enough to have him scooch up onto the pillows.

"Stay with me," she'd asked. "I would love your arms around me through the night."

From then on, it was simply the way of things. Sometimes they spoke in low voices until sleep claimed them, sometimes they reached for each other in the dark, content to share warmth and closeness and passionate kisses even if they had yet to take the final step. For Ivy, the intimacy of it was enough, more than that even. His steady breathing in the dark, his arm falling over her, his weight at her side, all brought her immeasurable peace.

Claire, for all her usefulness, remained unsettled in her own way. Ivy noticed the glances she and Ciaran exchanged when they crossed paths—swift, apprehensive, not friendly at all. Yet, so far as Ivy knew, they had hardly spoken a word. The air between them seemed stretched taut, a string waiting to be plucked.

Beyond the walls, late summer gave way to full autumn. The days shortened, the air grew sharp, while the trees on the slopes burned red and gold, a fleeting brilliance before the gray of winter would come.

It was in the quiet, one evening while Lily slept at her breast and the fire snapped in the grate inside her chamber, that Alaric said, very simply, "We'll need to move soon."

Ivy lifted her head, brows knitting. "Move?"

"To Braalach."

She blinked. "To...what?" The word—the name—struck a nebulous memory. Braalach?

"Home," Alaric said simply. "The MacKinlay keep. Further north, tucked against the hills by the loch. Strong walls, guid people. A place built to withstand winter and war both."

While the idea thrilled her—he'd said *we*—Ivy's gaze dropped to Lily, tiny mouth parted in sleep, and her heart squeezed. Images crowded in: the endless days in the saddle, the bone-deep fatigue of their marches, the cold and rain seeping through every seam. She could still feel the ache in her body from that journey, and she had only carried herself. What would it be like with a baby in her arms?

And then came the darker memories—the clash of steel, the cries of dying men, the battles she and they had stumbled into. She shivered. She wasn't afraid for herself, not truly, but for Lily. A babe so small had no defense in such a world.

She looked up at him, torn between the thrill of going where he went and the fear of what the road might hold. "But Alaric, she's so little still. Couldn't we wait until she's a few months older, a little stronger for the journey?"

Alaric shook his head. "Nae. We must ride before the snows. Once the passes close, we'll nae be able to get through. I'll nae have us trapped, either here or in the open."

Her stomach turned. She had seen enough of his determination to know he would not be swayed—but still she tried. The words tasted bitter even as she spoke them. "Then...perhaps Lily and I should remain. At Caeravorn. Until after the winter—just until Lily's older, stronger."

His scowl was sharp, his voice harsher than she'd expected. "Remain? While I—" He broke off, heat flashing in his eyes. "I'm nae going to leave my wife and daughter behind while I move on."

Ivy's heart lurched. "Your...wife?" she repeated, her voice barely above a whisper.

He paused, staring at her, his expression unfathomable. His words, however, were not. "Aye. Ye are. And it'll be made official once we reach Braalach."

At some point—possibly only recently—she'd told herself it was enough that he protected her, that he accepted Lily without question, and that he stood between he and a world she barely understood. But now...now he had named her something else, something she had never dared let herself imagine.

They hadn't spoken of love, or anything even close to it. Yet she knew, with a certainty that made her chest ache, that what she felt for him ran deep. It was in the way her pulse leapt when he entered a room, the way she leaned unconsciously toward his voice, the way she measured her days by his presence, how she ached for his touch.

Her throat tightened, and she blinked hard, afraid the tears would spill. She searched his face, that steady, unflinching gaze, the one that said the matter was already decided.

A laugh threatened to break loose, unsteady with joy. She bit it back, her lips trembling instead into a smile. She nodded. "Yeah, that sounds nice."

Alaric grinned at her. "Aye, verra nice."

***

The column stretched long and slow along the rutted track, a ribbon of steel and horseflesh winding northward. The air was colder now, the hills bristling with autumn color, the sky low with gray that promised harsher weather to come. Hooves struck hollow on the frosty ground, wagons creaked and jolted, and the breath of men and beasts smoked white in the crisp air.

Ivy sat on the bench of one of the wagons, bundled in cloak and plaid, Lily swaddled in her arms. The baby slept warm against her chest, her small breaths soft as feathers beneath Ivy's chin. Beside her, Ewan kept the reins loose in his hands, the sway of the wagon as familiar as the saddle it seemed.

Gone a day, they'd been, and she missed Claire so much already.

She'd wanted Claire to come with them, had already gotten Alaric's permission, but Claire had shocked Ivy by declining.

"Come with us," Ivy had begged days ago, after Alaric had announced his intention to depart Caeravorn. Ivy had expected to see instant relief and a thrill at the invite on Claire's face.

Instead, Claire had looked down, twisting her hands together in front of her.

"I think I'll stay right here," she said evasively. "Caeravorn suits me." Then, with an awkwardness unusual for Claire—and a comical little wince—she added quickly, "Of course, I'll have to ask Ciaran."

Ivy had been stunned. She hadn't doubted for a moment that Claire would want to go wherever she and Lily were bound. But then, despite her own days being consumed with Lily and Alaric, Ivy *had* noticed the looks that passed between Claire and Ciaran. Smoldering, intent—too reminiscent of the way Alaric had first looked at Ivy. And Claire, for all her composure, was hardly subtle in return. More than once Ivy had caught her friend's covert, lingering glances, a flicker of longing in them that spoke plainly enough.

It hadn't been lost on Ivy that Claire had left a husband behind in another century. And she appreciated that now, that life felt impossibly far away, like a book closed and set back on a shelf. Ivy could hardly blame her for responding to what was in front of her, tangible and immediate. Still, she'd been compelled to remind Claire of the man's existence. "Claire...what about your husband?"

Claire had drawn in a deep breath and exhaled. "I know. I know! But," she'd said, and her shoulders had sagged. "He doesn't love me, hasn't for a long time. That doesn't excuse or condone anything, I know, but...." She'd shrugged again, help-lessly.

Ivy had nodded. "But you might never see him again, might be here... for the rest of your life."

"Funny, isn't it?" Claire had mused. "My response to such a suggestion *should* be an emphatic, *Hell no*. And yet, it's not," she explained simply.

Ivy had laughed, shifting Lily higher in her arms. "That, I to-tally understand," she'd remarked. "And honestly, I don't think Ciaran's going to let you just walk out the door."

Claire's cheeks had flushed, her head ducking in sudden shy-ness. A moment later she'd lifted her gaze, her expression almost pleading for understanding. Something was there between them—undeniable—and Claire wanted to stay, to see what it might become.

Remembering how her own heart had clenched at the thought of being parted from Alaric, even in those early days, Ivy understood. "Claire, I completely understand. But know this—you'll always have a place at Braalach, if ever you should need it."

Still, the parting had been hard, and though Ivy hoped that Claire found whatever she was looking for, hoping for, with Cia-ran, Ivy herself hoped that she and Claire would be reunited again.

Now, the pale sun rode low, its weak warmth doing little against the sharp bite in the air. The company pressed onward, the wagon wheels creaking steady over the rutted track. By mid-day, Alaric reined his horse close, exchanged a few low words with Ewan, and climbed up onto the wagon bench himself. He took the reins and settled in next to Ivy, guiding the team with a flick of his wrist.

Amused despite the cold, Ivy remarked, "I didn't know lairds drove wagons."

"I'll do whatever's needful," Alaric replied.

For a time, they rode in companionable quiet. Ivy was pleased for Alaric's presence for more than just the obvious reason. She was able to feed Lily under her cloak, nothing exposed, but it would have been so much more awkward if Ewan had been sitting beside her.

"Can I ask you something?" She asked while her daughter nursed.

His eyes stayed on the road. "Ye've never held back yet."

"Well, I still think you believe me to be lying," she said carefully. "About, well, you know what. So, I'm left to wonder and I have to ask, why do you want me with you?"

He glanced at her, briefly, then back to the road. For a long moment he said nothing. At last, his voice came low. "Because ye are mine. I'd nae have left ye behind to fend for yourself—even at Caeravorn—nae when the world is full of wolves. But aye, it's more than duty. Something in me recoiled at the idea of letting ye go. Simply the idea of it left me...less. I dinna ken why, only that when ye're near, the weight I carry is nae so heavy. And when ye're far, it is twice as much. So, I want ye close."

Warmth unfurled in her chest. In truth, her heart soared at these words. God, that was super sweet, poetic even.

"Thank you, Alaric," she said. "That satisfies my question—and so much more." Recalling her intention here, she continued. "All right, so let me ask you this: do you agree that anything is possible?"

He considered it only briefly. "Aye. Anything is possible. But nae everything is reasonable."

"Oh, I wholeheartedly agree," she said with a smile. "But unreasonable doesn't make it untrue. Or *im*possible. Right?"

Perhaps he assumed where she was going with this, and thus only grunted a response.

Ivy surprised him, she was sure, by not following through there, but by forging ahead. "I'd like to make a deal with you, Alaric."

"Hm?"

She turned toward him more fully, emboldened. "We're going to make a deal. I'll tell you something you cannot possibly know, and when it happens—because it will—you have to promise to open your mind to the possibility that I am not lying about where—and when—I come from."

He gave a skeptical grunt, his lips thinned. "And what vague thing will ye tell me?"

"Not vague," Ivy said, smiling smugly. "I'm telling you that Robert Bruce will be crowned king of Scotland in March of next year. At Scone. March, 1306."

Alaric snapped his head toward her, eyes narrowing. His expression was one of stunned disbelief, the same that might have been worn on a modern man's face, just before he asked her what she was smoking.

"Crowned?" he repeated. "Bruce? 'Tis folly. He has nae army, is still shoved up Edward's arse—he's sworn fealty to the English king. He'd nae dare it, nae so soon."

"If you're so sure, then that's an easy bet to make, right?"

He stared at her, his brow lowering, as if he suspected her of some treachery but couldn't figure out the angle yet. Abruptly, he gave a harsh scoff. "Yer tongue weaves riddles. I'll nae believe a word of it."

"Fine," Ivy said, settling Lily more firmly in her arms. "But will you make the deal with me?"

His jaw worked. He said nothing for a long time. "Aye, I take that deal."

"Fabulous. Thank you." She smiled with satisfaction. "Remember, in March, you have to open your mind to what I've been telling you."

"Ivy, lass," Alaric said, turning a steady stare onto her. "I ken ye, and that is enough. Ye dinna ken where I come from, havenae seen Braalach, dinna ken my kin, my history, what I've done. But here ye are. It's nae different for me—it dinna matter to me from where or whom ye hail. I ken *ye*."

His words struck her still. She hadn't expected such certainty from him, so blunt and absolute. For a moment she could only stare, overwhelmed by the beauty of it.

She blinked rapidly, undone by his words. And she knew then in that moment, what she'd suspected for some time, that she was in love with him.

"I don't know what I've done to deserve that kind of faith," she whispered, her voice unsteady, "but I'm thankful for it. I feel the same. I *know* you, Alaric. And it's enough. It's more than enough."

By the time the sun dipped low, casting long golden shafts across the hills, the road bent sharply, and Braalach came into view.

Ivy drew in a sharp breath. The keep stood high on a rise, its high gray walls crowned with towers, banners snapping in the wind. The castle was tall, reaching up toward the expanse of open sky, and the loch in the foreground spread wide and gleaming at its feet. Beyond, the hills rolled away in every direction, vast and unbroken, as though the world itself opened here.

It stole Ivy's breath.

Beside her, Alaric straightened in the saddle, pride unmistakable in the set of his jaw. "Home, lass," he said quietly. "At last."

Something in Ivy shifted, deep and certain. The moment her eyes settled on it, she felt it—the same ache in her chest she had carried as a girl when she believed she'd touched the edge of heaven.

"Alaric," she breathed, her voice trembling. "This—oh, my gosh, I just got goosebumps." A laugh broke out of her, half-sigh, half-wonder. "When I was a kid at my grandparents' house, I used to run barefoot through the soybean fields. The sky stretched on forever, no end anywhere I looked. The sun was warm, and the air smelled of earth and growing things. Back then, I thought that was as close to heaven as anyone could ever get." Her lips parted as she shook her head slowly, unable to look away from the keep—home. "But just now—just looking at Braalach—I had that same feeling again. That vastness. That anything was possible. I...I was wrong back then." She swallowed, clutching Lily closer, her eyes shining. "This, here—with you, with Lily. *This* is as close to heaven as I'll ever get."

Epilogue

1315

One year after Bannockburn

The courtyard rang with the sound of children—shouts, laughter, the heavy thud of boots too large for small feet. Ivy stood in the arch of the doorway, her arms folded, watching with a smile that deepened the creases at the corners of her eyes.

Alaric was at the center of the chaos, as he always was when the children tumbled out of doors. He shed his mantle of laird as easily as his cloak, striding after his sons with mock ferocity. Eight-year-old Duncan squealed as his father's hand closed around him and lifted him bodily from the ground, swinging him up and onto a broad shoulder. Beside him, six-year-old Malcolm shrieked with delight and charged in to rescue his brother, a wooden sword clutched tight in his small hand.

Alaric bellowed in mock outrage, staggering back as Malcolm thumped at him, then let Duncan slide down to wrestle free. As entertained as she was warmed by the sight, Ivy shook her head—two boys bred for endless energy and mischief, matched only by their father's patience, and the boyish enthusiasm that made him such a great father.

Near the steps, Lily sat with her little sister Elspeth, carefully twisting her long strawberry blonde hair into two long braids. At ten, Lily had the long-limbed grace of girlhood, and her face was still soft with a child's openness. Elspeth, four years old, fidgeted, her small feet restless against the stone, though she bore her sister's attentions with a long-suffering sigh.

271

Ivy's gaze lingered on Lily. For the longest time, it had been just the three of them—herself, Alaric, and Lily. The two miscarriages that came after Lily had left Ivy raw, yet they had bound Alaric to Lily all the tighter. He had never once let the girl believe she was anything but wholly his. And Ivy knew they would never tell her otherwise—not the truth of her birth, not the secret of Ivy's strange journey through time. That knowledge lived only in the hearts of four: Ivy, Alaric, Claire, and Ciaran.

Ivy stepped down into the courtyard. Lily glanced up to catch her mother's eye, her smile bright. Ivy returned it, tenderness swelling in her chest, as she sat with the girls. Elspeth glanced up, her face wrinkled against the sun, and then casually laid her arm across Ivy's lap.

Alaric spotted her then. He was on all fours at the moment, with Malcolm on his back, and Duncan pulling at his leg—can't let the dragon reach the steps.

Her husband grinned, boyish in the moment, grimacing a wee bit as Malcolm bounced heartily atop him, trying to slow down the dragon. "Ye've come to save me, love?"

She laughed, shaking her head. "I doubt there's saving you from those two."

"They'll make ye bluidy again, Da," Lily predicted, her eyes on her task, referring to the nosebleed Duncan had caused just last week, in a similar circumstance.

"We're headed out for the bilberries in a moment," Ivy called out. "Do you boys want to come? Or are you happy slaying the dragon?"

Before they might have answered, Alaric found a surge of strength and fought off the *knights*. While still on his knees, he dumped Malcolm off his back, and then was able to rise to his feet, doing so in exaggerated fashion, in slow-motion with his arms flexed and while roaring. Ivy knew what would come next, had seen it dozens of times. Duncan and Malcolm clambered to their feet, each latching onto their father's strong arms. Obligingly, Alaric flexed even harder, growled louder, and raised his arms until the boys' feet rose off the ground.

"Dragon wins again," he said, walking the boys over to the steps. He winked at Ivy, "I ken we'll all get to the bilberries." He lowered his arms, depositing the boys just in front of Ivy and her daughters. He muttered then, "*Jesu*, it's got to be kinder to my bones than this."

Five minutes later, they headed outside the gates, toward the berry patches up near the ridge, close to the graveyard where Alaric's parents, Gwen and her son, and other MacKinlays were buried.

Alaris walked ahead, Elspeth on his shoulders now, Lily holding his hand, skipping at his side, telling him about today's lesson.

"Mama told me a story today about a girl named Joan who led armies. A *girl*, and she wore armor, and the men followed her. She was called the Maid of Orléans, and she fought the English and never ran from them."

"A fine warrior, by the sound of her," Alaric allowed.

"Da, at one point, she traveled over three thousand miles in less than two years!" Lily exclaimed. "I want to be a warrior just like the Maid of Orléans."

"Aye, ye can be anything ye set your mind to, lass, whatever path ye choose." Then his voice dropped, firmer, though no less warm. "But ye'll walk that path here, close to Braalach. Far and wide is for others. My daughter's place is at home."

Seeming none the worse for having her wings clipped so neatly, Lily carried on, relaying more details about Joan of Arc's triumphs.

So often, during her lessons with Lily and Elspeth, Ivy wished she could recall more—details, dates, and particulars. She wracked her brain for fresh ideas, content worthy of their little classroom, even exchanging letters with Claire for inspiration. Duncan and Malcolm had their own tutors, and Ivy was content to leave their schooling in other hands. The boys' education was steeped in numbers, land charters, the art of the sword, and the duties they would one day inherit—things Alaric insisted upon, and subjects Ivy could not pretend to master. But with her daughters, she felt a fiercer calling, to give them what the century itself would have denied.

She walked behind Alaric and the girls, with Malcom's hand in hers. He'd not taken naps in years, but he did slump in the middle of the afternoon, and leaned heavily on his mother's arm, his feet dragging. Duncan, tireless wonder that he was, was running through the tall grass that flanked the path, chasing anything that moved as was his way.

Ivy let herself breathe in the sight. The scene—anytime the six of them were together—never got old.

She rarely thought of the twenty-first century, hadn't in a long time now. That world felt thin and far away, a time and place that, in truth, she'd not fought too hard to hang onto. In the richness of this life—her children's laughter, Alaric's steady heart, the sure stones of Braalach—Ivy knew this was where she was supposed to be.

This was home. This was hers.

***

The keep slept, the stones hushed, save for the faint whistle of the wind outside the shutters. He ought to have been sleeping, yet his mind wandered as it often did in the still hours. Years of steel and blood had left their mark, not only on his body but on the darker corners of his spirit. He had seen men fall, break, shatter, hopes undone, had felt the gnaw of doubt that even victory could not soothe. War was hard, and aye, sometimes love—joy itself—was chased into a darker place. Invariably, inevitably, Ivy snagged him from the depths, pulled him back toward her, toward their bairns.

She lay now on her stomach, the furs tangled about her hips, her back bare to him. The fire's glow caught along the curve of her shoulder, the sweep of her spine. With his back against the headboard, he lifted a hand and traced idle patterns across her skin, the pad of his finger stirring gooseflesh in his wake.

It was a game between them, one begun long ago. He traced, he asked; she answered. Or sometimes she did the tracing, and the questions were hers.

"Ye have a favorite child?" he asked quietly, following the line of her shoulder blade.

Her voice was languid, thick with drowsiness and the sated glow of their lovemaking. "I do not. Do you?" A little laugh slipped out. "Would you admit it?"

"The questions are mine, and nae yers at this time," he rumbled.

"Fine." He saw the ghost of a smile touch her profile.

He drew a slow circle at the small of her back. "Ye have a favorite laird?"

"I might." She gave a negligent shrug, her smile widening.

"Only truth while the finger traces the back," he reminded her, echoing words she had once spoken years ago, when she first drew her fingertip across the scars that ridged his skin.

"Fine," she sighed, feigning huffiness. "But he totally looks like a man who could—and possibly has—turned feelings into felonies. And sometimes—well, I hate to admit this—but sometimes he leaves in the morning and forgets to kiss me goodbye. And that hurts. Otherwise," her voice softened, "he's nearly perfect."

Alaric's chest tightened, the jest turned truth, and he tucked the information away. He would not forget again.

He traced lower, his touch gentling. "Do ye ken we'd have even more bairns, if war dinna call me so oft?"

Her sleepy laugh answered him. "We'd need a bigger keep, I fear."

Silence stretched easy between them. His finger slowed, stroking rather than drawing.

"Do ye ken ye're closer to heaven now, love?" he asked at last.

She stirred, rolling onto her side to meet his gaze. In her eyes shone love, and perhaps a touch of wistfulness, that he had remembered what she'd once said.

"Alaric," she whispered, lifting a hand to his cheek. "This life—here, with you, with the children, at Braalach—this is everything. This *is* heaven."

He bent to kiss her, slow and deep.

And aye, so it was.

The End

*Don't miss what comes next—Ciaran and Claire's unforgettable
journey in* **I Loved You Then***.*
Enjoy a free sneak peek of the prologue below

***

Dunbar, 1296

The air stank of blood and smoke. Ciaran Kerr picked his
way across the trampled fields, his boots sinking into churned
mud slick with the bodies of men who only hours ago had stood
shoulder to shoulder. Groans rose from the ground in places,
broken cries from those not yet dead, mingling with the caw of
circling crows. The English had been thorough. Their steel had
cut through Scotland's hastily gathered host as if through grain
at harvest.

Ciaran had thought himself ready. He was Kerr-born,
trained with bow and blade since boyhood. But nothing in his
twenty-two years had prepared him for this—the weight of silence after battle, the ruined faces, the sheer number of fallen.
His stomach turned as he stepped around a Highlander with his
throat laid open, the man's eyes glassy and unblinking toward the
gray sky.

He wanted to run, to blot it from memory. Instead, he kept
walking.

At the edge of the field, where the heather began again, he
caught sight of yet another body. A woman lay crumpled among
the bent grasses, her ash-blonde hair matted dark with blood,
part of her skull crushed. There was a large gash in her back
as well, though the axe that had made it hadn't remained. At
first he thought her only another of the fallen, but then she

moved—fingers clawing weakly at the earth, dragging herself a hand's breadth as though sheer will might carry her away from the carnage. Ciaran's chest tightened. She was no soldier, no armored knight struck down in the press. Her gown, once pale, was torn and muddied, the hem snarled in the brambles at the field's edge. One slipper hung loose from her foot.

He approached slowly, almost warily, as though afraid that touching her might make the last spark of life slip away. His own breath caught in his throat. He had seen men gutted open today and had managed not to flinch, but something about this lone woman's struggle made him falter. She seemed both fragile and defiant, determined to crawl from death's reach even as it claimed her.

He dropped to his knees beside her, his hands hovering, unsure if he dared touch. At last, with a careful breath, gently, he eased her onto her back. He made to lift her; he would carry her and lay her with the other wounded, maybe she could be saved. Or she would not die alone. He wedged his hands under her shoulders and legs.

But then her eyes fluttered open—startling gray, sharp despite the certainty of death. The force of her gaze staggered him. Inexplicably, his strength failed, and instead of rising he sank back onto his heels, cradling her in his arms, rigid with some unknown sensation, riveted by her gaze.

She drew a ragged breath, and when he tried to stand again, she gave a faint shake of her head. He froze, still holding her, his arms braced around her slight frame.

For a long moment they simply stared at each other, the noise of the field falling away. Something passed between them—he could not have named it, only that her gaze held no fear. It was as though she saw him in a way no one ever had, stripping him bare with nothing more than her gray eyes. It was as if she knew him, but he did not recognize her, knew so few souls this far south. The battlefield around them ceased to exist; the cries of the dying, the stench of smoke and iron, all faded until there was only her and the steady pull of her gaze.

Ciaran felt it then—a strange, inexplicable bond to this woman he had never met. He should have been thinking of his kin, of the horror around him, but instead he was gripped by the certainty that this moment mattered. That she mattered. His heart thudded unevenly as if she had reached into his chest and laid claim to it without a word.

Slowly, the tension in her face eased, and a calm stole over her, as though she had found what she'd been searching for, what she had been crawling and scratching toward at the edge of the trees.

Her lips moved, the words barely more than breath. "I've been waiting for you."

The sound of it lodged in his chest. Before he could ask what she meant, her eyes fluttered closed. Her body grew heavy against him. A bitter scowl twisted his features. She was gone.

Ciaran remained there, stunned, staring down at her still face. He had no answer to the question pounding in his head. Who had she thought he was? And why had her dying words pierced him so?

It was a long time before he wrenched his stricken eyes from her face, before he moved again.

***

I Loved you Then will be released October 2025

Highlander: The Legends

The Beast of Lismore Abbey
The Lion of Blacklaw Tower
The Scoundrel of Beauly Glen
The Wolf of Carnoch Cross
The Blackguard of Windless Woods
The Devil of Helburn by the Sea
The Rebel of Lochaber Forest
The Avenger of Castle Wick
The Dragon of Lochlan Hall

Heart of a Highlander Series

Heart of Shadows
Heart of Stone
Heart of Fire
Heart of Iron
Heart of Winter
Heart of Ice

Far From Home: A Scottish Time-Travel Romance

And Be My Love
Eternal Summer
Crazy In Love
Beyond Dreams

Only The Brave
When & Where
Beloved Enemy
Winter Longing
Stand in the Fire
Here in Your Arms
So Close to Heaven
I Loved You Then

The Highlander Heroes Series
The Touch of Her Hand
The Memory of Her Kiss
The Shadow of Her Smile
The Depths of Her Soul
The Truth of Her Heart
The Love of Her Life

Sign-Up for My Newsletter
and hear about
all the upcoming books.
Stay Up To Date!
www.rebeccaruger.com

Printed in Dunstable, United Kingdom

66925193R00170